P9-DKE-219

HER OUTLAW HEART

Center Point
Large Print

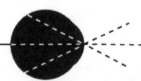

**This Large Print Book carries the
Seal of Approval of N.A.V.H.**

HER OUTLAW HEART

Samantha Harte

CENTER POINT LARGE PRINT
THORNDIKE, MAINE

James L. Hamner Public Library
Amelia Court House, Va. 23002

This Center Point Large Print edition
is published in the year 2016 by arrangement with
Diversion Publishing Corp.

Copyright © 2016 by Samantha Harte.

All rights reserved.

The text of this Large Print edition is unabridged.
In other aspects, this book may vary
from the original edition.
Printed in the United States of America
on permanent paper.
Set in 16-point Times New Roman type.

ISBN: 978-1-68324-040-2

Publisher's Cataloging-In-Publication Data
(Prepared by The Donohue Group, Inc.)

Names: Harte, Samantha.
Title: Her outlaw heart / Samantha Harte.
Description: Center Point large print edition. | Thorndike, Maine :
Center Point Large Print, 2016.
Identifiers: LCCN 2016014681 | ISBN 9781683240402
    (hardcover : alk. paper)
Subjects: LCSH: Girls—Wyoming—Fiction. | Outlaws—Wyoming—
Fiction. | Large type books. | Wyoming—Fiction. | GSAFD: Western
stories.
Classification: LCC PS3608.A7871596 H47 2016 | DDC 813/.6—dc23

For Laura, Robert and Kathleen,
Justen, Jason, and Emma.
Wishing everything good for my dear ones.

• • •

A very special thank you to my agent Abby Saul
whose hard work made all this possible.
And my editor Randall Klein for his expert
advice. You make dreams come true.

One

The Wyoming Territory
1879

Jodee woke to the shattering sound of gunfire outside the cabin. Her first thought was to jump to her feet and run, but she didn't remember where she was. She dragged her father's heavy pistol from the tangled folds of the knapsack pillowing her head and scrambled into a corner.

Heart racing, she watched her father's long-time friend, Cloyd Rike, and his three mangy sons awaken with curses and scuttle from their blankets to crouch beneath the single window. It was scarcely dawn. Now Jodee remembered—she was hiding with these men. High in the mountains. Too stupid to know what else to do with herself.

And her father . . . her father was dead.

One of the Rikes fell back, shot dead not five feet from where Jodee huddled in the litter of the abandoned cabin. Covering her face, she screamed until her throat went raw. She shouldn't be here. This shouldn't be happening to her. When the gunfire stopped abruptly, all four Rikes lay dead. Jodee couldn't take it in. She clenched her eyes shut until they ached. She felt sick, and dizzy. What should she do?

7

She heard Burl Tangus, the worst of the bunch, cussing across the room. Startled to think he was still alive, her eyes sprang wide. She saw him crab on his belly toward the far corner where the floor was rotted through. Headlong, he dove through the hole. That runty weasel. He was getting away! She reared up—

Something slammed her against the wall.

As Jodee's mind cleared, a burning sensation in her right shoulder claimed her attention. It felt like a hot coal under her skin. Her stomach lurched. She went limp and gave out with a moan. Weakness spread over her like hot water. At the sound of approaching voices and cautious footsteps outside the cabin, her attention snapped into focus with a stab of terror. There was no place to hide. Whoever was out there would kill her, too.

The cabin door flew wide and slammed against the wall. A brilliant slice of dawn sunlight fell across the gritty floorboards, stinging Jodee's eyes and outlining dead outlaws lying all around. In the far corner, the jagged hole in the floor lay in shadow. With sick determination, Jodee steeled herself for the final shot. It would be all right, she told herself. She'd join her father in the hereafter. The nightmare of her existence would be over.

As the silhouette of a tall, broad-shouldered man filled the doorway, Jodee's heart leapt with dread. Gingerly he stepped inside, pistol drawn, its long barrel glinting as he moved closer. A shiny badge on his grey shirtfront showed behind his open coat front and stopped Jodee's breath in her throat.

Lawman.

She scrabbled backward and her shoulder blossomed with heart-catching pain. Several men crowded in behind the lawman, gawking at her as she cringed on the floor. *Posse,* she thought. *Go ahead. Kill me! Get it over with!*

The lawman crouched in front of her, his face only an arm's length away. Jodee didn't have the strength to lift her father's pistol to shoot him. She saw dark brows draw low over shadowed eyes. A two-day growth of whiskers darkened his jaw. They had been following from the nearest town most likely. That must be how they found them so fast. His rosy lips tightened around a puzzled frown. He was trying to figure out what she was doing there. *That was a face to remember,* Jodee thought, growing light-headed. His cheeks bunched upward as if he didn't like what he was looking at.

Plucking the pistol from her limp grasp, he shoved it into his gun belt. Then he tugged off her slouchy hat. She felt her long hair tumble free. Squinting, he smoothed his hand over her head. She pulled away. The gesture made her throat tighten. Was there any hope he might show mercy?

Glancing at her britches that had become snug over the years, and her broken-toed boots that were too big for her feet, the lawman cupped her chin and turned it into the dawn light for a better look. His touch stung her with its tenderness. She met his puzzled stare and saw flecks of gold and black in the dark coffee brown color. Eyes full of worry. Eyes fraught with loneliness.

What did he say? She couldn't hear anything. Her ears were ringing. She felt too exhausted to think, too sick to fend off his fingers tugging aside her shirt collar where the pain blazed. Her head fell back. Her eyes drifted closed. She smelled blood. *Dear God,* she thought. She was gunshot.

After a few minutes, Jodee felt herself being gathered into the lawman's arms and lifted. Tarnation, that hurt. This was more than she could bear, being found in this place, with these dead outlaws, and gunshot, too. The lawman had trouble steadying her as he grabbed up her knapsack and blanket.

Outside, in the golden brilliance of morning, Jodee gazed at the lawman holding her so close, at his chestnut hair curling beneath his broad-brimmed hat, at the strong sunburned neck. And those eyes glancing at her as he picked his way across the rocky dooryard back to horses and men waiting on the trail. Honest eyes, not pity-me eyes like her father's. Not squinty, scheming weasel eyes like Burl's.

But this was a lawman. Maybe he was good. Maybe he wasn't. Maybe he wouldn't hurt her. With eyes like that, he couldn't. Could he? She let herself fall limp in his arms.

Thirty feet behind the cabin alongside a steep, boulder-choked creekbed, Burl Tangus crouched behind dry brush and watched the posse lash the Rikes belly-down over their saddle horses. All four dead. That was a helluva morning's work for one lawman, a deputy, and six deputized store-keeps, he thought.

Like shootin' fish in a barrel. *Didn't get me, though, did you, lawman?*

Burl should've cleared out in the night, but his horse needed rest. Now they'd flushed him so fast he'd gone down the hole without his loot bag. It was tucked under the corner of girlie-girl's blanket. Soon as the posse cleared out, he'd go back—

He clenched his jaw, groaned, and instantly relaxed his bite. The whole side of his face ached. All the way up to his hairline. Burl wished he'd had time to take back the Rikes' shares. Damn fools, bobbing across their saddles like carcasses. He saw the lawman carry girlie-girl from the cabin. Was she dead? Her knapsack dangled from his elbow, her blanket trailed in the dirt.

Damn! Burl stopped himself from jumping up. He pressed a fist to his jaw. *Goddamn!* Two deputies propped her upright while the lawman mounted his horse and then took her onto his lap. Burl half stood for a better look. Was she alive? Any chance she had seen his loot bag and kicked it into the hole?

Burl dropped down, breathing hard, his thoughts racing. His head swam with curses. Every part of this damnable robbery had gone wrong. He should've cut out, but Lee and Witt had been behind him, making sure Jodee followed. Old man Rike and Mose with the strong box had been in front, leading the way. They would've killed him rather than let him make off with the loot he'd taken off the passengers.

But when they found the cabin to hide in and started to divide the loot . . . Burl shook his head. Unbelievable. Groping in his pants pocket, his fingers touched the slip of paper he'd taken from the pocketbook. Maybe he didn't bust that snake-bit safe open, but he knew a combination code when he saw one written down and hidden under a leather flap. *Didn't see me palm that, did you, boys?* He handed over the cash to be divided like he was so fair. Someday he'd stroll into that Ashton Babcock Stage Office and open 'er up like a can of peaches.

It felt like somebody was hitting him in the face with a rock.

He rubbed his jaw. It was that cash box tucked down in the strong box that had clinched it.

Nobody had seen the rich gal clutching the ribbon around her neck. Burl pulled the ribbon from his shirt pocket and kissed the key hanging from it. Peeking around a boulder, he watched the posse start single file down the steep, narrow trail. Those stupid Rikes had been snoring like bears when he had unlocked the cash box during the night. What the hell had that rich gal been doing, traveling with so much cash?

Hunkering down, forcing himself to remain calm, Burl waited. When all was quiet, he made his way back up the boulder-choked creekbed. No need to squeeze back up through the rotting floor. He walked right in the cabin door.

Blood stains everywhere. Abandoned blankets kicked aside. Holstering his pistol, he looked around. A holey sock. No gold eagles in it. A rusted straight razor. The diamond brooch. He pocketed that. The Rikes had stashed the greenbacks in their boots, damn them. The posse had retrieved the strong box Mose broke open. Not a splinter left behind. A dozen spent cartridges. Old man Rike's dented tin flask.

Burl drained the flask into his mouth and held the whiskey over his rotting molar. He prowled the corner where Jodee had slept. Goddammit! It was gone.

Jodee woke to heavy snow-spitting grey clouds overhead. She was jolting on her back with the sound of horses' hooves clomping along the trail. She lay on a travois woven from pine branches hitched to a horse. They were on a rocky road lined with dense pines towering on both sides. And it was as cold as Christmas.

She twisted around and saw the broad-shouldered back of the lawman riding a big horse. At first she felt relieved, but then she sank back, shivering with dread. She wanted to climb to her feet and run, but a stabbing pain in her shoulder made her whimper. Her body felt like deadweight.

They'd taken her somewhere. A settlement? There'd been some kind of wheezing doctor. Yesterday? A week ago? She couldn't remember. Her eyes drifted closed.

The travois scraped to a stop. Gritting her teeth against the pain, Jodee listened to the creaking of saddle leather as the lawman dismounted. When he loomed over her, he seemed as tall as the sky. Jodee's hunger-hollow belly knotted. Why'd he scowl at her like she was ugly or something? Was he feeling even the slightest scrap of pity for her? She didn't sense friendship in that granite gaze. The stubble on his jaw looked darker, more frightening. She shrank back, unsure of him. Some lawmen were just as bad as outlaws.

Crouching, he tugged off his big buckskin glove and laid warm fingers against her chilled cheek. Something comforting spread through her body, something like warm honey. Oh, that felt nice, to be touched with kindness. She held her breath. He put his hand on her forehead. His dark brows drew together. Faint wrinkles formed at the corners of his eyes. A body could forget a lot, looking at a face like that.

"We're almost there," he said softly.

Her throat tightened. She swallowed hard.

"We have a real doc in Burdeen, not a bone-cracker like that one in Kirkstone." He tucked the blanket around her. Her shoulder responded with a thunderbolt of pain that made her flinch and gasp. "Won't you tell me who you are, miss?"

Miss? She thought of Burl's warning after the holdup. *You better come with us, Jodee-girl. If a posse catches us, we'll go to jail, sure. You, too.*

They didn't put innocent girls in jail, did they?

She heard one of the posse men call out as if he were in pain, "Patsy. Patsy!"

With a jerk of his head, the lawman straightened. He hurried along the mounted men to one slumped in his saddle. This was her chance to escape, Jodee thought. But she felt so weak, she could scarcely hold her eyes open.

After a moment the lawman stormed back to his horse and threw himself onto the saddle. They headed on at a faster pace. With each jolt of the travois, Jodee's shoulder blazed afresh. The lawman glanced back once to scowl at her. Did he care that he was hurting her? No, he looked

15

like he hated her. Jodee clenched her teeth, hating him back.

Soon the rocky trail widened. She saw storefronts and rough-looking saloons lining a steep rutted street. The snow came down heavily. She hadn't been to a town in years. Her father always steered clear of civilization. It felt strange to see folks walking along and wagon traffic going by and hammers echoing against the pine-clad mountainsides. Side streets sported newly built houses, real houses, not cabins or shacks. She couldn't tell if she felt excited or afraid.

Schoolboys playing in stacked lumber paused as the posse plodded by. They started running alongside Jodee's travois, reminding her of dirty-kneed schoolboys who once taunted her. *Yer pa's an outlaw. Ya got bad blood.* She wished they'd leave her alone. She looked from side to side, past signboards that read *Ellis Brothers, Boots, Shoes and Leather Findings; Stanley Holt, Seller of Whiskey and Cigars;* and *Munjoy's Fine Furniture and Coffins*—she had trouble reading them—the procession passed an Ashton-Babcock stage depot. A black crepe mourning wreath hung on the door. That was Burl's doing, she thought, looking away. The Rikes and Burl had held up an Ashton-Babcock stagecoach. The driver got himself killed, Burl said, his weasel eyes snapping like killing a man was nothing.

And her father.

Jodee couldn't breathe. Her father was dead. His body had been left behind on the stage road. He'd been taken away and buried by strangers. She didn't know where. She'd go crazy if she didn't find out. All she could remember from her last morning with him was how he looked, riding away, holding his hat high in the air. "This is the big one, Jodee-honey. Last time."

Jodee stifled a moan. Last time meant last robbery, not dead.

The lawman halted the procession. Townsfolk flocked down the street to stare at her before moving on to greet the posse men. He dismounted in front of a stone-built jailhouse with a shake roof and plank porch. There was a pine addition built onto one side, making it the ugliest jailhouse Jodee had ever seen.

She watched a skinny lad vault out of the jailhouse door and lope around to halt and stare down at her.

"You got 'em all, Marshal? Every last one of 'em?"

Rubbing his eyes, the lawman gave a sigh. "I got errands for you, Hobie."

"Yes'r. Who's this here?"

"Wish I knew," the lawman said. "Owen thinks she might be wife to one of the Rikes. I thought she might be a sister."

What a horrible idea, Jodee thought, wanting to protest, but the lawman—the marshal—scowled

17

down at her so darkly she shrank from him. She feared she might throw up.

Snowflakes swirled around his head. "I wanted to bring them in without a fight." He glared at the posse men dismounting along the street. It looked like his face hurt. "I had to shoot or risk more men. Tangus wasn't there. Or he got away. I don't know which. I couldn't take time to look for him. I had to get Virgil and this one to that quack in Kirkstone." He shook his head, dark eyes blazing. "Waste of precious time."

The lad's eyes followed the line of trail-weary horses to the end where the outlaws hung face-down across saddles. He looked stricken. "Virgil's shot?"

The marshal took his hat off, brushed snow from the crown, and clapped it back on his head hard. "I'll be in the stage office, wiring Cheyenne City. Get Roy Trappe over here for pictures. Tell Isaac I need four pine boxes."

Before the marshal could give another order, a female's screaming wail brought his head around. A red-haired woman in calico came running from the mercantile. She was about as pregnant as a woman could get and still move. She threw herself at the wounded deputy where he stood propped up by his fellow posse men. Sobbing, she covered his face with hysterical kisses.

The marshal looked away, his mouth a bitter

18

gash. Finally, he glared down at Jodee where she lay on the travois. "I must know who you are, miss."

Was he making fun of her? Nobody called her miss.

He gave the lad an exasperated look. "She won't tell me her name."

When had he asked her name? She couldn't remember him asking. She didn't dare answer. She didn't trust her voice. She didn't want him to know how scared she was.

The lad hunkered down to look at Jodee eye to eye. His eyes danced. Blue as mountain lake water. "I ain't never seen a girl outlaw before. Was you maybe a captive of them thievin' men?"

With all her strength, Jodee held back tears. She wasn't going to cry in front of this boy, or the marshal or the gawking people standing around. She shook her head and whispered, "He was my pa."

"Who, Cloyd Rike?" the marshal demanded.

That old buzzard, she thought in disgust. "T. T. McQue," she said, sounding a bit stronger than she felt. "He was my pa."

She watched a strange stiffness settle over the marshal's face.

The lad rocked back on his heels. "Well, howdy-do, Miss McQue. How old are you?"

What did that matter? she wondered. She wished she were dead. All she could think about was how her father had looked that final night, winking at her from across the campfire, bewhiskered and grinning, wrinkled as an old shoe. After the holdup the following morning when he didn't return with the others, Burl threw it in her face that her father had been stupid and gotten himself shot dead. She hadn't believed it. She couldn't believe it. She didn't know what to do. She wasn't going back home. That was certain. Desperate, she had followed Burl and those hated, mangy Rikes to that mountain cabin.

Now she was gunshot and too weak to think straight. She felt like she was going to bust open.

"How old are you?" the lad asked again.

"Twenty in the summer," she mumbled. It was a lie. She had turned eighteen the fall before.

He extended his hand but realized she didn't have the strength to shake it. He gave her a sympathetic smile. "My name's Hobie Fenton. I'll be sixteen come summer. Fell out of the barn loft when I was four. Broke my arm. I ain't never been gunshot. Does it hurt?" He craned his neck to view her wound. It was covered with a bandage.

The marshal pinned Hobie with a ferocious frown.

"Yes'r, Marshal?" Hobie straightened with a hint of embarrassment in his rosy cheeks. A gust of snowy wind ruffled his badly barbered hair.

"When you get back from Munjoys, sweep

out the north cell. I'll put Miss McQue in there."

Hobie's mouth fell open to reveal crooked teeth. "Uh, but . . . uh, y—yes'r."

Jail? Jodee fought to sit up. She wouldn't go. He couldn't make her. She hadn't done anything. Didn't he understand that?

Taking off at a run, Hobie disappeared into a nearby store bearing the ornate signboard, *Photographs*. Moments later a man in a blue vest trotted out carrying a wooden box camera on long spindly legs. Hobie followed, carrying a T-shaped contraption on a stick.

A stocky man strolled from the nearby restaurant, wiping his mouth with the back of his hand. He wore a deputy's badge but had weasel eyes like Burl's. "I kept the town buttoned up for you real tight while you was gone, Marshal."

The marshal stepped closer to Jodee, almost as if protecting her. "Prop the outlaws' bodies over there, Hicks. For photographs."

"You did a bang-up job, all right, bringin' 'em back alive." Hicks sauntered away. "I'm real impressed."

The marshal watched the man, his eyes narrowed to slits, his lips white.

Jodee watched Hicks prop the bodies against the jailhouse porch. There lay old man Rike, his long grey beard fluttering in the wind. And his three mangy sons, ugly as butchered hogs. It was too much to comprehend. She wasn't sorry the

Rikes were dead, not a whit, but it was jarring to see men she had known for two years frozen in eternal sleep like that, all four of them. Stiff as cord wood. The photographer stuck his head under a black drape on the back of the box camera with legs. A blinding explosion came from the contraption Hobie held. Townspeople closed in for a better look at the dead outlaws.

"Show's over, folks," the marshal announced. "Go on about your business."

A portly man with a handlebar mustache pushed forward from the crowd. He shielded his eyes from swirling snow. "Hungry, Marshal?"

Pressing a hand to his belly, he looked disgusted at the thought of eating. "But get a meal together for Miss McQue here, if you would. She hasn't eaten in two days or more."

When he turned back to scowl at her, Jodee averted her eyes.

"Is it true you're T. T. McQue's daughter?" he asked with disbelief.

Forcing herself to meet his dark stare, Jodee told herself she must never trust him because she couldn't gauge what kind of man he was. If he knew her fear, he might use it against her. Even abuse her, maybe.

She studied the way his tanned skin lay so smooth across his cheekbones. His chestnut hair tossed in the wind. She felt like she was drowning in those coffee dark eyes. It took her breath away to have him stare at her like maybe he could read her thoughts easy as print. Something akin to heat lightning went through her body. But he was taking her to jail. He hadn't even asked if she'd done anything to deserve it. He had to be a bad man. She had to expect the worst from him.

"Can you stand, Miss McQue?"

Determined to get away by whatever means possible, Jodee used all her strength to swing her legs over the edge of the travois. They felt like logs. She would dash to that alley over there, run into the shadows—but her muscles betrayed her. They felt like jelly. She struggled to push herself upright, frightened by her weakness. Her knees wouldn't hold.

Before she collapsed, the lawman swept her into his arms. Her shoulder went molten with pain.

Despite her feeble protests, the marshal drew her close to his chest, closer than need be, she thought, fighting him. She felt one strong arm behind her back and another beneath her knees. She wanted to lay her cheek against his shoulder, but she held herself stiff as a plank while he carried her inside out of the wind. The jailhouse smelled of gun oil and wood smoke. She struggled to be set on her feet, but the marshal ducked through an iron doorway and maneuvered her inside a small cell.

"I didn't do anything." she whispered, pushing at his chest. "I didn't."

"I'm sorry if I'm hurting you, Miss McQue, but you can't stay at the hotel, and I couldn't see leaving you to freeze in the street." Gently he lowered her onto a canvas cot against the rear stone wall.

"I'm not an outlaw." She twisted away. He mustn't see her tears. They were blinding her now.

"Hobie," he called, watching as she tried to get off the cot. "Fetch that knapsack from the travois. Then fetch a blanket and pillow from the hotel. What I have here won't do."

Looking reluctant to miss the marshal's interrogation, Hobie plodded out. When he returned with her knapsack, Jodee tried to snatch it away but couldn't reach it. She felt faint. What was going to happen to her? Without her father to protect her, she didn't know how to act. She watched the marshal lift the knapsack's frayed flap and pull out a battered book from inside. Brows furrowed, he turned it over as if he had never seen a book before.

"*Freestone Third-Year Speller*," he read the title.

"I found it." Her voice sounded far away. She'd found that book alongside a road, she thought, years before. East Texas, maybe. Did that count as stealing? Did that make her a thief? Every stitch of clothing she was wearing—the shirt, the snug britches—she'd snatched from some farmwife's wash line because her old clothes had worn out. And the boots—

Tarnation . . . she *was* a thief! There was no more fooling herself about it. She gasped for breath. He thought she was bad because she was bad. She was every bad thing folks had ever thought of her.

Opening the speller, the marshal read the name scrawled on the flyleaf: *Jodeen Marilee Latham McQue.* She'd been playing schoolhouse the day she wrote that. She'd been, what, thirteen years old? How foolish that seemed now.

"This is your name? Jodeen?"

"Jodee for short," she said softly.

Putting the book aside, the marshal rummaged and pulled out a folded white handkerchief from the depths of the knapsack. Jodee tried to take it from him, but he held it out of reach, scowling suspiciously. Inside the folds was a round gold locket with a broken chain. "Is this yours or taken during a robbery?" His eyes drilled holes into her soul.

"Don't think to keep that," she warned in a gruff tone. "That's mine."

If only she could slap him, she thought, shivering with rage. What right did he have to go through her things? But she wasn't stupid. She watched him pry open the locket with his thumbnail and peer closely at the tiny likeness framed inside. That was her private memento, she thought bitterly. Her breath came hard and fast, making her dizzy.

"I suppose you're going to tell me this is your mother."

Her throat tightened. "Yes."

If she had her pistol she would've shot him dead—except she'd never shot at a man. Not even Burl Tangus. She balled her fists.

"Let me get this straight." He cocked his head and looked hard at her. "The outlaw T. T. McQue was your father. That makes you an outlaw's daughter in possession of a real gold locket that you claim isn't stolen." He raised his brows in question. "You're certain this is yours? Not some-thing bought with stolen money?"

"I was wearing that when—"

She bit back her reply. She didn't have to tell him anything. Her father said never to talk to the law. Lawmen assumed things, same as every-body she had ever known.

With a sigh of exasperation, the marshal snapped the locket closed. After a downcast moment he slipped it into his shirt pocket. He reached inside the knapsack and dragged out a wad of thread-bare muslin. He held it up like a rag. "Yours, too?"

She looked away, overwhelmed with shame.

Putting the knapsack out of reach, he straight-ened to his full looming height and shook out the fabric. It was a torn, stained bed dress about the size a child of twelve would wear. For years she wore it under a shirt of her father's until it became so snug it gave way under the arms.

Clenching his jaw, the marshal watched her, waiting for what he expected would be an unconvincing story.

When she finally met his eyes, she said with burning defiance, "The locket belonged to my ma." For some seconds she couldn't make another sound. She remembered finding it, taking it after the funeral. Finally, she choked out, "My grandmother made that bed dress. I was wearing them things when Pa came for me. I was twelve."

It looked like the marshal was turning the story over in his mind. He tipped his head down and glowered at her as if he could pull the truth out f her with the teeth of his eyes. "Twelve years old," he stated flatly. "What do you mean, when your father came for you?"

"I mean, I was living with my grandmother. Pa came for Ma, like he promised he would, except she was dead. He didn't know about me, so he took me instead. Carried me away on his horse. In the night."

She wasn't going to tell about peeing her bed dress because she was so scared of riding away with a man she'd never seen before. She couldn't say how her father laughed about it and kissed her out of pity and affection. And washed the bed dress himself in a creek while she hid in the bushes, shivering in his shirt. The marshal didn't need to know nothing about that.

"We tried farming for a while," she said, "Pa and me, but the soil was bad. We rented a little spread for a couple of years. The cattle got stole. I cooked for Pa, washed his clothes. Them others, Burl and the Rikes, they came later, after we run out of money and near to starved. Two years ago, about. I couldn't stop Pa from deciding to ride with them." She looked away. "I tried, but he wouldn't listen."

Crouching again, the marshal locked his eyes with her. *What now?* she wondered. The black part of his eyes got bigger. Reaching into her knapsack, pausing, eyes intense, he drew out a drawstring bag made of worn, stained buckskin. At first she didn't see what he had in his hand. She was looking into his eyes, feeling a shudder blossom deep, and steal through her body like—

From the corner of her eye she saw the bag. Rearing back, she hit the wall hard, trying to get away from it. She threw out her left hand, fingers spread, as if to ward off a blow.

"That ain't mine!"

The marshal dangled it in front of her, the ugly old thing, looking heavy and misshapen by its contents. He didn't say anything. He just stared at her.

"That's Burl's loot bag! I seen him with it a hundred times. It ain't mine. It ain't! I swear on my dead Pa—where'd you get it? It wasn't in *my* knapsack. I wouldn't touch the dirty ol' thing. He kept it down his pants. Always braggin' on it. Somebody else put it in my knapsack. You got to believe me, Marshal!"

He looked at her so hard she felt like she was falling.

She was about to launch into a tirade of hysterical self-defense when he stood abruptly, still holding the bag, and ducked out of the cell. He slammed the barred door closed with a resounding clang.

She looked after him, startled and terrified. He didn't believe her! "I ain't done nothin' to be locked up for! They didn't give me Pa's share. I don't have a thing. I swear it on my mother's grave!"

He stabbed a long iron key into the square iron lock and twisted. "Until I know different, Miss McQue, I have to assume you took part in that holdup that got the Ashton-Babcock stage driver killed."

Two

"Hobie," the marshal barked, causing Jodee to flinch.

The lad rushed inside, his face red with cold. He'd been waiting on the porch. "Yes, sir? It's snowing hard now, Marshal. I better get home."

"Fetch Doc on your way. Miss McQue needs her wound tended."

After Hobie ran out, Jodee watched the marshal pluck a printed circular from a stack of papers on his desk.

"Do you know this man, Miss McQue?" he asked, pointing to the drawing on the paper. "Burl Tangus was part of your father's gang. Was he at the stagecoach holdup at Ship Creek Crossing? Did he shoot at Avinelle Babcock?"

Her anger gave her strength. "I wasn't there," she snapped back. "I never went along on hold-ups. I stayed in camp. Always. I cooked for Pa. I listened to his stories. I washed his clothes, but I never robbed nobody. Pa wasn't an outlaw for most of the years we were together, not until them others came along, the Rikes and Burl Tangus. And it wasn't Pa's gang, not like you mean. It was Burl's. You want to know who planned the holdups? Burl planned them." She fell back, holding her blazing shoulder. She hoped Burl had fallen off a mountain. She hoped he lay dead in a gorge. "Marshal, I don't feel right."

The marshal slammed outside, leaving the jailhouse door open. Cold air swept in and blew wanted circulars all over the floor. What was he so mad about, she wondered. She was the one behind bars.

With him out of sight, Jodee didn't have to hold

30

back her tears. As she wept helplessly, she felt ashamed for being so afraid. Her hair was a tangle, her britches dirty, her shirt torn and bloody. "Prairie rat," Burl liked to call her. That's what she was, all right, grinding her fists into her eyes.

"He's a good man, the marshal," Hobie said, closing the door against the cold and gathering up the scattered circulars. "He's gone over to the stage office. He won't keep you in jail long. He's just being careful."

Jodee had forgotten the lad Hobie was still there. She dashed away her tears.

Then the restaurant owner pushed inside, carrying a cloth-covered tray. Snowflakes stood on his freshly oiled hair. "Out of my way, boy. It's snowing to beat the band out there." He winked at Jodee and kicked the door closed. "The name's Artie Abernathy. Miss McQue, is it? Knock me over with a plank. Ain't nobody ever heard of ol' T. T. McQue possessing a daughter. I remember hearing his name way back, ten years maybe. You're a daughter, you say? Not a little filly friend?"

He placed the tray on the floor in front of her cell door and then stood grinning at her expectantly, his paunch straining against his apron.

Jodee didn't like knowing her father had been an outlaw during the years he'd been apart from her mother. She didn't like knowing they'd lived on stolen money those first few years together. And she'd told him so when she figured it out. She wished she had the strength now to climb from the cot. She wanted to kick the tray. Filly friend. Is that what they thought of her?

Realizing she was not going to respond to his humor, Abernathy exchanged a few words with Hobie and plodded outside, shaking his head.

"Thinks he's the funniest man in town," Hobie grumbled. He poured Jodee a cup of coffee and added several pinches of sugar from a cloth sack. Bringing it to the cell door, he set the steaming tin cup on the tray. "I make the best coffee in town. Even Ma says so."

The savory smells tantalized Jodee. She couldn't remember when she had last eaten. Painfully, she climbed to her feet and stood a moment, trying to maintain balance. Her head spun. Did Hobie have to humiliate her like this, watching her? Then she realized her shirt was torn half off her shoulder. A strip of cotton cloth stretched across her chest and around her back, holding a bandage in place over her wounded shoulder. A tantalizing patch of pale flesh was exposed above her breast.

Hobie's face turned scarlet, but he didn't look away.

With her left hand, Jodee clutched her shirt closed and forced herself to focus on the food. *There would be time enough to think about getting away,* she told herself. She had to get her strength back.

"I'd bring the tray inside to you, Miss McQue," Hobie said, sounding sheepish, "but the marshal would skin me alive if you got out."

Miss McQue, indeed, she thought. They didn't fool her. To them she was trash. From the time she had been very small, folks had considered her trash. "My name," she said in a gruff tone, "is just plain Jodee."

Sinking to the floor in a cross-legged heap, she waited until the explosive pain in her shoulder subsided. With her left hand, she plucked away the napkin covering the tray. *Oh,* she gave a cry at the sight of the food. Pan-fried chicken. A wing and a drumstick, golden brown to perfection. Smelling like pure heaven. Feather light biscuits dripping in butter. Three of them. Mashed white potatoes, swimming in cream gravy. And a misshapen sugar cookie sparkling with crushed sugar.

Jodee could scarcely breathe for the choke of tears in her throat. Like a starving child, she grabbed the chicken leg, inhaled the aroma of it and then bit, savoring the first splash of flavor flooding her mouth. Memories assailed her. The farmhouse kitchen, her pretty mother sitting across the kitchen table from her, the smell of chicken sizzling in her grandmother's iron skillet. Jodee felt as if she were five years old again, safe and sound, with her mother's love protecting her.

Unable to endure Hobie's rapt stare, Jodee twisted away. As she chewed, tears poured down her cheeks. It was the first decent food she'd eaten in six years.

As dawn brought pale light to the inside of Burdeen's jailhouse, Jodee dragged herself from a troubled sleep. She found herself covered with a fresh-smelling hotel blanket. Through the iron bars she could see the marshal's desk. Behind it stood a wooden shelf sagging with stacks of paper and books. No curtain hung at the shuttered window. The chair beside the door had one short leg. She studied how the iron bars stood between herself and an outhouse and wondered where the marshal was.

It seemed strange not to have morning chores awaiting her, no campfire to rebuild, no coffee pot to scrub clean with creek sand. There were no shaggy horses to tend, no outlaws snoring in bedrolls, no plans for holdups to aggravate her, no loot for the Rikes and Burl to squabble over.

No father to wake.

A rage of grief swept over Jodee so overwhelming she couldn't stand it. From the moment Burl and the others had ridden into camp without her father after the holdup, she hadn't had a moment to think. They fled westward up the nearest trail, and she'd been driven to follow because she couldn't risk being caught by a posse. They rode their horses near to death and then found that tumbledown cabin. Now she was in jail, gunshot and helpless.

With her mind reeling in anger and fear, Jodee heard a soft sleepy snort. She got hold of her panic and wondered if the marshal was sleeping nearby. A strange, not entirely unpleasant flutter went through her stomach as she thought of the marshal lying in bed in the jailhouse addition. What kind of life did a man like that lead, sleeping in a jailhouse?

Rolling over, she reminded herself she hated him.

But he had put a roof over her head . . . and she'd had that meal the night before. She'd slept under a clean blanket with a real feather pillow. Nobody had pestered her in the darkness. All winter she'd lived, cooped up with those worthless Rikes, sleeping in a dirty shack, listening to their crude talk and dodging their sly looks. And Burl Tangus had made no secret of what he thought she was good for.

Another snort.

Jodee sat up, shaking.

What if it was that sly-eyed deputy asleep in the other room? She heard someone throw off cover and climb to his feet with soft rustling sounds. Then she heard the thump of boots and finally footsteps crossing almost stealthily to the door. A door just out of sight swung wide. Jodee's heart stood still. She saw a man's shadow in the dim morning light as he moved into the main room. Her heart began thundering.

It was the marshal. Jodee sagged with relief. She watched him prop up the inside window shutter with a stick and push the outside window shutters open. Cold, fresh-smelling air tinged with the pleasant aroma of wood smoke rushed in. She watched him breathe deeply and stretch his arms wide.

Glancing back, he realized she was awake and watching him. "Didn't snow much," he said, looking taken aback by her stare.

She thrilled to the sound of his deep voice. Was there ever a more wonderful face than that? She couldn't tear her eyes away. Sleep had softened his expression to something kinder than the day before. Perhaps he'd just been tired.

Pulling up a heavy plank bar from the door with a rope he hooked to the side, the marshal was about to go out when he glanced sidelong at her. A peculiar expression crossed his face and reddened his neck. Quickly he went for the key hanging next to a rack of rifles. He unlocked her cell and held out his hand. "Excuse me, Miss McQue." He glanced at the unused chamber pot beneath her cot. His ears got red, too.

Jodee's face grew hot, as well. She should've guessed he would've provided all she needed, but damned if she'd use the convenience in so public a place as a jailhouse cell. She climbed to her feet, relieved to feel stronger. Her broken-toed boots stood at the end of the cot like two drunks. On her feet were thick white store-bought socks. She didn't own socks. Hadn't in years. She wiggled her toes.

"I'm glad to see you can stand," he said as he watched her poke her feet into her boots. Then he grasped her hand and took a steadying hold of her left elbow as she faltered while coming through the cell's doorway. "Take it easy. It'll take a while for you to get your strength back."

She didn't remember anyone taking her boots off. Or putting socks on her feet. Maybe he was looking for hidden money. She couldn't remember the last time someone had done her a kindness like that. Not even her father. She wondered what the undertaker had found in the Rikes' boots. She wondered if she should say something about it, but held her tongue.

The marshal kept a firm hold on her as they crossed to the door. She felt like an invalid. He probably expected she'd try to bolt. Instead, all she could manage was to put one foot in front of the other.

Outside, Jodee shivered in the cold. The snowy street was marked with wagon tracks and footprints. One set of footprints came straight to the jail's porch, then on to the next building, disappearing among wheel tracks down the street.

Frowning, the marshal looked up the street and down, into alleyways and open spaces between buildings, even at the roof of the stage office across the way, his body tensed, his palm settling on his holstered pistol. Then he started along the porch, still holding her elbow. He scarcely seemed to know she was there as he considered the tracks.

Was Burl rock-brained enough to come to town? Jodee wondered. She looked around uneasily, too.

"They're burying the Rikes this morning," the marshal said. "Will you want to go?"

"I got no feeling for them outlaws, Marshal," she said, still using her gruff tone. "It's on their account my pa's . . . ." She couldn't say the word. Feeling light-headed with the risk, she finally said, "Somebody checked their pockets, right? And their boots? You? The undertaker?"

He nodded, his expression thoughtful.

Relieved, she followed him around to an outhouse in back near a plank fence. Beyond the fence was the back of a two-story hotel flanked by the backs of saloons. A woman stood in an upstairs window brushing out long brown hair.

"Why, Marshal," she called in a sultry singsong. "Good morning to ya!"

He shot Jodee an irritated, possibly embarrassed look.

"Who you got there? I ain't never seen a cowhand with long yaller hair like that."

"Mornin', Rella," the marshal muttered. He rubbed the back of his neck.

Jodee shut herself inside the outhouse. Did the marshal know that kind? The woman was still watching when she came out.

"You must be Burdeen's new female desperado I heard tell of last night." The woman howled with laughter. "Everybody's talkin' about you, honey. She looks mighty dangerous, Marshal. Are we safe in our beds?"

"Pay her no mind, Miss McQue," the marshal said softly.

"Hey, little desperado," the woman called more loudly. "There's work for you here whenever you need it. When he lets you out, come on over."

"Pipe down, Rella."

"It must've been hard, sleeping near that wildcat all night, locked up so tight in her cold little cell." Rella's laughter echoed. "Did you warm her up, Marshal?"

The marshal took Jodee's elbow and steered her back around to the front of the jailhouse. "You all right?"

"How can I prove I never took part in holdups?" Jodee asked, trying to jerk free.

He didn't let go. "That's for the judge to decide."

"Judge! But I—"

39

"Miss McQue," the marshal said with exaggerated patience. "There was a stagecoach holdup. You were found with the outlaws who committed that holdup. To my way of thinking, that makes you look mighty suspicious. Until I have proof different, you'll stay in my jail."

"You're no better than a bullheaded outlaw yourself if you can't see I never done a wrong thing in my life except get myself born to an outlaw."

He studied her until she felt so squirmy she had to look away. How did he manage to make her feel so worthless? She twisted free of his hold.

Before he could take hold of her again, the pregnant matron from the afternoon before shouted from across the street, "Marshal Harlow, I want a word with you." Holding a shawl around her shoulders, she stepped into the melting snow and mud and waddled across the street.

The marshal looked like his face ached. "Won't you come inside, Patsy? I must get my prisoner back to her cell."

"Prisoner—" The woman gaped at Jodee. "From now on I am Mrs. Virgil T. Robstart to you, Marshal Harlow. You're no longer a friend of mine." She preceded the marshal inside the jailhouse.

Hobie arrived just then to lay a fresh fire in the heating stove. His hair was damp, combed back from his forehead. "Mornin', Marshal. Miz

Robstart." Then he fastened his eager gaze on Jodee. "Mornin', Miss McQue."

"You can't keep a female prisoner in this jail," Mrs. Robstart went on indignantly. She turned her attention to Hobie. "And you certainly can't keep a female prisoner with an impressionable young boy like Hobie Fenton hanging around."

"I'm not hanging around, Miz Robstart," Hobie exclaimed. "I work here. It took weeks to convince Ma to let me."

"I'll just see what your mother thinks when she finds out the marshal is keeping women in here. Get yourself to school before I skin you alive."

Hobie stood his ground.

"Now, Patsy—" the marshal began.

Like a rattler, she swung on him. "I spent a desperate night with Virgil. I didn't want him to go on that posse. You knew that. Then you bring him back to me, shot. You said you'd bring those outlaws back alive to stand trial, but you brought back four dead bodies and a female outlaw." She squinted at Jodee, took a few steps closer and gasped at the gaping rent in Jodee's shirt. "Are you all right? Has the marshal mistreated you?"

"I'm not an outlaw, Ma'am," Jodee said in her most polite tone. She wondered if there was any hope the woman might take pity on her. "At least he got me to the privy in time."

Mrs. Robstart sputtered. "The town will be in

41

an uproar, Corbet! Git, Hobie, or I'll speak to your mother."

"Don't you go costin' me my job, Miz Robstart," the lad said. "Ma needs the cash money I earn. Miss McQue ain't gettin' out of jail while I'm in charge—I mean, w—when the marshal goes on his rounds. No girl outlaw is goin' to turn my head to the wrong side of the law."

"Oh, for heaven's sakes, Corbet, listen to him."

The marshal's forehead lifted into furrows. "Virgil wanted to go on the posse."

"Doc says there's infection. Virgil won't be able to work for weeks. He could die. Didn't you ever think of that? Didn't you give me a thought? Or are you so dedicated to your precious job—and by that I mean to say dedicated to Avinelle Babcock, that you—"

"Virgil's a grown man and a damned capable one," the marshal cut in. "I took him along because he was—is—my best deputy."

"I hold you responsible, Corbet." Mrs. Robstart jabbed a finger at Jodee. "And you. Your people shot at Avinelle Babcock, killed a driver. It makes a body sick."

"If anything happens to Virgil," the marshal said gravely, "I'll look after you and the baby."

"If anything—now isn't that just dandy. If my husband dies you'll take care of us. Well, thank you very much, but I'd rather have my husband.

Alive and well!" Mrs. Robstart turned on her heel, her voice betraying rising tears. "Maybe it's true what folks say." She stalked out, leaving her words hanging in the air.

The marshal rubbed the back of his neck again. "What do folks say about me, Hobie?"

Jodee watched the lad's cheeks redden. "Aw, Marshal."

"Just tell me. I won't hold it against you."

The lad edged toward the door. "I'd best be gettin' to school." At the last minute he turned back. "I'm proud to sweep your floors, Marshal. Folks don't know you like I come to. Any night of the week some rowdy could shoot you dead. It ain't easy to leave that behind and go to a church social and be all polite and friendly to the ladies. It isn't the way of a lawman."

The marshal's mouth twisted into a rueful smile. "Thanks, Hobie." He clapped the lad on the shoulder.

Abruptly the marshal followed Hobie outside. Jodee couldn't hear what he said. For several minutes, the lad paced as if on guard. She heard a stagecoach rattle past with its six-horse team flinging muddy snow behind the big rear wheels.

"That's the early stage, Miss McQue," Hobie called inside to her, pointing. "Headed back to Cheyenne City. Ma says I'll be on it someday."

"I could be on it right now and gone forever,"

Jodee said back, thinking the lad might be persuaded to help her get away.

Returning, the marshal pushed past Hobie and came inside. "Got money for a ticket, Miss McQue?"

Jodee wished he hadn't heard her.

Before he could be scolded again, Hobie loped off to school. "I left enough wood to last the day, Marshal. I'll bring in more after school."

The marshal slammed the door against the cold. "How were you planning to ride out of town, Miss McQue, holding the driver at gunpoint? Have you and your kind ever considered work?"

Jodee turned away. What did he know of her life? As far as she could remember, she had worked every day of it. And in the shadow of her outlaw father. She sank onto the cot, too overwhelmed to hold her shirt closed over the bandage. No wonder her father had taken to thieving, she thought. Sometimes stealing was the only way to survive.

The marshal was just bringing a wash basin and water pitcher to her cell when the woman called Rella barged in.

"Ready to scrub up your little prisoner?" Rella called, grinning. Holding up a wad of flowered fabric, Rella winked at Jodee. "This here marshal come over to my place just now to say to me that you need a hair comb and something girly to wear. This might do." She pushed the flowered silk dressing gown between the bars. As it slithered to the floor, Jodee glared at it. It smelled of cigar smoke and whiskey.

After the marshal placed the basin on the floor beside the cell door, he handed Rella the key. Quickly he retreated outside

Rella gave a hoot. "Would you look at that, all gentlemanly and foolish-like. Don't you just love him? Big damn fool. He don't come near me or my girls. Too good for the likes of us, I reckon."

Jodee stood from her cot, grabbed up the dressing gown and stuffed it back through the bars. "I don't wear such like."

Rella fished a comb from her pocket. She stopped grinning. "Well, ain't you the prickly one. You'll find out, honey. Ain't a person in this town will ever accept the daughter of a stage-robbin' outlaw." Rella tossed the comb and key into Jodee's cell. "When you're desperate enough, honey, just give me a shout. I'll help you. I'll set you up right nice. Room of your own. Clean bed sheets. In a year you'll be rich."

After she waltzed out of the jailhouse, Jodee stared at the key. She was still standing there when the marshal came back in.

"Just 'cause my pa was an outlaw," Jodee yelled, picking up the key and handing it to him, "don't mean I'm her kind."

The marshal stared at her.

Taking the comb, she staggered back to the cot

and dropped onto it, exhausted. She began working at her tangles with the comb. Her right arm felt molten again, worse than before. Rella had been right. She'd never be accepted, not here, not anywhere. And she'd never go home. What was she going to do?

Three

Usually, by two o'clock in the morning, Marshal J. Corbet Harlow had finished his last circuit of Burdeen's streets and alleyways. Then he liked to sleep until eight or nine o'clock the next morning. After finishing Hobie's jail-brewed coffee he might go for a shave at Hamm's barbershop and make another round before lunch at Abernathy's restaurant. But on account of having Miss McQue in his jail, he hadn't gone out the night before. He didn't want to leave her alone in case Tangus tried to break her out. Tangus was a dangerous man. Corbet wanted him in custody, alive. Jodee, too.

Feeling irritable, Corbet sat at his desk, studying Ben Nobley's battered gold pocket watch. Miss McQue sat on her cot, still struggling with her tangled hair. After a few attempts she let her left arm drop. Patsy was right. He shouldn't keep a female in his jail, but what was he supposed to do?

He thought about the items already recovered from the outlaws he'd killed and brought back to town. Depot agent Ben Nobley's nickle-plated watch and pocketbook. The Ashton Babcock agent from back east—Chester M. Clarkson—his engraved gold pocket watch, stick pin and pocketbook, torn. No sign of his sapphire pinkie ring. Avinelle's cash box, still locked, and most of her jewelry. Her mother's things. The cash was at the bank, some still missing, but he'd figure that out soon enough. He scooped everything into his desk drawer and locked it.

Miss McQue needed the doctor, he thought, pocketing the desk key. Stronger men than that scrap of a girl had died of gunshot wounds. He couldn't just turn her loose. She might yet tell him more about Tangus.

When Abernathy arrived with another tray, Corbet seized his chance. "You're in charge—I'll be right back." He grabbed his hat. "If you see Hicks, tell him I need him here, and sober."

Before Abernathy could protest, Corbet was out the door. He plowed headlong into a homely stranger scarcely taller than Hobie. The man grabbed his bowler hat and grinned, "Whoa there, Marshal." His pock-marked face sported a day's whiskers. His trousers and coat were green plaid, dull as dead cactus. He carried an imitation leather sample case.

A half dozen drovers swarmed past, too, boldly crowding Corbet into the street. There had been a time when Corbet knew every face in town.

There had been a time, he thought, glowering at the drovers, *when folks showed him respect and stepped aside when he passed.* Now families arrived from the southern states and back east. Cow hands, salesmen, and telegraph linemen packed the streets, but Corbet rarely encountered troublemakers now. He had enough money saved he could buy a few acres north of town if he wanted, but he hadn't signed his name to a bill of sale yet. Buying land meant staying. Staying meant Avinelle Babcock had him in a harness.

He could do worse, he reminded himself.

At the stage office, Corbet came up short. He should've asked that green-clad drummer's name. Just because he pictured Tangus as tall and wearing pistols didn't mean he should ignore bandy-legged strangers in ill-fitting bowler hats.

After sending his morning's telegraph messages, Corbet scanned the street, spotting the cactus green among the brown and dusty black that townsfolk wore. He veered toward the cluster of ladies surrounding the grinning, talkative stranger displaying his wares. Button salesman. Annoyed by the distraction, Corbet hurried on, dismissing the man from his mind. Moments later he found the doctor's office closed. *At the Robstarts,* was scrawled on a slate hanging alongside the locked door.

Taking chalk dangling on a string, Corbet wrote, *Come to jail soon as you can. Urgent!*

He stormed on toward the barbershop. What was he going to do about Miss McQue? He had no reason to hold her. He himself found the buckskin bag on the cabin floor when he lifted her into his arms. At the time he'd thought the bag must be hers. He'd stuffed it in her knapsack, but he believed her now when she vowed on her dead parents she hadn't been part of the holdup. Besides, Nobley and Clarkson both swore in their statements in Cheyenne City that six men robbed them, not seven. Jodee McQue would've made seven.

Should he turn her out? What would she do then, serve hash to cowhands at Artie's? Dodge drunkards at the Whitetail Saloon? "Board" at Rella's?

He caught sight of himself in a storefront window, a tall scowling man with no friends. He admitted to himself why he was keeping such a close eye on his female prisoner. To him, the most important thing was to protect those too weak to protect themselves. In doing his bang-up job as marshal, he had shot a defenseless girl.

Well, she hadn't been entirely defenseless. She'd had that heavy old pistol and plenty of spunk.

Corbet plunged on, racked with regret. She looked so darned cute in those britches that clung to her backside like his hands wanted to—he immediately banished that thought. He'd never seen a woman wearing pants. The sight tended to keep a man awake at night.

It wasn't only that. It was her sun-colored hair, wild around her face like she'd been romping in a haymow. It was those eyes, big and blue and baffled by the cruel world she'd been born to. And that tear in her shirt wasn't helping matters. Best send her on her way. Buy the ticket himself. Good riddance.

At the barbershop Corbet sank into the cracked leather chair that stood prominently in the single front window, affording barber Walter Hamm a full view of the street.

"I need a trim, too," Corbet said.

"Glad to see you back from your man-hunt, Marshal. Glad them outlaws is gettin' planted today, too. I hear Virgil Robstart is crazy with fever."

"If you see Doc, tell him I got a wounded prisoner who needs attention." He wanted to quiet the barber so he could think.

Walter's eyes flashed. "I hear she's a regular spitfire."

Corbet wouldn't have described Jodee McQue quite like that, but then, he hadn't known her long. She seemed more like a lost kitten. "Who said that of her?"

"It's all over town she rode with them hell-rakes like she was born to it. Would make quite an attraction, hangin' a female in this town."

Corbet pushed the barber's razor from his face. "A *man* shot the stage driver, Walter, not a woman. She wasn't there. Nobley and Clarkson as well as Mrs. Ashton and Mrs. Babcock said so. Sworn statements. The first I knew of her was when I waded through outlaws I gunned down and found her bleeding on the floor. She hasn't done anything to be hanged for, for God's sake."

Grabbing a towel, Corbet wiped the lather from his face and hurled himself back into the morning cold without his shave. Hang her? Where did this town's sudden blood thirst come from? This was not what he had been planning to do when he'd headed west. It certainly wasn't what he was going to be doing for the rest of his life. Maybe it was time to move on. Let some other puppet dance at the end of the Ashton-Babcock tether.

With relief, Corbet saw the doctor trudging up from the direction of the Robstart's cabin. "You better head for the jail, Doc," he called in a none-too-pleasant tone.

The weary man looked up. "Delirious?"

"No, but she needs that dressing changed." Corbet's belly knotted. Virgil must be bad off.

The doctor passed Corbet. "Change it yourself. I have to get to my office for more supplies. I'll be catching Patsy's baby tonight if she doesn't let up."

The man from the restaurant stood watching Jodee so intently she couldn't go on trying to comb her hair. What was his name? Artie? Sitting on the cot with her head down, her hair thrown forward because she had been working at the knots in back, she muttered, "What's so interesting to look at?" Maybe her gruff tone would put him off.

Artie Abernathy looked to be around Burl's age, late twenties, Jodee thought. His hairline receded to ginger curls. His mustache was a clumsy attempt at a handle-bar style which accentuated the pale fullness of his face, but he looked nice enough.

"I've been cooking around here almost four years," he said grinning. He settled his haunch onto the corner of the marshal's desk, tipping it slightly. "Started out cooking in a tent. You know, I can't believe it's in a woman's nature to run with outlaws. You were forced into it, ain't that right, Miss McQue?"

Before Jodee could answer, the hard-eyed Deputy Hicks sauntered in. "What the hell'r you doin' here, Abernathy?"

Artie straightened and brushed the front of his apron. "You weren't here, so the marshal asked me to watch over Miss McQue."

Deputy Hicks rolled his tongue around his teeth. "Well, I'm here now." He winked at Jodee.

Jodee shrank back, loathing the sight of the man.

"Anything special you'd like for lunch, Miss McQue?" Abernathy shuffled toward the door.

Jodee shook her head. As Abernathy went out, she noticed a man in a black bowler hat passing by outside. The man looked in, straight at her,and then strutted on. She didn't recognize the clean-shaven face but she knew that walk. Shaking, and feeling sick, she pressed herself against the wall. That was Burl! But clean-shaven and wearing a green suit? It couldn't be. Was he crazy? Surely Burl was a hundred miles away by now.

When she opened her eyes, Hicks stood at her cell door, blocking the view of the open door.

"What's ailin' you? In them britches, a person'd take you for a saddle tramp, excepting for that long hair. And certain other things. Need some help combing that hair?"

When she didn't reply, he kicked the bars with a dirty boot.

"I'm talking to you. Ever been down Cheyenne City way?" He spat a stream of tobacco juice into the corner.

Jodee knew better than to speak.

He pulled a flask from his hip pocket and took a long pull. Whiskey that early in the morning meant nothing but trouble. "I used to frequent a gal down Cheyenne way had hair like yours. You got any connections with that line of work?"

She hoped she looked fierce. Gun shot and without a weapon, she had no defense against a man like him. At the slightest sign of weakness, the deputy would have her cell door unlocked, doing what came natural to vermin.

"Come to think of it, you smell like you ain't had a bath in a year. Ten dollars says I meet up with you at Rella's one of these nights. You'll smell better then."

Jodee twisted away. She had cleaned up at the hideout camp, but that had been days ago. She'd traveled many a mile since. She listened while the deputy rifled through the marshal's desk drawers and yanked hard at one that was locked. She heard him saunter into the sleeping room and browse through things he had no business touching. She felt indignant on the marshal's behalf.

Finally the deputy dropped onto the chair behind the marshal's desk and tipped it against the wall. When the jailhouse door opened, Jodee's hopes lifted.

"Hard at work, I see, Hicks," a stranger said.

"I do more work than you any day of the week. Sniffin' out a story, are ya', Inky? Well, there she is, our very own lady outlaw, but you'll find little to grab the attention of readers. She's as boring as slop and about as pretty."

"How would you know what might interest my readers?"

Warily, Jodee sat up. She pushed her torn shirt back into place.

The newcomer was an attractive man in a striped shirt and high-buttoned coat jacket. He swept off his hat. "I hope I'm not disturbing you, Miss McQue. I'm George Hatcher, *Burdeen City Dispatch*. It's only a one page newspaper, but I have ambitions. May I ask a few questions? I promise to be fair."

"Fair about what?"

"Why, in presenting your case to the public. How is it you came to be riding with those outlaws after the holdup?" Moving closer to the cell, he plucked a tablet from his breast pocket and stood poised with pencil, ready to write. "You might make a name for yourself back East if your story's interesting."

"Better make one up then, 'cause it ain't."

Hicks snickered. "Spoken like a real lady."

"Tell me where you hail from, Miss McQue," Mr. Hatcher said. "I heard you were born of a red-haired lady of the evening in San Francisco."

"Who told you that?"

"I hear you're every bit as violent as the men you rode with, that you helped plan robberies and even pulled a few yourself dressed as a schoolgirl."

Jodee struggled to stand. "That's a lie!"

"Then tell me your story so I can set the record straight. I can't begin to describe the harm you're doing to your reputation, staying in this cell without benefit of a lawyer. If you're innocent, why're you being held?"

She glared at the newspaperman, knowing she dared not trust him. But what could she do when folks were spreading lies about her? The lies sounded like things Burl Tangus might say just to be mean.

"I was born in Arkansas." She watched him scribble. "How do I know what you're writing?"

"I'll bring a copy of the story straight from the press. Can you read, Miss McQue?"

"Of course I can read. I went to school. I attended Sunday school, too, if that matters to you. I can recite and cipher and sign my name."

"And you're a dead shot with a pistol, they say."

"A body gets hungry enough, she can shoot near anything." Jodee could only manage to sit primly on the edge of the cot. "I grew up on a farm. I hunted eggs. I was learning to darn socks."

"Then one night outlaws raided your sleepy hometown, shot your family and captured you. You've been their prisoner ever since. Is that right, Miss McQue?"

Deputy Hicks kicked the chair by the door. "She weren't no prisoner, Inky. She is Miss McQue, as in T. T. McQue's own born daughter. That innocent-looking face of hers don't fool ol' Jimmy Hicks, here. You print that story—

eggs and Sunday school—I'll tell everybody it's a fool lie."

They didn't believe her. Jodee wilted. "You print lies about me," she hissed, "I'll come gunnin' for you." Too late she realized she sounded like an outlaw!

Before the newspaperman could retort, the door swung wide. By the thunderous expression on the marshal's face, he'd been listening on the far side of it for some time.

Ducking his chin into his collar, the newspaperman looked embarrassed to have been caught questioning the marshal's prisoner without him present. "I was just leaving, Marshal, but if you please, Miss McQue, one last question. Which man shot Willie Burstead during the holdup? The stagecoach driver."

"I don't know! I wasn't there."

"We hear Burl Tangus rode with your father and the Rikes. Nobody's seen him. Where is he? Is he coming for you?" the newspaperman asked.

Balling her fists, Jodee flinched as her shoulder blossomed with pain. "I ain't nothin' to Burl Tangus, so why would he come for me?"

She hoped Burl was gone, but she feared he was in town, following her, making up stories about her, waiting to break her out and steal her back to the outlaw life she hated so. Why would he bother?

"That's not what I heard. I heard you and him

had an understanding." Mr. Hatcher cocked his head, one eyebrow raised. "You're his girl."

Jodee struggled to her feet. The cell spun in front of her eyes, unsettling her stomach. Trembling, she advanced on the newspaperman, whose face lit with excitement. He stood poised on the other side of the bars, ready to write.

"I ain't nobody's girl, but I have to wonder who you been talking to. Maybe Burl Tangus hisself? Did he promise you a good story if you pestered me?"

Sputtering, Hatcher made his excuses to the marshal and fled the jailhouse. The marshal followed him outside. Jodee heard a heated exchange. When the marshal returned and sent Hicks away, he wore a turbulent expression. "Just tell me one thing, Miss McQue."

"Oh, please," she snapped. "I'm weary of all your polite talk. Just call me Jodee."

"Jodee," he said more gently, approaching her cell like she was a dangerous mountain cat. "What does Tangus looks like?"

Making her way back to the cot, she dropped onto it. "Runty man. Stringy dark hair, dirty beard, weasel eyes. Thinks he's as smart as a whip. Walks like he owns everything."

"Any chance he might be in Burdeen?"

Her heart leapt into her throat. Why would he ask that? Did she dare say what she suspected? "Honest, Marshal, on my ma's grave I ain't nothin' to Burl Tangus. He ain't nothin' to me. He turned Pa back to outlawing and ruined what chance we had for a decent life. I wished him dead more'n once, and that's a fact. That night when we were hiding at the cabin, I heard him brag that he shot the stage driver. They was laughing at him on account he couldn't bust some safe open. When he shot at it he claimed a bullet ricocheted and near to hit one of the ladies. He bragged how it made her jump and scream. She isn't dead, is she?"

The marshal pulled a telegraph message from his pocket. "The bullet tore through her clothes, she writes. Something like that would surely upset a woman like Avinelle Babcock. She was probably wearing something new. You say Tangus' face is pock-marked?"

He was baiting her, and she knew it. What a snake. "I never seen Burl without a beard. Don't you listen? He never took pains to look decent." She thought about the man she'd seen strutting past the doorway earlier. That couldn't have been Burl. Just a curious passerby.

The marshal unlocked her cell. She shrank from him, fearing her clothes smelled dirty like the deputy suggested.

"Take it easy, Jodee," he crooned, crouching. "I need a look at your wound. Doc's been up all night with my deputy and his wife, so I have to look after you myself."

59

Jodee shook her head. *I can't bear for you to touch me.* "I'm fine. Please."

He was so close she could see the flecks of gold and black in his eyes. Something melted inside her, leaving her tingling in ways she had never felt before. He looked back at her, caught momentarily, and he swallowed.

Oh, Marshal, she thought. *You are the damndest looking man I ever saw.*

"I'm keeping you here for your own safety, Jodee. You understand that, right? Until I have Tangus in custody, you're at risk."

"Burl don't care about me, I tell you."

"But you saw him shoot the driver." He held her gaze with electrifying intensity. "Your testimony could send him to the gallows."

"I told you," she said, with equal intensity. She fought to keep her lips from quivering. "I wasn't at the holdup. I didn't see him do nothing. I heard him talking about shooting the driver. Afterwards. At the cabin. Burl's in Cheyenne City or Denver by now, looking for some other fool like my pa to follow his schemes. He can't do things by himself. He needs men stupid enough to help him. To make him look big. I saw you got most of the loot back. Burl won't come after it. Why would he? He's gone. Even if he broke in here, I wouldn't go with him. I hate him. I've always hated him."

The marshal stared and stared and stared at her

60

until finally, blessedly, his gaze softened. "All right. Settle down. You're right. I've recovered almost everything taken during the holdup. Lay back. Let me see." He pulled aside the bandage and sucked in his breath. Did it look that bad? He was just doing his job, she told herself. He didn't care about her. He wasn't worried.

"You let me out of here, I'll take myself away," she whispered. "You won't have to bother with me anymore."

He shook his head, his eyes pinched with pity. "Where would you go? Is there really a family farm back in Tennessee?" He was so close she could've kissed him.

Her face went hot. Looking away, she bit out, "Arkansas!"

"Anybody still there?"

"I don't know. Ma used to tell me that when Pa came for us we were going to go off with him no matter what, so when he came, even though Ma was gone six years, I went with Pa. In all the years I been gone, nobody ever came after me. I figured they were glad I was gone."

"Who?"

"My grandmother," Jodee said, surprised that she still felt hurt after so long. "Aunt Mardee, Uncle Jeb." So few people to care about her, Jodee thought. She felt so alone. "Grandmother was too old to come after me, I reckon. Aunt Mardee had my young cousins to tend. Uncle Jeb had the farm. They didn't want me. Really, they didn't."

"What happened to your mother?"

"She took sick. I was six. Then Granddaddy died . . . out in the barn, during a storm. Times got hard. I was a burden." Jodee couldn't say more. She watched the marshal's coffee brown gaze. He was listening, but she couldn't tell if he believed her.

"I just want you to know, Jodee, me asking Rella to help you was not meant as an insult. I'm not much use to you. I felt you needed a woman's help. I don't want you to consider her kind of life."

"I ain't turning into no fancy woman, Marshal. I know good from bad." To cover her embarrassment, Jodee gave a laugh. "Just look at me." She meant she was not pretty enough to become a fancy woman.

Abruptly the marshal stood. "With your shirt torn like that, Jodee, maybe you'd like one of mine to wear."

She clutched at the torn fabric and shook her head. She longed to be covered, clean and decent, but felt ashamed to accept something belonging to him. "I couldn't."

The marshal went out of the cell, leaving the door open wide, and returned moments later with a folded blue shirt with no collar. He brought the water pitcher and basin from his sleeping room. By the furrows in his brow, he looked like he thought she might be dying.

When he left her alone at last, she pressed the clean shirt to her face and breathed in. It smelled of washing soap and reminded her unexpectedly of her mother. A flood of anguish rushed over her. Ma, gone so young. Now Pa. She was an orphan. In jail. She might end up in prison for something she hadn't done.

All she had ever wanted was a decent life, she thought. She wanted to hear her name held in regard. She wanted a cabin to keep tidy and a family to love and love her back. She wanted neighbors, church socials, book learning, friends, and a clean bed to sleep in. She wanted a bath, a cook stove, and white dimity curtains.

With the last of her strength, Jodee pulled the marshal's shirtsleeve up her aching right arm and over her blazing shoulder. Then she lay down to sleep, wrapped in the marshal's clean scent.

The remainder of the morning Corbet worked at his desk, finishing his report of the stagecoach holdup while Jodee slept. At noon she woke to eat and wash her face. With her hair slicked back she looked no more than fifteen years old. Corbet was stunned by the simple beauty of her delicate features. He hadn't suspected she'd turn out to be so sweet-looking. It complicated matters.

He'd better get her out of his jailhouse, but

quick. She hadn't been at the holdup—he was certain of it—but Tangus had killed Willie Burstead. Corbet belonged on the trail, tracking Tangus, not here, hovering over a bedraggled orphan. But he made no move to unlock Jodee's cell to let her go. He couldn't turn her out onto the street. She needed him. It was that simple.

Jodee was still asleep when Hobie came by after school. "Aw, Marshal, somebody spit in the corner. If you ask me, Hicks ain't fit to wear a lawman's badge. He drinks on the job, too. I want to be your deputy. I'll quit school. I got no use for college next year."

"By the time you're old enough to be a deputy, I'll be long gone," Corbet said, surprising himself when he said it. He'd thought himself ready to settle down. The prospect of starting over somewhere new filled him with dread. "College will make you a better man than me."

"You can't leave Burdeen, Marshal. There ain't a man in town fit to take your place. Mr. Robstart won't never be marshal now. Folks say he's crippled permanent. Besides, he wasn't never as tough or cold as you."

Corbet didn't like being thought of as cold. He remembered the look on Patsy Robstart's face when she opened the door to his knock earlier that day. Instead of being her stalwart friend, he'd become her enemy. Without a word she'd closed the door in his face. He understood, of course. It was on his account that Virgil's life was in jeopardy. But her blame hurt him worse than he liked to admit.

Folks were wrong about him. He wasn't cold. He just kept his feelings private. A man might suffer guilt and remorse, loneliness and longing, but a marshal couldn't afford such. This mess was his to bear alone. The McQue gang holding up that stage, and him following with a posse of overzealous townsmen . . . that had all been his fault. Now Virgil was riddled with fever. His fault, too. Patsy Robstart hated his gizzard. His fault. Jodee lay in her cell looking like a motherless calf. His fault.

Putting aside his report, Corbet thanked Hobie and urged him to run along. "First thing tomorrow, check the depot for telegraph messages. I'm waiting for information about Miss McQue."

A wily grin spread across Hobie's young face. His teeth were a scramble. "If you thought a telegraph message was coming, I'd be at the stage depot waiting right now. There ain't nothin' comin' on her, is there? Because she's innocent. You're goin' to let her go."

Corbet let his gaze settle on Jodee, sleeping on that narrow cot. His heart did a strange jig. Hobie was right. He had to let her go.

To go where?

"Keep your eyes open, Hobie. Early this morning I saw a man in a bowler hat. A button

65

salesman, carrying a case. If you see him, get back to me. I'd like to talk to him."

"You think it's Tangus?" Hobie gasped, his eyes wide. "Right here in Burdeen? Will there be a shoot-out? I remember that first one, Marshal. Everybody in town remembers. I was only twelve, but you—"

Corbet put up his hand to silence the lad. He didn't deserve praise for those first battles that settled the town.

"Will Tangus try to take Miss McQue?" Hobie gasped. "You can't let him! She don't want no part of him."

"Don't tell anybody about this, Hobie. I don't want a panic."

"Don't you worry. If Tangus is in Burdeen, I'll find him."

"That is not what I meant," Corbet exclaimed, alarmed at the lad's rash idea. "He's a dangerous outlaw."

"But think what the Ashton-Babcock reward would mean for Ma."

That damnable reward, Corbet thought, scowling at Hobie. He'd just found out about the two hundred cash dollars offered for Tangus by the Ashton-Babcock Stage Line. He took hold of the lad's shoulders. "You make the slightest effort to find Tangus by yourself, I'll fire you for good and all. Don't make me sorry I took you on."

"Sorry, sir. I didn't mean it." Hobie looked every bit his fifteen years as he fought disappointment.

Corbet sent the lad out the door into the late afternoon sunlight. The snow had melted, but the temperature was dropping. The muddy ruts in the street were freezing. He liked that boy. If anything happened to him he would never forgive himself.

When Artie brought the dinner tray a half hour later, Corbet noticed Jodee scarcely roused long enough to take more than a few bites. Eating his own dinner, Corbet fumed. Hicks hadn't returned. Corbet couldn't go on rounds. Every word Patsy Robstart spoke earlier haunted him. Jodee McQue's presence in his jail complicated everything.

As dusk fell, Corbet could do nothing but sit and watch his prisoner sleep. How could he let her go, a lone girl dressed in ragged men's clothes? He grew full of urgency looking at her and knew, suddenly, that he was attracted to her in a way he must never reveal or indulge.

It was late when Corbet felt ready to turn in for the night. He'd searched his files, written a dozen letters and struggled to think of a solution to Jodee's predicament. He barred the door and latched the window shutters. He checked the locked gun rack. He sat a while on the edge of his low-slung bed, studying his hands, remembering slipping socks on Jodee's thin, cold feet the night before. It had been hours since Jodee had been awake. A whole day and still the doctor hadn't come. Virgil must be bad off. Patsy, too. If either died, he'd quit marshaling. Simple as that. Walk straight out of town. To hell with everything.

Pulling off his boots, he resisted what he wanted to do—check on Jodee. What if she'd died and he didn't know? His stomach rolled over. Taking a half empty bottle of whiskey from his bedside stand, he padded into the main room in his stocking feet.

"Jodee?" He got a clean kerchief from the drawer and the cell key.

He shouldn't go into her cell, he warned himself. That was the very thing folks suspected of him. What kind of man did they think he was? Didn't they know—he could picture himself gathering her into his arms—didn't they know how helpless she was? He shook himself. Didn't they know how important it was to protect the weak and friendless? He wouldn't let himself think of her lithe young body beneath his hands. He'd never take advantage. That wasn't the way of a real man.

Unlocking the cell door, Corbet stepped inside. What if someone came along and saw—the jail-house door was barred. An army couldn't get in.

"Jodee," he whispered.

His body responded to the nearness of her, to

the faint, musky fragrance of her, to the sight of her slim body lying so still in the darkness under the hotel blanket. He hadn't felt such urges in a long time.

She didn't stir.

Sick with dread, Corbet moved aside the tray on the floor with her partially eaten meal on it. Then he crouched beside the cot and gingerly touched her shoulder. He was braced for the shocking feel of cold and death. The astonishing heat of her body on the palm of his hand stunned him. She blazed with fever.

Corbet laid the back of his hand against her cheek, then on her scorching forehead. It felt like the worst fever he'd ever known. His hands began to shake. She lolled onto her back, nearly rolling off the cot into his arms.

Scooping her up, he carried her quickly into his sleeping room. Appalled by the waxy hollow look of her face, he laid her on his bed. Wetting his kerchief in the wash basin, he wiped her face, feeling immense relief when she twisted away. He wiped her slim throat—she was so fragile-looking—and then pushed aside the collar of his blue shirt that she was wearing over her own torn and bloody shirt. The dressing had come loose from her wound. It looked bad. Soaking a fresh kerchief in whiskey, he laid the dripping cloth over the puckered hole in her skin.

Jodee writhed and moaned.

"I'm sorry."

Her eyelids fluttered and then, slowly, she opened her eyes and looked at him. Beautiful dark blue.

Corbet's heart began thundering. He couldn't think. Could she see him?

"Marshal," she whispered so softly he almost didn't hear her. It was the most arousing sound he'd ever heard. She looked at him with eyes glassy with bewilderment. Before he could think, she lifted her left hand and encircled his neck. She pulled him close. "Marshal."

He couldn't believe she'd been able to keep herself innocent for so long in the company of outlaws. Maybe she'd tell him where Burl was hiding. He leaned close enough to feel her breath hot on his face. Her hand burned his neck, sending tingles of arousal through his body like heat lightning. Without warning she arched up to place her sweet, hot mouth on his.

It was the most tender kiss he'd ever known. It was the kiss of a girl, the kind of sweet kiss he'd dreamed of as a boy. It was a kiss of longing and loneliness. Corbet felt Jodee's tenderness flow into him straight to his heart.

"Marshal," she whispered against his mouth, her breath hot.

His response was frightening in intensity. This mustn't happen. He watched tears gather in her eyes. What if everything she'd said was true? What if she really was completely and totally innocent?

Jodee's lips told Corbet all he needed to know. This was her first kiss.

And she had bestowed it upon him.

Four

Corbet held the whiskey-soaked kerchief to unconscious Jodee's enflamed wound. With her hair smoothed back, he could see the delicate expanse of her forehead, the sweet arch of her brows and the slim straightness of her nose.

And that mouth. *What tenderness lurked in that gentle curve, plus a hint of hurt and pain and sorrow,* he thought. Had he seen her smile yet? He couldn't remember.

Open your eyes again, he said to her silently.

To be certain she was still breathing, he watched for the imperceptible rise and fall of her chest. He wished someone would, indeed, come along so he could safely leave her to go for the doctor. He couldn't do this alone.

When his legs began to cramp from crouching, he stood. He bathed Jodee's face again with water, but this time she didn't stir at all. Adjusting the whiskey-soaked kerchief over the wound, he sank to the floor. Leaning back against the pine bedframe, he wondered what would happen when Avinelle came home from Cheyenne City.

What was taking her so long? Avinelle and her domineering mother wanted him to run the stagecoach line. It'd be so easy to trade his marshal's badge for the brocade vest and gold pocket watch of a businessman. It didn't seem to matter to them that he didn't know how to run a business. More to the point, he didn't want to.

But for two years, since her husband's death, Avinelle Babcock had done everything possible to attract Corbet's romantic attention. Why he resisted, Corbet didn't know. It was more than the fact that he didn't love the woman. He never expected to love any woman. Love was for other men, men with a place, men with a means to make a living.

He had nothing to offer a woman, and yet all he needed to do was turn in Avinelle's direction and he'd be planted as deeply in the town of Burdeen as those Rikes had been planted out at the cemetery. Burdeen could be his home. Avinelle could be his family. The stagecoach line could be his living. He could smoke the best cigars, surround himself with little ones, although it was difficult to imagine Avinelle mothering babies and small children. He wanted a home. He wanted little ones. He just didn't want them wearing velvet with lace collars.

Why didn't he want it?

Corbet looked at the young woman lying unconscious on his bed. *Jodee McQue, his little*

72

desperado, he thought. He pushed a tendril of pale hair from her cheek. Another inch and that bullet would've shattered her collar bone. Lower down, the bullet would've pierced her lung. *If she survived this night, she'd be all right,* he told himself.

What then? Put her on a stagecoach and let her disappear from his life?

Corbet closed his hand into a fist and rubbed his knuckles over the furrows on his forehead. He longed to gather Jodee into his arms. To a woman like Avinelle he'd be a puppet. To a girl like Jodee he'd be a god. He didn't want either. He wanted a woman in his life, but he wanted a life that was his, a place that was his, and a family that was his.

That farm, back where he grew to manhood, might have been his, but the offer to stay had come too late. He'd realized he couldn't waste his life in that desolate place with only cows for comfort. He'd had to leave.

Sitting on the floor beside Jodee as she began to shiver with chills, Corbet realized that sometime in the past year his youthful loneliness had melted away. It was time for something more, something settled. Burdeen was beginning to feel like home.

Getting to his feet, Corbet fetched his extra blanket and covered Jodee to her chin. *There had been no church socials for this poor girl,* he

73

thought. She'd had no beaus unless one counted that lout Tangus. She claimed there was no attachment. Corbet remained skeptical. If no one had searched for her in six years, her family had to be dead. What kind of people let an outlaw carry off a twelve-year-old child and didn't search for her? He looked at Jodee's shabby shirt and britches. Avinelle wore a new dress every week and reminded him as often as possible that she had once enjoyed the cultured life in New York. What did Jodee McQue have but him?

Damned if he didn't want to lean over and kiss Jodee's cheek. He remembered kissing little Jenny Harlow long ago. He'd been perched on the milking stool which made him about the same height as his little friend when she stole into the barn to flirt with him. She'd giggled and blushed. Jenny had been his only childhood friend. By taking her father's surname, Corbet had made himself like her brother.

He didn't feel like Jodee McQue's brother.

"Come on, Jodeen," Corbet murmured. He hunkered down to study the curve of her cheek. He could be tender when no one was looking. "Don't give up." He laid his hand on the side of her face and wondered why some people had to have it so hard. Jenny Harlow shouldn't have died at the age of ten, and Jodee McQue didn't deserve to die, either, and certainly not in jail.

His decision came so simply he was taken

aback. Straightening, he clutched at his hair and felt an easing in his gut. In the morning he'd set Jodee free. Once he had Tangus behind bars in Jodee's place to stand trial for the murder of Willis Burstead, he'd turn in his badge. Then he'd buy that land. He wanted to protect people, but as marshal all he'd managed to do was help his friend Virgil into his deathbed. Such a thing wasn't going to happen again. He'd run cows, grade streets, or build houses, but he wasn't going to be responsible for killing any more people.

Jodee woke to the sound of male voices raised in argument. She felt like a child again, waking in the night to hear her grandmother shouting at her father in the downstairs parlor that long ago night when she was carried off and her life changed forever.

Frightened, Jodee struggled to sit up but could scarcely turn her head. It was alarming to discover herself so completely incapacitated. A tall man appeared in her line of vision. She tried to figure out where she was. The man looked so tired, his smile was limp.

"Miss McQue, I'm Dr. Trafford." He stepped into the room. "The marshal says your fever broke about five o'clock this morning. Will you allow me to have a look at your wound? I apologize for taking so long to get here. While the marshal sat up with you last night, I delivered Mrs. Robstart's baby. Almost lost him, too, but he's a strong little fellow. Not much bigger than a new puppy."

He moved his hands from Jodee's eyelids to her throat and finally to her shoulder where he frowned at her wound. He touched her so gently she could only stare at him in dreamlike fascination. At last she realized where she was. She was still in the jailhouse, but now she was in the marshal's own sleeping room, on his bed, not in her cell. The scent of the marshal was all around her.

"Am I dying?" she whispered.

"Healing from a bullet wound, even one as shallow as yours, is no easy task, my dear. I suspect this was a ricochet shot. Slow and glancing. It's to be expected you should suffer fever. I'm pleased to see you're on the mend, no thanks to me." With tenderness he cleaned and dressed her wound. Even so, it burned enough to bring tears to her eyes. "You'll feel better soon. You'll never wear a low-cut dancing dress, but you'll dance again, I promise."

She shook her head. "Never danced."

The doctor raised his brows. "Well then, you have something to look forward to. Stay put. No running off. Marshal Harlow said he found no warrants against you. No witnesses placed you at the holdup. When you're able, we'll get you situated in a new life. That's what you want, isn't it?"

A new life? Why would anyone help her with that? "Is the deputy's wife all right?" she asked.

"I wouldn't be surprised to hear Patsy's up already cooking breakfast. I'll tell her you asked." He closed his bag and left without a goodbye.

Jodee struggled with tears of relief. The moment she sensed someone new entering the sleeping room, she tried to hide her wet face.

"Miss McQue, can I fetch you anything?" It was Hobie.

"Water," she choked out, turning to give the lad a grateful smile. "Thank you."

When he saw the tears standing on her cheeks, he blushed scarlet. He was back moments later to hold a tin cup of water to her lips. His hands shook so badly, water dribbled down her chin to her neck as she drank the sweet coolness. His eyes glowed as he leaned in close to help her.

"That'll be all for this morning, Hobie," the marshal said, watching from the doorway.

"But I want to sweep her cell—"

"Miss McQue won't be going back to her cell. She'll rest here until we find her a place to stay. Mrs. Brady's boarding house is full, apparently, but don't worry, Jodee. We won't run you out of town. Hicks is heading out to that cabin to track Tangus. You'll be safe here in town. You're no longer under arrest."

Jodee didn't know what to say. She was free to go?

Hobie edged out of the room. "Hope you're feeling better soon, Miss McQue."

The marshal regarded Jodee with a closed expression. That was when Jodee remembered kissing him. Surely it had been a dream. She'd never kissed anyone except the whiskered cheek of her father.

"Hungry?" the marshal asked, rubbing his neck. He seemed skittish. "Artie brought another tray. He can't seem to get enough of feeding you." His words hinted at amusement but his eyes remained hooded. "I think he's taken a shine to you. Hobie, too."

She answered hesitantly. "I'm not hungry . . . I don't think."

"I'll be here working in case you need anything." He pulled the door closed and left her to consider her astonishing new fate.

She slept soundly most of the morning. Just before noon she woke feeling ready to eat everything in sight. Artie brought chicken broth and freshly baked bread for her luncheon. She had no idea what had become of her uneaten breakfast. Then she remembered that had probably been a day or two ago. The newspaperman stopped by for an update on her condition, but Corbet didn't allow him to visit.

Around three o'clock, Jodee felt well enough to take a turn behind the jailhouse to the privy.

Rella's windows were shuttered against the late afternoon sun. Although Jodee didn't have the luxury of watching the marshal work at his desk, she relished listening to the rustling of his papers and the scratch of his pen. Two men came to talk to the marshal a while, but Jodee couldn't catch what they said. She thought she heard the marshal unlock his desk drawer. The doctor stopped by late. Her wound was better, he said with an easing of his pinched eyes. Mrs. Robstart was up, tending her tiny newborn son whom they had named Henry, after Virgil's father back East, he told her. Virgil was sitting up in bed, taking broth. The worst was over.

Jodee slept the remainder of the evening feeling as if the world had come to rights again. She didn't wake again until after dark. It was late when she heard the marshal give instructions to a deputy for evening's rounds. It wasn't Hicks. She spent a peaceful night dreaming things she couldn't remember come morning.

The early stagecoach rattled through town as Jodee woke the following morning. When she sat up she felt as near to normal as she had since before the shootout. Her shoulder ached, but she could move her arm without fainting with pain. She flexed her elbow, wrist, and fingers, relieved to discover she could still move them.

Swinging her legs off the bed, she found she

could stand without assistance. How wonderful it felt to be nearly well again. She breathed in, smelling fresh coffee in the main room.

There was a small barred window in the sleeping room. Jodee looked out at the busy street and watched three men struggle to lift a heavy black safe with gold lettering on the door from the rear boot of the stagecoach. They lugged it into the stage depot.

Jodee closed her eyes. "Oh, Pa," she whispered. "Why'd you leave me to this?"

On the far side of the stagecoach someone helped a woman in a magnificent blue traveling dress step down to the rutted street. Another woman wearing a hat with black plumes climbed from the stagecoach, too.

It felt so amazing to watch the goings-on of the street without feeling the need to hide. Trying to forget her grief, Jodee reminded herself they were going to help her start a new life. She might never again be sick enough to steal a kiss from the marshal—that's what it had been, stolen—but at least she had the memory of it. Her father would've wanted her to start over. She had to try, for him.

Thinking she should tidy the bed, Jodee realized the two women were coming across the street to the jailhouse. She edged back where she wouldn't be noticed, peeking out the window of the marshal's sleeping room. She heard the women step up to the porch, arguing in hushed tones. Behind them, a surrey with fringes around the roof rolled to a stop beside them. The driver brought parcels and two carpetbags from the stagecoach and loaded the things onto the surrey.

The older woman climbed aboard the surrey and fussed with her black skirts.

Jodee heard the jailhouse door open.

"Why Corbet Harlow," came a young woman's sweetly scolding voice, "We expected you'd greet us at the depot just now. Didn't you get my telegraph message?"

"Avinelle! Weren't you due tomorrow?" The marshal's voice sounded strained.

"When we got your message—you recovered my cash box—we had to come right away! You can't know how grateful I am. Oh, but you do look surprised. All right, I'll forgive you, but only this once. Won't you at least give me a kiss hello? You look—well, really, Corbet! Aren't you glad to see me at all? I'm back after my horrifying ordeal. Mother has been a trial, you can be sure, but then . . ." She lowered her voice. "Mother always is."

In the sleeping room, Jodee's heart sank. She dropped to the edge of the bed and sat listening. So, the marshal wasn't as alone in his life as she liked to imagine. This was why he so relentlessly followed Burl and the Rikes into the canyon. The woman on the stagecoach was his sweetheart.

81

Feeling like a fool, Jodee fought a jumble of hurt and hopeless feelings. She heard the marshal cross the floor and pause. Was he kissing his visitor hello?

"You're all right then?" he asked. "That first message sounded as if you'd been killed. You weren't wounded, not at all?"

The woman gave a laugh, but she spoke with a pout. "It was terrifying! They ordered us out of the coach. We had to stand there at gunpoint like, like . . . It became ridiculous. They were a passel of fools, arguing over that safe. The lout couldn't open it. Dropped it. Threw it against a boulder. Shot at it. The bullet ricocheted, ripping through my clothes. I could've been killed!" She lowered her voice. "The cash box, Corbet?"

Jodee heard him unlock his desk drawer.

Their voices dropped so low Jodee couldn't hear anything more for some seconds. She feared he was consoling her, holding her, kissing her.

No longer able to contain her jealous curiosity, Jodee balled her fists. It was stupid to reveal her presence in the marshal's sleeping room, she knew, but she couldn't stop herself from pushing the door open and facing the woman who was the reason her father had been killed.

At the sight of Jodee emerging from the sleeping room, the woman's mouth fell open. She clutched a small, flat metal box to her bosom and backed away. She was the most beautiful person Jodee had ever seen. Her complexion looked like her grandmother's porcelain teacups. Her closely-set eyes blazed with astonishment. She wore skirts drawn back into complicated folds and pleats. Over the dress was an elbow-length cape of plum-colored fabric that caught the morning sunlight. She wore an elaborate hat with ribbons trailing over a cascade of gold curls.

Jodee stared at her until her eyes went dry. The marshal had his hand on her elbow as if he had just kissed her.

Jodee watched his neck redden as he stepped back.

To think she'd fantasized about the marshal taking a shine to a bedraggled desert rat like herself, Jodee thought, feeling like a jackass.

The woman's eyes darted over Jodee, from her sleep-tousled hair to the overlarge blue shirt she was wearing and her worn denim britches that hugged her long legs. She gawked at Jodee's stocking feet. Drawing herself up, she seemed like a rattler ready to strike.

Jodee imagined herself swaggering forward, twirling her father's heavy pistol on her finger like Burl liked to do. She wanted to say something gruff—aw, but wasn't that just the stupidest thing she had ever thought of? Acting like an outlaw would only impress another outlaw. Jodee suddenly felt every bit the rough outlaw's daughter she was. She wished she was somewhere else, anywhere else, and anyone but herself.

"Corbet?" came the woman's strained voice. "What is the meaning of this?"

Corbet let his shoulders drop. What a formidable figure he cut when he glowered like that, Jodee thought, beginning to tremble.

His voice came out as impersonally as if he were addressing a stranger. "If you'll take a seat, Avinelle, I'll explain what's been happening while you were recuperating in Cheyenne City."

"I shall stand, thank you."

"Well, then, Jodee, this is Widow Babcock, co-owner of the Ashton-Babcock Stage Line. She's the woman who was nearly shot during the holdup at Ship's Creek Crossing last week. She's the woman the stage driver died defending." Turning to the young widow, the marshal said with exaggerated formality, "Avinelle, this is Miss Jodee McQue, daughter of the outlaw also killed during the holdup."

Widow Babcock's eyes rounded. "Your father was one of those outlaws? Then, what are you doing in there?" She gestured to the sleeping room.

The marshal explained how Jodee came to be wounded and in jail.

"She nearly died of fever two nights ago," he added. "I had to put her in my room so I could tend her."

"And just where was Dr. Trafford?"

While he explained about his wounded deputy, the man's wife, and their new baby, Widow Babcock shook her head in disbelief.

"But Corbet, you can't have a woman in your sleeping room. People will think—" Her mouth contorted with an effort to hold back emotion. "This looks very unseemly, Corbet. Think of your reputation. Think of mine."

"This is where you can help," the marshal said with rising animation. Interrupting himself, he indicated the chair behind his desk. "Jodee, you needn't stand. You're still weak."

Jodee's cheeks flamed with embarrassment. He was concerned about her? She doubted that. She shook her head. She dared not sit in the presence of this woman.

"Exactly how might I help, Corbet?" Widow Babcock asked with open sarcasm.

"If you would, Avinelle, please help me think where Miss McQue might stay until she's well enough to work. She wants to go home, but she must earn her fare. I tried taking up a collection but—"

"Work, you mean here, in Burdeen?" The widow's face paled. She glared at the marshal, her tortured feelings for him naked in her eyes. "If this is what you want, Corbet, I shall certainly give it my complete attention." Tottering a little, Widow Babcock made her way to the door. She paused, looking flustered. "I came in to invite you for dinner Sunday. Mother plans something special."

"Honored, as always," the marshal said. "You wouldn't happen to have a dress Miss McQue could wear?"

Jodee backed away. "That ain't necessary, Marshal!"

"Anything else? Hat? Parasol? Corbet, you must excuse me, Mother's waiting. I'll do what I can, but you mustn't allow this person to return to your sleeping room. Does anyone know she was in there?"

"Doc Trafford. Hobie. George Hatcher. It's no secret."

Clapping her hand over her mouth, the pretty young widow lurched out the door, her expression stricken.

"If I'm free to go, Marshal, I'll go now." Jodee started for the door, but her head began to swim. She grabbed the desk for support. *I'm not even strong enough to cross the room,* she thought with disgust.

Corbet was quick to lend her his arm.

From the doorway, Widow Babcock watched with narrowed eyes.

"Doc wants Jodee to get a week's bed rest," he explained as she hesitated. "Jodee actually *was* shot, Avinelle. You needed a week to recover a bullet hole in your cloak."

The widow sucked in her breath. "Corbet Harlow, you cut me to the bone. I—I shall return within the hour. Miss McQue," she said in a condescending tone that left Jodee bristling, "I am *filled* with regret over your predicament, but you must not go back in that room." She swept out, leaving behind the crisp fragrance of silk.

The marshal sighed.

Jodee felt like cussing.

When the marshal met Jodee's eyes she expected him to order her to his chair, but instead he pulled it around and urged her to sit. "A word from Avinelle Babcock and folks will line up to help you, Jodee."

She resisted him. "I don't want her help, Marshall. The hotel's fine, the livery stable, anyplace. I'll work off the cost and be gone as soon as I can."

"Call me Corbet, please."

Jodee just wanted to flee. "I—I couldn't."

With all her heart Jodee yearned to sidle up to him, slip her arms around his neck, and lay her head against his chest. Lest he see the longing in her eyes, she dropped her gaze.

"Jodee," Corbet said softly. "I'm sorry I put you in jail. Let me make it up to you. You need help returning to decent society."

She shook her head. It had been easier living with her father, apart from all that. She missed her father so much that she suddenly felt overwhelmed. With Corbet watching, Jodee felt her heart roll over in anguish. Finally, with a huff of exasperation, she dropped into the chair.

He smiled. The way his lips curved back over his teeth made Jodee's heart soar. It was the first time she'd seen him look pleased. The effect was dazzling. She felt a blossoming inside, of longing and hope.

The moment Avinelle climbed into the surrey, her mother snapped, "What went wrong this time?"

Balling her gloved fists, Avinelle tucked her cash box into the folds of her skirt, fighting the urge to curse her mother.

Corbet had looked as if he'd rather wrestle rattlesnakes than dine with her. And that Jodee whatever-her-name-was . . . Avinelle felt elderly compared to that fresh-faced young thing, standing in his sleeping room doorway! Not a wrinkle around her eyes, not a blemish on those apple cheeks. Long, tousled hair. Just the sort of waif big dumb men like Corbet Harlow found appealing. The little urchin looked as if Corbet had just ravished her.

"Get going, Bailey," Avinelle snarled at their driver. "This wind is unbearable."

Two years before, when she was first widowed, Avinelle thought, Corbet had showered *her* with his solicitous attention. He'd been nothing more than a shotgun messenger at the time, working on her late husband's stage line. Tall and muscular like that, who wouldn't have noticed him. Her mother certainly had. Her mother had used her influence, too, to get him hired as city marshal. Corbet proved so capable that her mother decided he'd make an even better business manager, and Avinelle's next husband. Avinelle gritted her teeth.

"Well?" came her mother's grating query.

"What *is* it, Mother?"

"Whatever is bothering you now? I see you have your cash box. Empty, I suppose."

Avinelle's mind reeled. *Yes, indeed, I have it back, Mother,* she thought. She said nothing of its contents. Let her mother think whatever she wished. *If I possessed an ounce of courage,* Avinelle thought, *I might be on my way back to New York right now.* But no, she took pity on her mother, gave in to her fear of returning to a life less prestigious than this one. Richest widows in Burdeen City? So what? Avinelle was losing her mind with frustration.

"Corbet has an outlaw's daughter recovering in his sleeping room. That's what's bothering me, Mother. Bailey, if you repeat a word, I'll fire you. You should've seen the way Corbet looked at her. He wants me to find her a place to stay, and to work."

The surrey lurched forward. Moments later it stopped in front of the Ashton-Babcock house a block from town. Avinelle fought her skirts, scrambled down, and charged up the flagstone walk, her ankles aching. She hated Burdeen City, and she hated this house. No one cared that she had nearly been killed during that holdup. She'd expected Corbet to fetch her from Cheyenne City and fall on his face in his efforts to comfort her tattered nerves. She and her mother had waited and waited. He hadn't come. Now she knew why.

Avinelle felt like a laughingstock.

Her mother followed her into the entrance hall. "Maggie," her mother called to the maid, "this place needs airing. Where are you? Old fool. Probably in her room, mumbling to herself."

"Mother, what am I to do?"

"So you caught Corbet with a harlot in his bed."

Avinelle watched as her mother spied a piece of mail waiting on a silver tray and snatched it up. Her mother answered absently, "Turn a blind eye. Men have their needs."

"I will not."

Their maid scurried into the entry, her graying hair untidy. She escaped a scolding by hurrying into the parlor to throw open the windows. Avinelle watched her mother tear apart the envelope and read, eyes widening with alarm. What was it this time? A lost mail contract? Higher taxes?

Jamming the letter into her pocket, her mother

said, "The answer, Avinelle, is pitifully obvious. Corbet's hussy must stay with us. Whoever helps Corbet's little protégé will earn his gratitude. That must be you."

"What if she robs us while we sleep?"

Her mother's lips curved into a cunning smile. "Then she will prove herself unworthy of our help. Away to prison she goes. Problem solved. Corbet marries you, as planned."

Avinelle stormed up to her room and slammed the door with all her strength. Throwing the cash box onto her bed, she tore into the bottom of her wardrobe. In her late husband's humidor she grabbed up his pocketbook and plucked his copy of the cash box key from the hidden compartment.

Taking the cash box and dropping cross-legged onto the floor, she jammed the key into the key-hole and lifted the cash box lid. Her breath went out. She couldn't believe her eyes. It was all there. Her entire hoard, intended to get her back east. There was still hope of escaping this damnable prison called home.

Five

Waiting for Avinelle's return, Corbet paced the jailhouse porch, thinking how Jodee had looked moments before as Hatcher stopped by to present his single-page newspaper sheet. Spying the article about herself, Jodee's eyes snapped with fire. Corbet was impressed with her gumption.

At the sound of Avinelle's surrey approaching, he felt relief and went back inside. He wanted to know what Hatcher had written, too. Jodee still sat at his desk, reading aloud but sounding little better than a schoolchild.

FEMALE OUTLAW JAILED

Returned safely from his desperate manhunt, Marshal Harlow has detained Jodeen McQue, daughter of wanted outlaw Timothy Titus McQue, upon further investigation as to her innocence or guilt. T. T. McQue was shot dead during the Ashton-Babcock stagecoach holdup at Ship Creek Crossing last Friday afternoon along with William R. Burstead, driver out of Cheyenne City. Ashton-Babcock station agent Benjamin T. Nobley, Burdeen, company agent Chester M. Clarkson, Philadelphia, co-owner Theia Ashton, and her daughter Avinelle Babcock of Burdeen were robbed at gunpoint. As reported in our last issue, Deputy Virgil Robstart was wounded during the shootout which ended the reign of terror perpetrated by the McQue gang. Cloyd Rike and his three sons, Mose, Witt, and Lee, were killed dead by Marshal Harlow and his posse of Burdeen's finest and most courageous townsmen. Burl Tangus, a known associate of the McQue gang, remains at large. It is not yet known if Miss McQue partook in her father's thieving ways, but it is said she is a crack shot and accomplished at attending the needs of renegades.

Corbet cringed. The townspeople would surely wonder just how Jodee McQue "attended" renegades.

Jodee threw the paper down and twisted away.

Avinelle charged into the jail, breathless in fresh silk. "I'm sorry to be so long, Corbet, but it was difficult convincing Mother."

Turning from Jodee, Corbet took the bait. "Convince your mother of what?"

Jodee rolled stiffness from her wounded shoulder, drew her right arm to her side, and held it there, her lips pressed together as if to keep everything she wanted to say from flooding out. Aside from the flinty gaze she gave Avinelle, Jodee looked pale.

"Miss McQue," Avinelle began with formality. "Mother has agreed to let you stay in our home. A short time. We'll help you find employment. Not with us, of course. We don't need more help."

Corbet's heart gave a leap of relief. It was a marvelous idea! Why hadn't he thought of it himself? He'd never seen Avinelle look so over-wrought, but he grinned nevertheless. He wanted to kiss her for helping him. "That's so generous."

Pinking prettily, Avinelle thrust a paper-wrapped parcel tied with kitchen twine at Jodee. "A dress. Go ahead, put it on. I give you permission to go into the sleeping room to change. You can't go out in public looking like that."

Reluctantly, Jodee accepted the parcel. "I'll pay you back, Ma'am."

"Nonsense. No repayment is expected, I'm sure. And please, call me Avinelle. We'll be fast friends. But remember to call my mother Widow Ashton. It'll take a while for her to get used to having someone like you in our home. We've been in mourning, you see." She made a pathetic smile. "For my late stepfather, *and* my dear late husband."

"I won't stay more'n a day or so."

"Doc will decide that," Corbet cautioned, beginning to wonder if Jodee would make it to Avinelle's house. He watched her totter back into his sleeping room. Quickly he grasped Avinelle's elbow and pulled her outside to speak to her privately. "You're sure about this?"

Avinelle leaned in close and gave Corbet her most captivating smile. She smelled of roses and looked irresistible. "I don't know why I didn't suggest it right away, Corbet."

"Well, I do appreciate this. I'll stop by once or twice a day to check on things."

"She'll be no trouble at all, really, Corbet. We'll

love having her. Why, in a week's time you won't know her. No one in Burdeen would want the daughter of an outlaw attending their children, kitchen, or parlor, but what people in Cheyenne City don't know will be to Miss McQue's advantage. We'll find her a job there." Avinelle patted his hand with lingering tenderness. "Then we can get back to normal and forget all about that horrid holdup."

Jodee discovered she actually liked the flowered blue calico she lifted from the widow's wrapping paper, but the garment was threadbare. Reluctantly she unbuttoned the marshal's shirt and tugged it from her aching shoulder. She removed her own torn and bloody shirt and tossed it aside. The doctor's fresh bandage around her chest felt tight. She longed to tear it off. Aware suddenly that she stood half naked in the marshal's sleeping room, Jodee quickly pulled the calico dress over her head, leaving her denim britches on underneath. This was no charitable gift, she was certain. This was a sample of all she would endure as Avinelle Babcock's house guest.

Grabbing the marshal's shirt, she pulled it back on like a jacket. She supposed she could refuse to go, but what else might she do? She had to get well. She had to start over somewhere. For two years she'd endured the company of outlaws. Before that had been loneliness and hardship.

A few days with two thorny widow ladies could be no worse.

Moments later, as Jodee walked out of the jailhouse a free woman, she asked, "When will I get my pistol back, Marshal?" She watched his eyes go over her and wondered just how awful she must look.

He seemed pleased, but worried. "You won't need your pistol at Avinelle's house. And you don't have to worry about Tangus. Cedric Bailey is Avinelle's driver. He'll stand guard over you."

Corbet watched Jodee's shaggy blonde hair lift on the breeze as she climbed into the surrey. As Avinelle drove away, he waited for a sense of relief to sweep over him, but it didn't come. With a sinking heart, he realized he was going to worry about Jodee McQue no matter where she went and no matter what she was doing.

He wandered into his sleeping room. Jodee's blood-stained shirt lay on the floor. Picking it up, he wondered what kind of man T. T. McQue had been to take his twelve-year-old daughter from the safety of her grandmother's home. How could he make Jodee follow him into horse stealing and stagecoach holdups?

Back in the empty main room, Corbet noticed Jodee's knapsack lying on the floor of her cell and retrieved it. He found several small stones in the bottom. They weren't gold or silver ore. He tried to imagine an adolescent girl living among outlaws, wearing tattered clothes and collecting rocks wherever they camped. He couldn't imagine the desolation of it, the danger.

Placing the knapsack for safekeeping in his sleeping room, Corbet headed outside, crossing the rutted street toward the jeweler's store. Later, at the stage depot, he sent another telegraph message to Cheyenne City's sheriff, asking after T. T. McQue's final resting place. He also requested a deputy with experience. He intended to fire Jimmy Hicks. Then he went to the cemetery where he looked down at four unmarked graves where the Rikes lay. He'd ended those lives without a thought. He supposed his quick action had saved his posse and helped the good people of Burdeen by preventing further holdups, but it was nothing to be proud of.

Back on the main street, Corbet wondered why Jodee's people let a twelve-year-old girl vanish into the night. Surely someone had mounted a search for her. A thousand terrible things might have happened to her. He felt indignant on her behalf and duty-bound to befriend her. Already he wanted to stop by Avinelle's to check on her. Did Jodee remember how to behave in a decent household?

Finishing his rounds south of town where the livery barns, horse corrals, and cattle yards spread, Corbet thought about his own bleak childhood. At nine years of age, and already tall, he'd been hired out to Willis Harlow, a dairy farmer who worked homeless lads like himself. For nine years Corbet had slept in hay mows, washed at a trough, and took his meals on a windswept porch.

As the newest and youngest farm hand, Corbet had endured beatings at the hands of the older boys. Isolated on that beautiful but lonely Wisconsin farmstead, he'd learned to fight for his right to exist. When years of farm work changed him from frail to formidable, Corbet defended new boys from the bullies. Most of the farm hands left by the age of sixteen. Corbet stayed two extra years. Eventually he, too, yearned to get away. Three years at a brewery in Milwaukee loading beer barrels brought him to full, broad-shouldered manhood. Hiring on as shotgun messenger on a stagecoach line carried him west.

Three years before, working for the Ashton-Babcock Stage Line, Corbet rode the stage into Burdeen each week, often encountering the owner's wife at the stage depot. He thought her the prettiest woman he'd ever seen. Later, after he'd been chosen as marshal, his natural kindness helped the pretty widow during the early months after her husband died. Too late, he realized how it looked, him a good-looking upstart, and she, co-heir to the stage line. Everyone expected he'd propose, but Avinelle proved difficult, given to tantrums and baffling changes of mood. Corbet's interest dwindled. Strangely, her interest doubled. Now he didn't know how to discourage her.

She liked to impress him with tales of the New York social scene she had once enjoyed. All he remembered of his childhood was hiding in alleyways. Who his parents had been, he never knew. How they came to their end, he couldn't remember. He adopted his initial "J" to give himself stature. *Corbet* was a word he heard at the orphan's asylum. J. Corbet Harlow become his own invention. He didn't appreciate Avinelle and her mother trying to shape him into something different.

With nervous anticipation, Jodee held her seat as the beautiful young Widow Babcock steered her surrey up the steep side street where Burdeen's quality homes overlooked the town. Widow Babcock stopped in front of a two-story house with ornate trim under the roof edges. As she climbed down with an angry jerk of her skirts, a balding man in suspenders and slouchy pants came around from the muddy side yard.

"Will you be needing the surrey any more today, Ma'am?" he asked, looking not the least concerned with Avinelle's ferocious scowl. He gave Jodee a nod of greeting. If he knew Jodee was the daughter of an outlaw, he gave no indication.

"Nothing more today, Bailey." The widow trudged up the flagstone walk to the porch. "Bring the tub. Our guest needs a bath." Absent was the dazzling smile the widow reserved for the marshal. "Come on, you," she called to Jodee.

All I need is a few days' rest, Jodee reminded herself, following the widow into the house. As soon as possible she'd be gone. As far as aggravation was concerned, Avinelle Babcock would be no match for Burl Tangus.

Jodee heard Burl jeering in her head. *"Aw, look at lil' miss prissy, sittin' all by her lonesome, eatin' beans and actin' so high like she's in some fancy parlor instead of sittin' on a rock by this here campfire. T. T., you ought to teach this girl she's a born criminal, same as you and me."* Jodee was certain nothing Avinelle or her mother might say would ever upset her as much.

From the dim hallway beyond the entry, a middle-aged maid in a homely black uniform scurried in. She looked up at Jodee with shy interest.

Avinelle pushed her aside. "Must you always look like such a worthless piece of nonsense, Maggie? Don't you have something you should be doing?"

All pretenses of good manners had been checked at the door like pistols, Jodee thought, startled by the change in the young widow's manner. Then she brought herself up short. She'd entered another world. She saw tables with funny legs, a hall tree with ornate hooks and knobs, and a ponderous tall clock with a swinging brass pendulum. The framed mirror on the wall looked as big as a store window. Avinelle was reflected in it, jerking off her gloves. Beside her stood a shaggy blond-headed vagabond with big eyes and a gawking expression.

Burl would find this place a wonder, Jodee thought bitterly, noting silver candlesticks, pictures in gold frames, and a silver tray with a calling card on it. There was probably a chest of silver flatware tucked away somewhere and a velvet-lined box overflowing with jewelry.

Jodee shook herself. Burl would never see this house.

Peering into the drawing room, Jodee saw long panels of white lace hanging at the front windows. Every piece of furniture was darkly carved, every seat tufted and edged with fringe. Delicate porcelain knickknacks on frilly white doilies crowded every surface. Heavy, framed pictures covered the papered walls.

Watching Jodee, Avinelle gave a nasty smirk and called in a simpering sing-song, "Oh, Mother. I'm back with our guest."

A pocket door behind Jodee slid open. Jodee was met by the icy appraisal of a woman scarcely five feet tall. Behind the woman spread a parlor even more cluttered than the drawing room. Ferns, fringes, peacock feathers . . .

Jodee brought her nervous attention back to Widow Babcock's mother's disapproving eyes. "Howdy-do, Widow Ashton," Jodee said, resisting the urge to dip a curtsy.

The elder widow's face remained frozen with distaste. "Come this way."

Widow Ashton led Jodee down the center hall past the staircase. They went into a plain kitchen to a door in a rear hall. Jodee turned in circles, trying to see everything. The house was so much larger than her grandmother's house had been.

"Bailey is bringing the tub. Hanna is heating your bath water." The woman indicated a rangy servant wearing a long white apron, standing at the cook stove. "You have no objections to bathing, I hope."

"No, Ma'am," Jodee said, bristling with indignation.

Jodee was shown into a small room no bigger than the jailhouse cell. Against the far wall stood a sewing machine on a table. Baskets of thread lined a shelf alongside folded fabric. Tiny gold scissors lay on the table. Jodee touched a finger to them and then snatched her hand back. Burl would have pocketed them without a thought.

Bailey staggered in, dragging a sit-style bathing tub. Jodee's grandmother had bathed her in a wooden laundry tub on the back porch. For many years, though, Jodee had simply bathed in creeks or rivers.

"You do know how to take a bath, do you not? Liberal amounts of soap." Widow Ashton managed to look down her nose in spite of her diminutive height.

Jodee clamped her teeth together.

"This is hair washing paste," the widow said, taking up a small round tin and twisting off the top. The scent of lilac wafted up. "Wash your hair three times. Scrub vigorously. Will you require a stronger preparation? Bailey can drive to the druggist."

Bitterly insulted, Jodee accepted the tin with a shaking hand. "Ain't nothin' crawling on my head," she hissed with restraint. The fragrance reminded her of spring afternoons at the scrubbing board with her mother and lilac bushes blooming in the yard. "I'm grateful for your kindness, Ma'am." She couldn't meet the woman's eyes. She put her left hand on the door, making it clear she expected both hostesses to leave her in privacy.

With Avinelle and her mother backing into the hall, astonished by her audacity, Jodee watched their servant Hanna carry in two kettles of steaming water. Bailey brought buckets of cold water to mix with the hot. Avinelle looked as if she were just realizing what she had taken on by inviting an outlaw's daughter into her home. Her expression was so filled with horror, Jodee almost laughed.

Unsure if she liked being feared so much, Jodee said, "Thank you, Widow Babcock. Widow Ashton."

Avinelle twisted away. "I asked you to call me Avinelle."

"If it's all the same to you, Ma'am," Jodee said, hoping she sounded dignified, "I'll stick to the proper."

Stripped of her snug jeans and the marshal's shirt, and the threadbare old dress, Jodee stepped into the bathing tub and huddled naked in the warm shallow water. Feeling vulnerable and ashamed, she scrubbed all over until her skin burned. How many days now had it been since she had been alone with no eyes upon her, she wondered. Not since the holdup when she waited with the pack horse, expecting to ride away with her father to a new life.

With that thought came the full weight of grief she'd been holding back. Her father was dead. She'd never see his smile again. Never hear his voice. Depend on his presence. Make him laugh. She missed him so keenly, she wondered if there was any point going on. What was the use cleaning up? Why find work? Why plan for a future without him? Wouldn't it be easier to die?

Like everything else, how would she even manage to do that. *Damn fool girl,* she thought, slapping the water, splashing the floor. Quickly she blotted up the spill.

She remembered those first months with her father when she was twelve. She'd known nothing about him except the stories her mother had told of the handsome drifter who rode into town with three other whips. They'd lolled around saloons, getting drunk, playing cards, and talking loudly, her mother had so often told her. Jodee always pictured her pretty mother at seventeen, sashaying along the boardwalk on her way to the mercantile.

She could imagine brash young T. T. McQue calling out, "Would you look-ee there, boys. Ain't that the prettiest hair color you ever did see? What hair color is that, young missy? Ain't it the color of morning sunshine?"

At that point in her mother's stories, Jodee's mother always giggled. "I told him, 'I am Haydee Latham.' And I said it right in front of the whole town. They couldn't stop me from talking to him. I never did what folks thought I should. Mother called me willful. Pa said I'd been a trial since the day I was born. What's the use in doin' what folks tell you to do if it ain't what you want to do? If it ain't fair or right?"

Jodee always pictured her handsome father, loitering by the saloon's hitching rail, hat cocked, looking rough and tumble. A scoundrel, they called him. A no-account with bad blood.

"He was all that," her mother used to say with perverse pride. "He didn't own a thing but his horse, his pistol, and his hat, but your papa had a smile as bright as a bonfire. His eyes were kindly. He treated me like a lady. One afternoon by the river he proposed on bended knee. We ran off that night and were married by Justice of the Peace Warren Carter in Texas. There's a certificate in my bureau drawer to prove it."

Jodee's mother always scrubbed a lot harder at the washboard when she spoke of such things. "When Timmy comes back for me, Jodee honey, he's going to be mighty surprised to find you, too. We're going to go away with him, you and me. Have you ever wondered why we stay here, doing laundry to earn our keep? If we left, Timmy wouldn't be able to find us, so we're staying and we're waiting for as long as it takes."

With that, Jodee remembered her mother laid out on the dining room table just the following year. Twenty-four years old. Her hair still like morning sunshine.

When her father finally did come, he rode away with a daughter instead of a wife. Terrified as she was, Jodee wanted him to carry her off. She never wanted to return to the loveless home of her childhood. Her father proved to be every-thing her mother promised, doting and good-hearted. He proved to be a fool, too, with impossible dreams. Jodee loved him anyway.

"Do you think your ma knows I came back for her?" her father once asked. They hadn't taken up with Burl yet, but times were hard.

"I heard Grandmother talkin' one day," Jodee recounted to her father. "I was listening at the window. 'In the end . . .' I heard Grandmother say, 'Haydee didn't even know me. Her fever was so bad. I prayed, Lord, spare her. I'll forgive her everything. Haydee rose up like she was seeing a vision and called out, Timmy! Timmy!' Honest, Pa. That's what I heard Grandmother say. Mama loved you to her last breath."

It was comforting to think her mother and father were together in the hereafter. Rinsing her face, Jodee scrubbed her hair with the fragrant hair washing paste. She scrubbed hard, as if to erase her grief. If she were to go home to Arkansas she'd have to spit in the eye of every do-gooder who drove off her father and broke her mother's heart. No, she'd never go back. She must think of somewhere else to go. Anywhere else.

Sweeping handfuls of water over her head, Jodee rinsed away the lather from her long tangles. Reaching for more hair washing paste, she froze, realizing the servant was standing in the doorway, staring at her fiery puckered wound.

"Doin' all right, honey? I brought you something to eat." Hanna placed a tray laden with milk and sandwiches on the table. "You're skinny as a drownt rat." But she smiled. Freckled, with several missing teeth, Hanna's was the kindliest face Jodee had seen in a good while.

Six

That afternoon, Jodee and Hanna sat behind Avinelle's house letting the wind dry Jodee's hair. It was chilly outside, but the warmth of the sun felt good. In spite of her throbbing shoulder wound, Jodee felt refreshed and ready to face her new life, whatever that might turn out to be.

Wearing only the shapeless blue dress Avinelle had given her, Jodee felt half-naked, perched on a low stool while Hanna brushed her long damp hair. The touch of the woman's hands was soothing.

"I been workin' for Miz Ashton and Miz Avinelle since they came to Burdeen four years ago." Hanna let Jodee's hair play through her care-worn fingers. "They're wearisome ladies, to be sure, but Miz Ashton can turn out a new dress in less than no time. Never heard of no lady could sew like that. You ask me, she weren't born to money like she wants folks to believe."

Only half listening, Jodee began to doze.

"Now Avinelle, she's spoilt clean through, been self-sorry since her husband got himself killed—it's a scandal we ain't supposed to talk about. Now, that outlaw . . ." She lowered her voice. "I can't believe a little thing like you was living with outlaws."

Jodee roused herself. "I was with my father, not the others. How can I make folks believe I wasn't like them? The marshal let me out of jail, didn't he?"

"You know how folks is, honey. They believe what they want, the truth be damned."

Jodee wilted. "Then there's no hope. I might as well be an outlaw for all they care what I've been through."

Avinelle appeared on the rear porch, her expression peevish. "Oh, there you are, Jodee." She called back into the house in her sing-song, "Miss McQue, won't you come inside? The marshal insists on seeing you," she added in a harsh whisper.

"I can't see him, not like this," Jodee cried, crossing her arms over the thin fabric of the dress.

"I'll fetch a shawl," Hanna said, hurrying inside.

Jodee followed her. Once in the kitchen, Hanna draped a homely knitted shawl around Jodee's thin shoulders.

"Thank you, Hanna. You've been so nice. I don't know how to thank you."

"Don't be scared now," Hanna said, teasing. "Ain't a gal in town prettier than you."

What a fool notion, Jodee thought. Avinelle was

the pretty one with that pert chin and dazzling smile. Jodee felt as rangy as a buffalo calf.

"Fact is, honey, your chances of marrying are better than finding work. You want a husband and family, don't you? Well, then, get yourself a big strapping man like the marshal." She gave Jodee a gaping smile.

Fragile lamps with crystal drops. Doilies on every surface. Whatnots that probably cost more than was decent—Corbet hated Avinelle's suffocating parlor. His jailhouse suited him better. Cold stone walls, iron bars—well, maybe the jailhouse wasn't the best fit either. Just anything but this.

Avinelle's aging maid told him Jodee was in the yard. If they had her doing laundry, he'd raise holy hell. She was supposed to be in bed, recovering.

At the sound of approaching footsteps, Corbet braced himself.

"Ah, Marshal Harlow." As usual, Widow Ashton didn't smile. "I was lying down. What more do you need of us today?"

Corbet felt like a schoolboy. "I stopped by to make sure you're managing."

"If you mean has Miss McQue robbed us yet, we have given her little opportunity. You may think it wise to set her free; I bow to your judgment. But I have my doubts. Avinelle could not rest, knowing the unfortunate girl was in jail, wounded, subject to public scrutiny and the riffraff you usually have installed there. She insisted we invite Miss McQue to stay with us."

Jaw tightening, Corbet didn't envy Jodee's time under this roof. He noticed a certain pallor around the widow's eyes, however, which suggested perhaps he was frightening her. He tried to soften his expression. He didn't purposely bully old women.

When Jodee appeared in the hallway, Corbet's breath went out. Already she looked better. No more was her hair a mop of tangles. Like corn silk, it fell in a cascade to her waist. She looked as shy and reserved as any proper young lady might.

"You wanted to see me, Marshal?"

He couldn't remember why he'd come. When Jodee gestured toward the knapsack he held, she came forward to claim it and retreated back to the hall. He realized she wore nothing under the dress but her lithe young body.

Avinelle crowded past Jodee and seized his elbow. "Have you had lunch, Corbet? Hanna would be happy to fix you a plate. I want to discuss that outlaw, the one you said got away. I don't feel safe unless you're near."

"Sorry, Avinelle. I just wanted to drop off Jodee's knapsack. I can't stay."

"But you must give us a bit of consideration," Widow Ashton put in. "We have had a trying

111

time this past week. And Miss McQue is not yet presentable. We allowed your visit nevertheless. I assumed you had—"

"—If this is too much for you ladies," Corbet interrupted, "just say the word. I'll take Jodee somewhere else."

Widow Ashton's eyes flashed. "You wound me, Marshal. The entire territory seems bent on provoking my daughter and myself, helpless widows at the mercy of thieves and murderers. If you wish to take Miss McQue away, then do it. We opened our home to her. My guest room is waiting. You cannot hold the decency of a bath against us."

A bath—Corbet felt like a fool. Perversely, he said, "Miss McQue, I'd like to just say your hair looks like morning sunlight." The moment he spoke he figured he must have lost what was left of his mind.

When Jodee collapsed to the floor in a heap, Avinelle and her mother looked so startled they didn't respond. Corbet had been waiting so many days for Jodee to faint he didn't need to think. He was at her side in a single stride and scooped her into his arms.

"Jodee?" he whispered. "Jodee!"

She didn't revive.

"I'll fetch Doc," Hanna said from the back of the hallway where she'd been watching. She vanished back into the kitchen.

112

Corbet drew Jodee tightly against his chest. The day had been too much for her. His fault. He was rushing things. His fault. Through the thin calico, he could feel the warmth of her legs and back.

"Upstairs, quickly," Widow Ashton said.

Corbet took the stairs two at a time. He was pleased to note the guest room smelled freshly aired. Widow Ashton turned back the coverlet and closed the window. He placed Jodee on the bed. Stepping back, he realized Widow Ashton was glaring at him. Avinelle stood in the doorway, wearing the same wounded expression she had often worn since her husband's death. He felt like a cad. Avinelle loved him, but he felt nothing in return. Now she knew it.

As Jodee stirred, Corbet held his breath. Blinking, she looked around until her eyes fell on him. He filled with her wide-eyed gaze. She was all right. He heaved a sigh.

"Jodee," he said awkwardly, "you're in good hands here. See you all Sunday."

He made it down the staircase without seeming to run. He didn't understand what had just happened. He wanted nothing more than to keep his town in order until he decided if he should stay or move on, but his thoughts were suddenly in chaos.

The memory of Jodee's eyes kept him moving. Corbet felt bewitched. He wasn't even sure where he was going.

· · ·

Jodee threw herself off the bed and backed away from it on unsteady legs. The abrupt movement made her dizzy. What was she doing on this fancy bed? Avinelle and Widow Ashton stood in the doorway, gawking at her.

The last thing she remembered—the marshal said something about her hair.

Jodee twisted away. She saw her reflection in a tilting mirror framed on top of a bureau of drawers. Was that her ma? That sun-browned face with the astonished-looking eyes was her own actual self, Jodee realized. With her hair clean like morning sunshine; she looked decent. Actual and for real decent!

Reluctantly, Widow Ashton touched Jodee's arm. "Lie down. You fainted."

"I can't take your room, Widow Ashton," Jodee exclaimed. "It's too fine for the likes of me. I'll sleep in the shed."

"Bailey sleeps in the carriage house, foolish girl. This is our guest room. My room is down the hall. Avinelle's is across from mine. The pitcher and basin are here for washing your face and hands in the morning. Hanna will show you where to empty the chamber pot. Lie down now. No more nonsense."

Downstairs there came a rap at the front door and then the sound of footfalls pounding up the stairs. Dr. Trafford burst into the bedroom, his hair windblown. "Hanna said there was an emergency."

Stepping aside, Avinelle bit out, "Mother, I must speak with you." She edged into the hall. "Thank you for coming so quickly, Doctor. It's Jodee, as you can see."

Widow Ashton looked about to say something but thought better of it. "I apologize for this infringement on your time, Doctor. Miss McQue is all right. Please join us downstairs for a refreshment. You look tired."

Ignoring the invitation, the doctor came at Jodee and tugged aside the neckline of her dress to examine the wound. This was Widow Ashton's first glimpse of it. She fled with her fingertips covering her lips.

Dr. Trafford looked relieved. "Why did you faint?"

"Oh, Doc, I'm just so gull-darned tired. Everybody keeps pulling at me. Go here. Go there. Do I have to stay here? The marshal said something about the hotel."

"No decent woman stays at a hotel unaccompanied, Miss McQue. If you had a decent upbringing, you'd know that. If you were to waltz out of here in that get-up, folks would chase you straight to Rella's. She'd paint you up, fit you with a silk dress that men would pay you to take off. Soon you'd be drinking whiskey to dull the shame of your life and end up smoking opium to make it through the night."

Had he lost his mind? "Why are you saying this to me? I ain't done a thing. What's the matter with you?"

"I haven't slept in days. That's what's the matter with me. I came over here thinking you were dying. Corbet's giving you this chance. You have to work now. You have to earn your keep. No more robbing or stealing. If you think life has treated you unfairly, you're probably right, but life has treated you no worse than Virgil Robstart or anyone else. You can't afford to stay in a hotel. You're lucky to be a guest here. Lying on that featherbed will be the easiest trial you'll have to endure."

Jodee decided she hated the doctor.

He glowered back at her. "You wouldn't be expecting a child, fainting like that, would you?"

"I am a virgin girl," Jodee snapped.

"You are no girl, Miss McQue. You are a woman grown. Start acting the part."

How could he think such a thing of her? Jodee wondered, pacing the guest room after he'd gone. She would've died rather than lay with one of the Rikes. Or Burl! Were they all crazy? Did folks really think that low of her? Well, she'd show them all. She'd earn her keep. She'd pay her way and walk out of this town free and clear same as she walked out of that jailhouse.

She needed a ledger to write down her mounting

116

debts. She owed Rella for a hair comb. She owed Artie for meals. She must return the marshal's shirt, washed and starched. She owed that newspaperman a swift kick in his shins, but she supposed she'd never collect that debt. She owed Avinelle for the ugly dress she was wearing, the hair washing paste, the hot bath water, the soap . . .

The list suddenly seemed awfully long. How would she ever earn so much? Looking around, Jodee felt grudging resentment and rising terror. The guest room looked like heaven with a four poster bed and a dresser with a doily protecting the marble top. There was a Turkish carpet on the floor beside the bed and another in front of the dressing table. There were flowered papers on the walls and a glass globe lamp on a spindly table beside the bed; her grandmother never owned such like.

Forgetting the doctor's insult, Jodee tiptoed to the window to examine the delicate weave of the dimity curtains. Pretty as petticoats. Would she ever look out a window of her own like this? She went to the bed and smoothed the linens. Not a stitch of mending. She couldn't bring herself to climb between the sheets.

There was an ornate metal box on the dressing table that she longed to touch. Up close, it looked to be pure silver. She smoothed her fingertips over the fancy design on top. What was in the drawers of the bureau? She longed to look but wouldn't let herself. Did any of them realize how hard she tried to make up for being born poor, and with bad blood? Her shoulder ached, reminding her this was no dream. This was her new life. She didn't know the first thing what to do.

Had she been in some hideout camp, she'd have water to fetch, firewood to gather, Burl and the Rikes to avoid. How easy it had been to dream of a better life while trapped in the old one, she thought. The doctor was right. This was her chance to show folks just what kind of person she really was. A decent person wouldn't itch to open the silver box or peek in drawers. Would they?

From the time she'd been twelve years old she'd been like a stick in a creek, swept away on the current with no will of her own. How did a lone woman stay decent? Was that why Avinelle tried so hard to win the marshal's affections? She needed another husband to keep herself decent? Did it matter who a woman married so long as she was married? Should Jodee consider finding a man instead of work?

She didn't want a husband! Who'd take her, ignorant as she was? The marshal? She drew in a ragged breath and let it out slowly. Morning sunshine indeed. What was he playing at? He'd put her in jail. Questioned her like a criminal. She wasn't sure why he'd let her go. It was probably a test. He no more cared about her than he would a stray dog.

But she was as good as anybody. Standing in this guest room was no different than living in a shack or hideout camp or jail cell. She stared herself down in the looking glass. *I am Jodeen Marilee Latham McQue. I was hard as rocks with outlaws because I had to survive. I can be polite as candy with do-gooder widows like Miss Avinelle and her mother. Easy.*

Easy pickin's. She heard Burl's sneering voice in her memory. "You won't never have a different life than this, girlie-girl. You're a born outlaw. That's all you'll ever be."

Jodee woke abruptly. She'd dreamed of sitting on the sharp points of an iron fence. On one side was a barking dog like the ones she'd passed on her way to school as a child. On the other side was her mother's washtub, but the clothes in it were frozen. It was snowing and she was cold. The dog had her sleeve in its teeth.

Struggling to sit up, Jodee remembered falling asleep on the floor, curled up on the carpet. It must be evening. She heard voices below, reminding her of being at her grandmother's, alone in her upstairs room years ago. Her knapsack lay on the floor near the closed door. On the dressing table lay a tray of food. Someone had placed the shawl across her legs.

Climbing to her feet, she ate a little of the food and rummaged in her knapsack. Holding her tattered old bed dress to her face, breathing in its musty scent, she summoned a memory of those first few months with her father. Those had been good days, honest days, even if they had come near to starving.

In the bottom of the knapsack she found her speller and the stones she'd collected over the years. This round one came from the creek behind that first farm. This white one came from the ranch in Texas. Other smaller stones were from camps and hideouts that ran together in her memory over the last two years. She ought to chuck them all. It was time to forget.

Then Jodee felt a charge of alarm. She rummaged through the knapsack but came up empty. Her locket wasn't there.

Seven

"That smells good!" Jodee exclaimed. The loaf of bread just pulled from the bake oven made her think achingly of home. Having slept well, however, she shook off the memory and grinned at Hanna as she came into the kitchen from the back stairs. "I'm going to town this morning. I'm going to trade my pa's pistol for better clothes."

"That's a good idea, honey," Hanna said,

pausing in her work, "but you can't go looking like that. Miz Ashton had that rag of a dress in the bottom of her oldest trunk for as long as I've worked here. I can see clean through it."

Jodee refused to be discouraged. "Maybe if I could keep your shawl awhile, I'll be all right."

She fetched her britches from the clothesline out back. Moments later she was in the sewing room, pulling them on under the thin blue dress. *Shopping!* she thought, trying not to think how awful she might look setting foot in a store. She was going shopping just like decent folks! She poked her feet into her boots. In a few hours she wouldn't look so awful.

With the cook's shawl clutched around her shoulders to disguise that she wore no camisole or corset under the dress, Jodee waved goodbye to Hanna and hurried out into the crisp morning air. She was so excited she almost broke into a run. She wasn't hiding with outlaws anymore. She didn't have to feel ashamed or afraid ever again.

In less than ten minutes she stepped up onto the jailhouse porch feeling bold as brass. Her heart pattered happily at the prospect of seeing the marshal again. She found him standing in front of the heating stove, frowning thoughtfully at the coffee pot. The sight of him made her heart thrill.

Hearing her come in, Corbet's expression

blossomed into a smile when he turned. "Jodee! What are you doing here? You look rested."

She ducked her head, pleased by his reaction. "I come for my pa's pistol." She explained her intention to trade it for new clothes. "It really is mine, you know. Pa had it long before he knew Ma. He didn't steal it."

Looking sympathetic, the marshal pulled Jodee's gun belt with its attached holster from his desk drawer. He took the pistol from his locked drawer. He'd cleaned it for her.

Oh, it cut her heart to see that big ol' gun again. She remembered her father teaching her to aim and shoot. Just as her father had done with her, she showed the marshal the scrollwork around the initials TTMQ. "Pa was real proud of this. Best gun he ever owned, he said. He gave it to me on my sixteenth birthday. I got good at bringing down jackrabbits. Even got me an antelope once." She relished the way Corbet watched her with those deep, dark eyes of his. "Am I free to walk around town by myself now, Marshal?"

"I should go with you, Jodee. Folks might get the wrong idea, you carrying a big shootin' iron like that." He gave her a little smile that said he was teasing. "There's a stop I'd like to make first."

With the smile still tugging at his lips, he extended his elbow. She didn't like him acting so proper-like. It put a nervous scare into her. He was probably still suspicious. He took her hand and tucked it into the crook of his elbow. With a delicious jolt of awareness, Jodee walked outside with him, arm in arm, her worries forgotten.

They strolled to a shop with a sign reading "Watches & Fine Jewelry" painted on the window. As she passed beneath the tinkling bell over the door, Jodee heard the marshal say softly, "I thought you were going to call me Corbet."

At the closeness of his voice, a thrill went through her. "What are we doing here, Mar—" She swallowed hard. "—Corbet?" It delighted her to say his name as if they were friends.

The jeweler appeared from the rear of the store. "Marshal, I have your item ready." The man took a wooden tray lined in green cloth from behind the counter. In it lay Jodee's newly polished locket, its chain repaired.

Jodee's eyes went dry staring at it. *He'd gone and had it fixed,* she thought. Why would the marshal do such a thing?

"This is a fine old piece, Marshal, maybe fifty years old," the jeweler said. "Quality workmanship with a lovely miniature inside. Yours, Miss?"

Jodee ached to touch it. She thought the marshal took it to keep. Fifty years old—did that mean her grandmother had owned it first, and gave it to her mother? She could sell it, too, but could she part with something so special? This was all she had left of the mother who had defied an entire town in the name of love.

When Jodee accepted the locket, Corbet tried to fasten it around her neck. She drew away. Unable to trust her voice, she closed her fist around the gold and tucked her fist beneath her chin. Of all the things her mother might want for her, surely it was for her to have a new start. Could Jodee give up so much?

"What do I owe you?" Corbet asked the jeweler.

"No charge, Marshal. Just a broken link."

"Thank you," Jodee whispered. Blinking away tears, she hurried outside.

Corbet caught up to her as she stepped blindly from one boardwalk and crossed to the next. "Are you all right, Jodee? You're not angry with me for taking it and having it repaired?"

She shook her head, still unable to trust her voice.

"Well, then. Which store would you like to try first?" He smiled with exaggeration as if hoping to cheer her.

How could she think? Her heart was in pieces. When she woke she'd been so sure that selling her valuables was the right thing to do. But she couldn't part with her father's pistol and her mother's locket.

Corbet's smile wilted. He searched her face. "Have you changed your mind? You must value this locket an awful lot."

"I do, but I need a new start." She looked down

at the threadbare dress she was wearing. She couldn't go through the rest of her life living off other folks' charity. "I need cash money for my new start." She dashed away a tear.

"And a ticket home," he said gently. "I know how hard this is, better than you can imagine."

Tarnation, Jodee thought. He thought she wanted to go home. He didn't understand what it had been like for her there. He didn't know she'd never go back.

But he looked so optimistic. She let him lead her into a small general store. The moment she stepped through the door, she felt her new life beckoning. Just the smell of the place gave her hope.

"Jodee, this is Smithfield Quimby, new to Burdeen City a few months ago. He comes to us all the way from London. Smithfield, this is Miss McQue. She'd like to trade two items of great value to her for some necessities. Would you be willing to accommodate a trade, as a favor to me?"

The slender man in sleeve garters regarded Jodee in her homely shawl and threadbare calico dress. "My dear girl," he said in an unfamiliar accent, "you are in dire need of a new bonnet. I know just the thing, shipped from Boston just last week and on sale for a remarkably low price of twenty-five cents."

Relishing the smell of leather, split pine packing crates and peppermint sticks, Jodee looked around with rising excitement. Hearing nothing of what the man was saying as he headed for a stack of untrimmed braid hats, Jodee could imagine how wonderful it might be to wear clothes of her own. Clothes that were clean. Clothes that fit her slim frame. When she met the storekeeper's eyes, she knew he was assessing her worth. She had no worth, she thought, momentarily flagging in confidence. Part of her wanted to run away.

The storekeeper glanced uncertainly at the marshal.

Gently, Corbet placed Jodee's battered gun belt and holster on the counter. He held the pistol out of sight behind his back.

"What have we here?" Mr. Quimby asked, going behind the counter. He regarded the leather belt with the extra holes gouged in it to make it buckle around a small waist. "I'm afraid I cannot offer more than seventy cents for this. Is this yours, my dear? Are you a shootist?"

"I reckon I am," Jodee said softly, ashamed suddenly of the way the old belt and holster looked. Lee Rike had given it to her, years before. Stolen, most likely.

She fought discouragement. This was hopeless. How was she ever going to get a new start, trading such worthless stuff? She spied a small pistol in a nearby glass case but spun away. She didn't need to defend herself any longer. Her life with outlaws was over.

"Shall I show him the pistol, too, Jodee?" Corbet asked. "You're sure about trading it?"

Her father's pistol, she thought with her heart thudding. She put her fist to her chest. Her dead father's engraved pistol. His gift to her on her birthday. She couldn't do it. She just couldn't part with it. What was she thinking?

Without waiting for her reply, Corbet placed the pistol on the countertop in front of Mr. Quimby's startled gaze. Jodee heard the man's sharp intake of breath. Glancing back, Jodee caught him hefting it, taking aim with it, turning it this way and that just as she had done on her sixteenth birthday—she had to look away again. She couldn't stand to see him touching it.

She made her way over to a brown paperboard box on a shelf labeled "Ladies Underdrawers." Dazzling white lawn drawers filled the box to the top. The topmost pair had wide lace around each leg. The price was two dollars. She began to worry in earnest. She couldn't even afford to buy herself a pair of drawers? How could she start over?

Mr. Quimby regarded her with skepticism. "This is also yours, Miss?" he asked of the big pistol.

"It was my pa's. Do you have any drawers that aren't so fancy?"

He laid the pistol aside as if it meant nothing and climbed a rolling stepladder to a top shelf.

He brought down a box. "Simple, economical. I recommend a half dozen."

"Will you take my pa's pistol in trade or not?" she asked, fighting tears. Her voice sounded anything but gruff.

"Jodee is interested in a complete outfit, Mr. Quimby," Corbet put in. "Because you had a difficult time getting established with two other mercantile stores in town already, I thought you might offer a good price."

Quimby went back to the pistol and scowled at it. "Five dollars."

That sounded pretty good, Jodee supposed, trying not to let on that she was considering his offer.

Corbet moved closer. "Look at the engraving, Quimby. Do those initials bring anything to mind, something you might have read about in the newspaper recently about an outlaw gang?"

The man squinted more closely.

"Some might pay a lot more than five dollars for T. T. McQue's own pistol. Miss McQue can't buy a complete outfit for five dollars. I see Wilson's Mercantile is open."

"Six and a half," Quimby said with haste.

"I mean to buy a few presents, too," Jodee said, her throat still tight, but she was feeling a glimmer of hope. At Corbet's quizzical expression, she added, "Hair washing paste for Avinelle. A hair comb for Rella."

"Ten dollars. No more." Quimby gave her a firm nod of his head.

Jodee felt giddy. Ten? With a trembling hand, she held out the locket. "What about this?" She couldn't hide the quiver in her voice. "It's real gold."

Snatching it from her, Quimby carried the locket to the front of the store where the light was better. "Four dollars and seventy-five cents. Not a cent more. It's old."

"An heirloom," Corbet put in, but he was smiling. "Tell Quimby everything you need, Jodee. You have a room back there where she can try things on, don't you?"

"Have we a deal?" Quimby asked.

Jodee hesitated. "Let's see what fourteen dollars and seventy-five cents will buy."

"My dear," Quimby said, "for some, that is half a month's pay. If you prefer simple things, I can outfit you from head to toe and leave you enough for gifts, hair pins, and a bar of my best Mother's Crème Toilette Bathing Soap. Gentle to the skin, and fragrant, too."

By the time Corbet returned from his morning shave, Jodee was nearly done with her shopping. Quimby had boxes open on every surface, displaying everything from handkerchiefs to toothbrushes.

Jodee stood in Mr. Quimby's back room with

her feet encased in agonizingly tight high button shoes. She wore a white muslin chemise at twenty-five cents under her snug "comfort-style" corset that cost fifty cents. She had on plain muslin underdrawers. They felt wonderfully soft after years of wearing only britches next to her skin. Over the drawers was a cotton belt with dangling button-garters holding up black ribbed stockings at ten cents a pair. Her muslin petticoat was a bargain at forty-seven cents and even had pin-tucks around the hem. Her blouse had twin pleats on either side of the band and long sleeves with a plain collar. It cost ninety cents. Her skirt was made of blue and white Olympia poplin, Mr. Quimby said. That didn't mean a thing to Jodee but seemed quite special to him. He let the item go for ninety-eight cents.

The high-button shoes reminded Jodee of long ago Sunday mornings struggling with her grandmother to get her shoes fastened in time to walk to church. She selected the cheapest pair at a dollar twenty-five. Since living with her father, she'd worn only men's boots. She felt quite the lady, sashaying in a circle, whispering, "how do" to a pile of blankets.

Before she chose a drawstring bag and wool shawl at forty-five cents, Mr. Quimby totaled her items. She had enough left to buy a bed dress for forty-two cents, a bonnet, hair pins, hair washing paste for herself, and a tablet to list her debts on. The tablet cost three cents. Mr. Quimby threw in a penny pencil for free.

She was done.

All her doubts were gone, her anguish forgotten. She felt as happy as a new puppy. She spun around and said, "If only you could see me, Pa." She knotted her hair and pinned it in place. Plopping the hat on her head, she went back into the main room. Customers took no notice of her. With breath held, she approached Corbet, who was thumbing through a mail-order catalogue while he waited.

When he glanced up, he sprang to attention. His eyes grew wide and his neck reddened. "Is that you, Jodee?" His smile spread across his face in a dazzling display. "You take to shopping like every female I've ever known. How do the shoes feel? Are they the right size?"

Doing a jig, she nodded happily.

Mr. Quimby busied himself wrapping her old things in brown paper for carrying home. He finished Jodee's tally and counted out her change, four dollars and sixteen cents.

Jodee could not remember being happier.

She looked decent. She felt decent. She was about to say so when Hobie trotted in, his eyes pinned on the marshal. Jodee held her breath, hoping the lad would notice her and exclaim, too.

As if she were a stranger, Hobie tipped his cap but said to the marshal, panting, "I've been looking everywhere for you, Marshal. A telegraph message." He offered a folded paper.

Jodee's heart gave pause. Was it about her?

Hobie looked away. "And I'm s—sorry, Marshal, but I can't sweep up for you no more. Got to go. I'm late for school." He fled the store before Corbet could ask for an explanation.

Hobie hadn't noticed her. Jodee felt crushed. She was about to ask what the telegraph message was about, but Corbet left the store without speaking. She felt abandoned.

"I am proud to have been your outfitter, Miss McQue," Quimby said. "I will keep your father's pistol in my own private collection. You will tell folks you purchased your wares from my store, I hope."

"Where'd the marshal go? Why'd Hobie have to quit working for him?" Jodee asked without thinking the storekeeper would know.

"A lad that age should not be exposed to the rigors of a lawman's life," Quimby said in a sanctimonious tone. "His mother is a widow, you know. She probably let the lad work for the marshal in hopes of attracting his interest. Women are clever creatures. Yourself included, no doubt. You needn't worry. The marshal will find another helper."

Hobie had lost his job on her account, Jodee was certain, and she felt ashamed. She might look decent now, but the change was only on the outside. She was still unwelcome outlaw trash cluttering up the town. Nothing had changed. Corbet was still a marshal, and Burl was still out there somewhere. She might walk out the door in her fine new duds but she might run straight into Burl. Or she might look out her bedroom window some night and see Burl waiting for her in the dark. Burl might come after her, and she'd have no pistol to keep him at bay. It wasn't too late to take everything off and put her rags back on, she thought. She'd been born to an outlaw after all.

Setting her jaw, Jodee sidled over to the counter where she'd seen the little two-shot pistol displayed under the glass. "How much for that there little pistol?" she asked in her old gruff tone.

Looking startled by the change in her manner, Mr. Quimby plucked the pistol from the case. It was a perfect size for her new hand bag.

Jodee hefted its slight weight and took aim at a wash tub. "How much?"

"A d—dollar ten, my dear. Cartridges are nine cents for a box of fifty." The man looked alarmed.

She counted out the price from the change he'd given her moments before. Then she dropped the little pistol into her bag. Her hand was trembling, but she felt strangely better. "I'll tell everybody how kind you've been."

She marched out of the store, shoe heels clattering satisfyingly on the wooden porch. *This gull-darned town isn't going to lick me,* she thought, gritting her teeth. A couple more days in this sorry place wouldn't wear her down. The moment she felt strong enough, she'd be gone.

She felt so angry she momentarily forgot her determination to start over decent. Ten dollars' worth of new duds didn't change her. If Burl could see her putting on airs, he'd laugh. She wanted to shout every bad word she knew. Hobie hadn't been hurt by her being in that jail, she wanted to shout. She wasn't a bad influence on anybody. She wanted to scold Hobie's mother for taking him from work he liked. Hobie's heart must be breaking.

No . . . no . . . simmer down . . .

Jodee slowed. Decent women didn't march down boardwalks like pistol-toting troublemakers, blazing with thoughts of vengeance. She had on new clothes. Now she needed to find decent work. She needed money. Money she had to earn.

And she was hungry. She had two dollars and ninety-seven cents left. She shouldn't have bought the two-shot pistol, she thought, her fit of temper giving out. Money didn't come easy when a person was decent.

Crossing the street, she noticed strangers tipping hats to her. She dared not return their greetings. It wasn't seemly for a lady to take notice of strangers.

She spied Artie Abernathy's restaurant and

hurried inside. Twenty men sat at a long table, gobbling and jabbering. Silence fell like a thunderclap as they all turned to stare at her. Artie hurried forward, a comic expression of solicitous concern on his round face. *It felt darned strange to look different,* Jodee thought. He seemed to think she was a stranger. A woman alone.

"Good morning, Mr. Abernathy," Jodee said in a clipped tone reminding her of Avinelle in one of her fits of temper. Oh, tarnation, she didn't want to sound like that snippy thing. She gave Artie a more agreeable smile.

Taken aback, his handle-bar mustache twitched. "Good morning! Do I know you, Miss?"

Almost giggling, Jodee felt tempted to toy with him but realized she mustn't encourage the man. "We've met, yes, Mr. Abernathy."

The man's face flooded to such an alarming shade of scarlet that Jodee became suspicious. She knew that look. The Rikes used to look like that when they came back from a night on the town. They liked fancy women.

Jodee's smile went sour. Did she look like a fancy woman? She felt sick to think she might've chosen the wrong sort of clothes.

Artie's eyes skittered around the restaurant and then raked her from head to toe. He seemed ready to order her from his place when recognition dawned.

"Miss McQue?" Looking dumfounded, he

stepped closer. "My, but you do turn out nicely. I heard you were out of jail. What can I do for you this fine morning?"

"Feed me breakfast?" she said inelegantly. "I can pay, if the price ain't too high. I grew partial to your biscuits while I was . . . uh . . . at the marshal's."

Behind her, the door swung open. In surged Corbet, looking flushed. "I thought I'd lost you, Jodee. You're all right? Table for two, Artie." He took Jodee's parcel of old clothes and put it on the floor. "I assumed you'd eaten before you left Avinelle's. I'm sorry. You must be starving!"

She sank into the nearest chair and rolled her aching shoulder. "I was in a hurry when I went out this morning." She tried to draw a deep breath but couldn't. Her new corset was too tight.

He leaned in close. "Are you all right? You look feverish."

Grabbing a fistful of her new blouse, she worried about her heart pattering in a way she didn't like. "I guess I shouldn't have come in here alone. I'll get the hang of being in a town again, and wearing decent clothes. Give me a day or so." She closed her eyes and concentrated on breathing. She didn't want to drop over in a faint again. "How do women go about their chores in these contraptions?" Then she squirmed. What a fool thing to say in front of a man.

She opened her eyes.

Corbet grinned with all his teeth showing. His was the most wonderful face. How could she feel upset when he was around? He placed his hand, warm and gentle, on top of hers. Her body reeled to his touch.

"You'll be all right, Jodee. Just consider this. Days ago you were in the jailhouse, dying of fever. Now here you are, all decked out. You might wake feeling fine, but you need to realize you're not strong yet. Doc's going to box your ears for getting out of bed so soon. You should be resting. All day. For several days. No chores until Doc says it's all right. I should've made you go back the moment I saw you this morning—let me finish—except you needed outfitting. I knew you'd feel better wearing things of your own. As soon as we're done here, I want to take you back to Avinelle's. We'll decide about finding work another day." He leaned in close. "All right? You're not well enough to work yet. You know that, right?"

"But I'm running up debts! I got to start working right away, or I'll get in so deep I'll never get out." She felt overwhelmed suddenly. It was more than that. She was afraid she might run out on her debts like her father had always done. Or be tempted to steal something to pay for them. She was an outlaw's daughter, after all. She had bad blood. She wanted to run now. "I'm upset about Hobie, too."

Artie brought flapjacks swimming in butter and syrup.

"Hobie leaving his job with me wasn't because of you," Corbet said when they were alone again. "Hobie's mother wants him to go to college this fall. He needs to concentrate on finishing school. Now eat."

With Corbet carrying her parcel of gifts and old clothes, and buoyed by a good meal, Jodee was able to walk slowly back to Avinelle's. Strolling alongside Corbet felt like a dream come true.

The late morning sunshine felt good on her face, although the air still held the cool tang of spring. She kept Hanna's knitted shawl around her shoulders. Concerned about her new shoes, she had to take care with each step. No wonder decent women were always mincing around, acting foolish and fainting. She giggled. They were suffocating and worried about dirtying their shoes.

Corbet turned to her. "What is it?"

"I feel like a fool, Marshal—Corbet." She shook her head. "I'm trussed up like a Christmas goose. I should've bought britches, a work shirt, and sturdy boots. How am I to cook or do washing or dust whatnots if I'm falling over in a faint every two minutes because I'm wearing a gull-darned corset?"

Chuckling, Corbet slowed his pace. "Do you always worry like this?"

Jodee side-stepped a wide expanse of mud. "I didn't notice all this mud on my way to town this morning." She might get mud on her hem, too. "I just walked along, free and happy. Now I got to be careful of everything I say and everything I do. I'm going to go crazy. I reckon I do worry, Mar—Corbet. Them fools I lived with, and Pa, they never had a sensible thought. It was always me figuring out what we'd eat from day to day. I had to pick our campsites or find us a shack. If I left it to the men, we'd be bedding down in a cactus patch or a dry gulch that might flood after a rain in the night. One of my first thoughts after waking up from being gunshot was about our packhorse with all our gear. You can't live without a skillet or coffee pot. Or beans. If I never have to eat another bean—you reckon anybody found that horse and took care of him? Poor old thing."

Corbet nodded. "We brought him back to town. Did he belong to someone, in the gang, I mean?"

She swallowed hard, remembering that last day. It seemed like a lifetime ago. She agonized over the truth. "He was . . . borrowed. I know you got work to do, Marshal. You don't have to walk me. I can get myself back to Avinelle's." She wanted to escape that stab of shame.

"And leave you to get run over by a passing wagon?" He gave a warning nod.

Looking over her shoulder, Jodee stepped back just in time. A six-horse team pulling a freight wagon bore down on her and then lumbered past. A bit of mud landed on her hand.

"I must've been out of my head to buy white. I ain't even had 'em on an hour and already I'm covered in dust—" She managed to laugh.

"It's not easy what you're doing," he said, his voice low. "Folks won't forget I had you in jail. I'm trying to make up for that. That day we got back, I wasn't thinking. I was tired, and upset about Virgil. Him getting shot was my fault. Putting you in jail was the only thing I could think of at the time."

She made a smile that only tightened her cheeks. He felt duty-bound, she told herself. Them walking together meant no more than that. He wasn't partial to her like she wished.

"Any person new to a town has a hard time of it," he went on. "I should know. I've been on my own a long time. Lots of new towns. Months proving myself. Folks are naturally suspicious. They have to be, with no-accounts like Tangus around. Give folks the chance you would want them to give you."

She nodded. "You're right, Marshal."

"Corbet, remember."

She said his name like a kiss. "Corbet." He

might be duty-bound to her, but she felt more than beholden toward him. She wanted to drink up his face. She wished she could kiss him again. "I got to give folks time," she repeated in order to please him.

"And yourself. You need time, too."

Her body responded with a thrill that flashed through her like a whirlwind. Her cheeks flushed hot.

When they reached Avinelle's gate, Jodee sensed someone watching from the front window and gnashed her teeth.

"Thank you for breakfast . . ." She couldn't bring herself to say his name again. She didn't want him to guess how foolish she felt about him.

The front door opened. There stood Avinelle wearing a pink confection of a dress. Her tiny waist made her look girlish. Quite an outfit for morning, Jodee thought. Her heart gave a painful wrench. If ever she had felt second class, it was in that moment.

"Good morning, Avinelle," Corbet called in a formal tone. "I trust you rested well last night. No worse for the wear after your ride home from Cheyenne City yesterday."

"Why, Marshal Harlow," Avinelle simpered. "Good morning to you. Who's that—" She swished onto the porch, her skirts moving like a cloud. Then her hand clapped to her mouth.

In a sing-song she called, "Mother. Mother! Do come out here. Jodee's back."

At Avinelle's nasty-sweet tone, Jodee went rigid. *Better be careful, Missy Prissy. There's a pistol in my bag.* Shocked by her own thoughts, Jodee edged closer to the marshal.

Widow Ashton came out onto the porch. The two ladies stared at Jodee. Jodee let them look long and hard, and when she'd had enough she took the parcel containing her old clothes from Corbet and bit out, "Thanks again." She started up the flagstone walk. She could see Avinelle's flashing eyes. Jodee cocked her chin at her.

Avinelle's mother eyed the pin-tucked blouse. "Where did you get these things?"

"Quimby's General Store. His stock came from England." Jodee wasn't sure where England was but it must be far away or she would've heard of it before.

"I wasn't aware Mr. Quimby offered credit. Did he offer you a job, as well, I wonder? I suppose you might clerk for him. If you can count. How much will this ensemble cost? Surely you do not expect me to pay for it." Widow Ashton's tone was plainly insulting.

It didn't seem that the cost of her clothes was any business of hers, Jodee thought. "I worked out a trade."

Widow Ashton's face drained to white.

What was so horrible about that, Jodee wondered. Didn't decent women trade with tradesmen?

Corbet came up behind Jodee. His face looked carved of ice.

"Did you help her pick out these things, Corbet?" Avinelle inquired ever so sweetly.

"She traded Quimby her two most valuable possessions," Corbet said, his words holding a subtle warning. "Her father's pistol and her mother's gold locket. All I did was make sure Quimby gave her a fair price."

"I see," was all Widow Ashton could manage.

"Can you come inside, Corbet?" Avinelle moved down the steps to take his elbow. "Hanna's breakfast was especially delicious this morning. Her coffee is perfection. I'm sure there's plenty left."

"We had breakfast, Jodee and I, but thanks, Avinelle. I have to be going. Did I hear you say you had gifts, Jodee?"

Avinelle pouted her way back up the steps but she looked at Jodee with new eyes. She and her mother stepped aside as Jodee climbed to the porch in her loud, new heeled shoes and entered the house. Corbet came as far as the door.

"Widow Babcock." Quickly Jodee tore into her parcel and handed Avinelle a tin of hair washing paste with a picture of an elegant buxom lady with long waving hair on the lid. "Mr. Quimby said this here is the best he has. It's from London. It smells like roses."

Looking dumfounded, Avinelle accepted the tin.

"That's my thanks for you helping me get cleaned up yesterday. And this here is for you, Widow Ashton. Mr. Quimby suggested a lady such as yourself would appreciate the finest tea in the world, English tea." She handed the woman a square tin with a funny looking house and twisted trees on the top.

Widow Ashton frowned as if unable to comprehend that Jodee was giving her a gift.

"And," Jodee said, looking around. "Hanna?"

Hanna appeared so quickly, she surely had been listening at the kitchen door.

"This is for you. I'd like to keep your shawl if you don't mind." She handed Hanna the new wool shawl, a lovely weave even to Jodee's inexperienced eye. The long fringe was especially beautiful.

"I ain't never had anything so fine, Miss Jodee. I can't—"

"Avinelle," Corbet interrupted the exchange. "Widow Ashton. Hanna." He tipped his hat and started away. "Good morning, ladies. Remember what I said, Jodee. No work until Doc gives the word."

When he disappeared down the street, Maggie closed the door.

An awkward silence fell.

"I don't care what the marshal says," Jodee said into that deadly quiet, "I need to learn housework right off. Maggie could teach me to dust and scrub floors." She realized she'd forgotten to buy a gift for the shy maid.

"Honestly, Jodee," Avinelle snapped with exasperation. "We wasted an entire morning worrying about where you went. We are responsible for you, you know. You should've asked if you were well enough to go out. Of course, I would've said no. Get upstairs. To bed immediately."

"Sorry," Jodee said softly, too tired suddenly to fight them. She heaved a heavy sigh and climbed the stairs. Being decent surely was a chore, she thought.

Eight

Maggie placed Jodee's parcel of old clothes on the bed. "There you go, Miss."

Jodee wanted to put the nervous-looking maid at ease but didn't know what was bothering her. She felt surprised at how tired she was after her morning of shopping. Sinking into the chair by the window, Jodee asked, "Have you worked for Avinelle and her ma for a long time?"

The maid looked as if the door might be listening. She ducked her head but her eyes shone with furtive excitement. "Yes'm." Just when Jodee thought that was all she was going to say, Maggie whispered, "I know everything."

"What do you mean?" Until that moment, Maggie had seemed uninteresting.

Maggie dashed to the bureau and lifted the lid of the silver box. Tinkling music filled the room. Seconds later, she snapped the lid closed and stood hunched and listening, her eyes wary. "A treasure," she whispered, "from long ago."

When Maggie started to open the wardrobe doors, Jodee cautioned her, "Don't do that! I don't want to know what's in there." That was a lie. Jodee longed to see everything in the wardrobe and bureau, everything in the house, truth be known, but she feared if she saw something she might be tempted to take something. It was a foolish fear but real nonetheless.

Before the maid could reply, they heard a buggy arrive out front. Maggie bolted downstairs to answer the door. Jodee felt amazed at how quickly the woman could move when she needed to. Jodee heard a male voice and let out her breath. It wasn't Corbet. It must be the caller Widow Ashton expected for luncheon. As voices moved from the entry into the parlor, Jodee pressed her door closed.

Unwilling to muss or take off her new clothes, Jodee sat by the window where she could look out between the panels of dimity. It was a good spot to watch for Burl. He was out there somewhere. Why, she didn't know. He was taking a crazy chance, hanging around when he was wanted for murder. She hugged her new hand bag. Inside it, the new pistol felt hard and reassuring.

An hour later, Hanna found her there.

"Silly child, sleeping in a chair. Are you all right, honey? Did Miz Avinelle or Miz Theia hurt your feelings? Don't you let them bother you. Them clothes are just fine."

Jodee roused herself, grateful for the woman's encouragement. She stood up, feeling a bit groggy and stiff. "Is there anything I can help you with?"

"You can watch me set the table." Hanna brushed Jodee's hair into a long tail, twisted it, and within moments had enough new hairpins stuck in to hold the knot at the nape of Jodee's neck. "If I do say so myself," Hanna said smiling at her handiwork, "you look ready to catch yourself a husband."

"Oh, Hanna, I told you I don't want a husband. I should've bought something more practical. When I start working, these clothes will get dirty."

"I got aprons."

They went down the back stairs. In the pantry, Hanna gathered plates and chattered happily as she spread a fresh lace cloth on the dining room table. As she worked she explained what each plate and piece of silverware was for. Then she parked Jodee on a stool and made certain Jodee knew how to peel apples. Happily, Jodee whittled them clean.

"Maggie has a room in the attic," Hanna said, keeping her voice low. "She hardly says a word, but she don't miss a thing. Now me, I have all my children. My oldest girl looks after the younger ones while I work. And Bailey, he sleeps in the carriage house. He used to drive for Mr. Ashton, you know, before he got sick. Bailey's too old to go back east, so I don't know what he's going to do. Burdeen was just a turn in the road when the Ashtons and Babcocks moved here to expand the stage line and open the depot. Mr. Ashton claimed Burdeen would be a metropolis some-day." She chuckled. "Big ideas. Lots of investor friends back east. My husband and me, we worked on a ranch near here. I was cook, he was a drover. Then Elmer—my husband—he got himself killed in a stampede. There I was, a widow with five children. I moved into town and found Miz Ashton desperate for help. I'll stay on a while, I guess." She shook her head, paused to think and laugh.

"What happened to Mr. Ashton?"

"Avinelle's step-father just up and died. Maggie won't tell me who Miz Ashton was married to before him. Some rich feller back east. Now Miz Avinelle, she was a bride when she first got here, but not a happy one. Hated Burdeen. Mr. Ashton took sick the first winter. You wouldn't expect it, but after he was gone Miz Ashton was beside herself. Now, Miz Avinelle's husband, he was no better than a chicken with its head off. All the time riding to Cheyenne City or Fort Laramie or Denver on business. My foot. He liked his faro, that's what. Miz Avinelle had to sell jewelry to pay his debts. He went off to Cheyenne alive one day, came back the next day in a pine box, shot in a saloon brawl. Now, remember, honey, you get caught touching anything, them two so-called ladies will toss you out. They're watching, you can bet. When they told me you was coming here, I thought they'd gone off their heads. Not on account of you just coming out of jail. On account of them two aren't the charitable kind. They like to think they're fine, putting on airs, but I know them better'n anybody."

"What about Maggie?"

"She's Miz Theia's pet."

Wearing a peculiar expression, Hanna darted from the kitchen to check the tall clock in the front hallway. "Plenty of time 'til dinner," she called loudly when she returned. Lowering her voice, she whispered, "Maggie was listening at the door. Don't say nothing around here you wouldn't want announced in church."

At supper time Hanna filled a hand-painted tureen with chicken stew from the cook pot. The apple pie was almost done. Its heavenly aroma filled the kitchen. Even Artie's fare didn't compare.

"I used to roll pie crust with my grandmother," Jodee said. "Used to sneak bites of dough. I haven't thought of that in a long time."

"I'll never forget when they hired Corbet as city marshal," Hanna went on. "Big strapping man. Folks laid odds he'd marry Avinelle in a month and take over the stage line, but he backed off." She gave Jodee a wink. "It'll take a smarter gal than Avinelle Babcock to get that man in harness."

Jodee turned away. She didn't want to think about Corbet and Avinelle together.

Hungry and looking forward to a delicious meal, Jodee realized, however, that Avinelle and her mother expected her to learn to serve as well as set a table. As a waitress, she didn't get to eat with them. All through the meal, Hanna, Maggie, and Jodee stood in the dining room at the ready, fetching fresh water, more bread, and another crock of corn relish from the cellar. Jodee wondered if the women deliberately dawdled to keep her on her feet.

Finally, blessedly, the ladies withdrew. After clearing the table, Jodee ate with Hanna and Maggie in the kitchen. Even cold, the food tasted wonderful. Jodee did the dishes so Hanna could go home. Without a word, Maggie vanished to her attic room. While Jodee put away the last of the dishes, she saw so many valuables in the pantry she couldn't help but think of Burl. Sterling serving pieces and heavy silver flatware, cut crystal, and fancy porcelain with gold around the edges. She almost felt as if she should guard the house.

In her room that night, Jodee put on her new bed dress. It smelled of peppermint. She turned back the bed's coverlet and allowed herself the luxury of crawling between the soft linens. She was only half done reviewing the day's remarkable events before she was asleep.

The following day she helped with chores and saw the doctor briefly in the afternoon. Avinelle and her mother took turns with the bathing tub in the sewing room after supper. Jodee stood by, fetching extra towels, scented oil, and velvet slippers, wondering how servants endured the boredom of housework.

Burl hunched at the rear corner of a smoky saloon, the town's newspaper sheet on the bar before him, rumpled and damp. The place was so dim he could hardly see to read.

The barkeep ambled closer. He gave a nod toward Burl's empty shot glass. Burl nodded. "One more."

"The barber charges four bits to pull a tooth," the barkeep said.

Burl pinned him with a black stare.

Shrugging, the barkeep filled the glass to the brim. "Anybody can see you're hurtin', friend. The whole side of your face is swolled up. Toothache's been known to kill a man. Doc can do it, but he'll charge more. He's educated."

Snapping one of the last of his stolen coins on

the bar, Burl rapped the newspaper sheet with his knuckle. "Helluva thing," he mumbled with effort, giving the near-empty saloon a furtive glance.

The barkeep snickered. "I hear they recovered near everything, so the marshal let her go. You in town long, friend?"

His question was too casual to take lightly. Burl extended his hand. "R. W. Preston out'a Nebraska. Buttons and sundries." Burl pretended interest in the barkeep's frayed sleeve garters.

The barkeep shook Burl's hand. Wiped the bar. Watched the door. It was late. He looked bored and tired.

"Where you suppose she went? Cheyenne?" Burl asked.

A man rose from his seat at a nearby table, clapped his hat on his head, and gave Burl a once-over. "Come over to my store Monday morning, Mr. Preston. I can always use more stock in buttons. I hear she's rooming with the widows. Helluva thing, all right. The widows get robbed at gunpoint and then they take the girl in. That's decent church-goin' women for you. I say she robs 'em blind 'for they know what for."

"That a fact," Burl said, taking more whiskey into his mouth. The pain eased. He closed his eyes and swallowed. Saloons were such informative places. "Barber, you say? Four bits? Then I'd better not drink away my salvation. Business has been slow. I better be gettin' back to the hotel."

He straightened, gave a nod to the barkeep and the stranger, and headed for the door. He only wished he had a room at the hotel.

"Preston?" the stranger said, detaining him at the door. He extended his hand. "Horace Wilson. My store's right over there." He pointed at the street lined with darkened storefronts.

Burl gave an impatient nod. "See you Monday."

At dawn Sunday, before Hanna had arrived to put on the first kettle, Jodee was in the kitchen laying the cook stove fire when a knock came at the front door. Maggie hadn't come down from the attic yet.

Nervously, Jodee opened the front door to a grizzled stranger in dirty overalls. She had no idea what to do. "Who should I say is calling?" she said, feeling silly. That was the proper thing to say, she hoped.

The stranger handed her a folded paper. "I got this here note."

Avinelle appeared at the top of the stairs. "Jodee? Who is it?"

"I'm jes' the marshal's new hired help. Grady's the name." The stranger tipped his hat.

Avinelle tumbled down the stairs in her frilly silk dressing gown and snatched the note from Jodee. She didn't look at the man. "Messengers to the back door."

153

As the man shambled down the steps, Avinelle read the note and then flung it aside. "Mother," she shouted, ignoring Jodee. She stormed back up the stairs. "Corbet's been called away."

Upstairs, a door slammed. Jodee heard strident weeping. Did Avinelle care so very much for the marshal that she would carry on like this? She returned to the kitchen, wondering if dinner would be cancelled.

Hanna came in. Upon hearing of the message, she made a bemused face and sank onto the nearest chair. "Mercy me, you watch, honey. Them two will be like two cats in a bag all the rest of the day."

Corbet reined his horse behind his deputy. It was mid-morning and cold in the mountains. He was supposed to be having dinner at Avinelle's in an hour, but instead he was miles away, looking at a body half buried in the pines.

"Over there," Hicks called, reining on the narrow trail and pointing through a dense stand of pine. "That's where I seen him. Laying just like that. I didn't move a thing."

Corbet saw a dark coat and what looked like soles of worn boots splayed beneath a thin blanket of dry pine needles. It was difficult to tell how long the body had been there. Dismounting, he prowled the area. If the man had fallen from a horse, his body would be closer to the trail.

He suspected the man had been waylaid, robbed, and dragged into the trees. Corbet's face felt taut with disgust.

No horses missing a rider had been reported in Kirkstone, Hicks claimed.

No sign of a bedroll, travel case, or saddlebags. Corbet bent to examine the body. The coat pockets were empty.

"It's Tangus," Hicks announced around a cigar.

Corbet wasn't sure. "Could be anybody."

"Cheap pistol. Old boots. It's him." Hicks hooked his knee around the pommel of his saddle.

If the dead man had been waylaid, why leave the pistol and the boots? Corbet wondered. "We'll bury him here."

They dug the grave alongside the remains. Corbet kept the pistol and coat to show Jodee. If she identified the items as Tangus', he'd take her word, but he dreaded bringing up the subject.

When the grisly chore was finished, he sent Hicks back to Burdeen to write the report. He went on to Kirkstone, where he spent two hours at the bath house soaking the smell of death from his hands. After a bad meal at the only restaurant, he asked around. No one said anything different than what Hicks had told him.

Corbet decided not to stop by Avinelle's when he got back to town, not even to check on Jodee. He didn't relish the scolding he'd receive when he eventually showed his face there. Instead, he reined his horse at the Robstart's cabin. Having a door slammed in his face sounded like a good way to end a depressing trip, he thought.

At his knock, Pasty Robstart yanked the door wide and glared. Scarcely five feet tall, she bore the red and swollen eyes of recent weeping. "Just the man I want to see," she snapped in a peevish tone. "Get in here, Corbet."

Startled, he saw Virgil propped in bed across the room beyond a blanket curtain. Virgil lifted his hand in a weak hello. Corbet felt kicked in the belly. Virgil looked worse than he could've possibly imagined. The cabin felt chilly and smelled of sour milk. The hearth fire was out. There was no kindling in the box. His friend wasn't mending.

Patsy pushed untidy red hair from her face. "I can't care for a colicky newborn, watch over a gunshot husband, and chop firewood, too. My mother says I made my bed, so now I'm lying in it. Well, I'm not sorry. I love Virgil, but he's no better, as you can see. I have to blame somebody, so I'm blaming you, Corbet." Her face split into a tortured mask of misery.

Corbet gathered her into his arms and let her sob helplessly, and heart-rendingly, against his chest. Over her head he saw Virgil's sad eyes cling to him. *Damn Tangus and all men like him,* Corbet thought. What he wanted out of life meant nothing in the face of this. All Virgil had wanted was a brief respite from the emotional storms of a very pregnant wife. By taking Virgil on the posse, Corbet had thought he'd been doing them both a favor.

Suddenly, Patsy punched Corbet's chest hard and tore free of his patting hands. "I need a few things from Papa's store. Would you stay? I couldn't leave Virgil."

Corbet scarcely had time to drape Patsy's shawl around her shoulders before she was out the door. She looked small, hurrying away, clutching her squalling baby to her neck. She was so proud, so stubborn. Corbet felt awash with pity and admiration for her.

Shedding his coat, he went outside to split kindling until he dripped with sweat. If Patsy had let him in sooner he might've been more help, but he didn't blame her for rebuffing her. When he'd stacked kindling to the roof poles and filled the wood box inside, he made fresh coffee, took note of Patsy's supplies and determined that if her parents failed to send what she needed, he'd send everything himself at his own expense.

By then it was full dark, and he was hungry. He built up the hearth fire until it roared. Then he sank into the rocking chair next to Virgil's bed where his friend lay so ghastly pale.

Virgil opened his eyes. "Trying to burn the place down?"

Corbet forced a smile. "You're looking better."

"I look like hell. Try not to mind Patsy. It was a difficult birth, Doc said. She's sore and she's tired. The baby feeds every two hours, so she can't sleep. I thought the baby would make her happy, but she's so touchy. Doc says new mothers get like that. I know she's worried. If I could get up, Corbet . . . but the . . . I try to hold the baby, but I got no strength." Virgil turned his eyes away.

To distract him, Corbet talked about Jimmy Hicks finding the body up in the mountains. He told Virgil about his new helper, old man Grady, and the new deputy, Charlie Malone, up from Cheyenne City. "I wrote for another deputy, one with experience, so I can let Hicks go. I don't know. Maybe I'll keep both." He left the remainder of his thoughts hanging, thoughts that he was considering turning things over to the new man, a man who wanted to be a lawman.

"I never should've married her," Virgil said as if he hadn't heard a word Corbet spoke. "I should've stayed on the ranch, but no, I saw that sweet face and started making up excuses to come to town to hang around her pa's store. They didn't want me for their daughter. Said I was no-account. I knew they were right. That's why I clerked for them as long as I did, trying to make up for taking her from them. To prove myself, I "guess." Virgil sounded drunk. His voice sounded as soft as death.

"Patsy loves you," Corbet said, fearing the defeated note in his friend's voice.

"I was no good at keeping accounts, or pressing folks to pay, but I was a good deputy. Wasn't I, Corbet?"

"The best."

Virgil caught Corbet's sleeve. "Look after her and the boy. See she finds a good man."

"Virg—" Corbet started an alarmed protest.

"I'm sorry about them times," Virgil whispered, "you brought me home drunk. She'd cry. I felt like a rotten dog, doin' that to her. She didn't deserve that."

Corbet laid his hand on his friend's fist. "Stop." He hadn't forgotten his shock the first time he carried Virgil home from Rella's. Virgil had a temper. He and Patsy had had fights. "She forgave you."

Hearing footfalls outside, Corbet tried to send Virgil strength with his voice. "You're not going to die." He watched Virgil take a deep breath and relax. Unburdening his mind had helped. Corbet felt better, too. Heavier, but better.

Pasty came in, her expression brightening at the sight of the blazing hearth fire. "Artie sent a pot of his best chicken broth."

She set a kettle on the table. Behind her ventured her mother holding the sleeping baby and her father with a carton of goods. There had been strain in the family since Virgil and Pasty ran off to marry without their blessing.

Corbet greeted Virgil's in-laws. He hoped there had been a reconciliation, but he seethed to think Patsy's parents had done their best to make this young couple suffer.

"Looks like you're in good hands, Virgil. I'll be going now, but I'll be back tomorrow to see what other chores need doing." He ignored Patsy's automatic protest.

Glancing at the squirming bundle waking in Pasty's mother's arms, Corbet thought he had seen bigger loaves of bread. Young Henry Robstart chose that moment to fill the cabin with a wail that sliced Corbet's ears.

"Get out of here," Patsy said, pushing him toward the door. "You take up more room than you're worth." She had nearly closed the door on Corbet's back when she paused to add, "I'm sorry. Thank you. I know Virgil begged you to take him on the posse. I can't keep blaming you for that. It could've been anybody getting shot."

Corbet had no idea what to say.

He spent the remainder of the evening prowling Burdeen's saloons, asking for information about Tangus and the body in the mountains. Had anyone heard talk of a missing man, a horse with no rider or a rough-looking stranger? He heard nothing useful. *It had to be Tangus in that badly dug grave,* he told himself.

He found his new deputy, Charlie Malone, asleep behind the desk when he entered the jailhouse late. Hicks had come and gone hours before. No report lay on his desk, just spittle on the floor and the faint bite of whiskey in the air.

Charlie stumbled off to his boarding house. Corbet wrote the report himself. The cells were empty. The heating stove was cold and choked with ash. When he was done writing, Corbet wandered into his sleeping room where only days before Jodee lay with her fearsome fever. He let himself think about that kiss she had bestowed on him. What was he so afraid of? It didn't mean anything . . . but it did. Otherwise why would he be so reluctant to think about it?

He went back into the main room and took the dead man's gun and coat from his saddlebags. The smell of death clung to them. No bullet holes in the coat. No blood stains. There were scratches on the gun that might be considered notches, except until the stagecoach holdup Tangus hadn't been known as a killer.

Corbet found no murder warrants on him among his collection. The dead man was just a clumsy highwayman with an old gun. The gun belt offered no information other than the wearer had been skinny. Corbet feared he'd never know who he buried.

Nine

Bracing himself for an onslaught of feminine emotion, Corbet delivered himself to Avinelle's doorstep the next morning and forced a smile. "Sorry to call so early—"

"Corbet!" Avinelle beamed. "Have you had breakfast? No, then you must come in. What was your emergency?"

She seized his elbow and dragged him inside. This was a pleasant, if suspicious surprise, Corbet thought. He had expected reproaches and tears. Avinelle pulled him into the dining room. Feeling like a bull at the county fair being led around by a nose ring, he plucked off his hat.

Avinelle's mother sat queen-like at the head of the table. At the sight of him, her expression registered shock. She tipped her head as if granting him leave to enter. "Marshal Harlow, how good of you to call so early and unannounced . . . as usual. Do sit down."

He declined. He was impatient to see Jodee, to know she was all right.

Avinelle took her seat. Fussing with her napkin, she flashed a peculiar look at her mother, irritating Corbet, because he couldn't guess what was beneath this feigned propriety.

"Since you had to disappoint us on such short

notice this past Sunday, we expect you to honor our invitation this coming Sunday, if you would be so kind, Marshal," Widow Ashton said.

There seemed to be a subtle change in the woman, Corbet thought, noticing a shadow of anxiety darkening her glinting eyes.

Before he could state his purpose, Jodee elbowed her way through the door from the pantry. She was wearing her new clothes. Her pale hair was tied back, making her appear thin and frail. She was pale except for blotches of color on her nose and cheeks. Hers was a natural beauty that didn't need a frame of elaborate curls or expensive lace. It was a relief to see her. Corbet suppressed a smile.

Seeing Corbet, Jodee faltered. She held a heavy-looking silver tray loaded with a platter of sausages and eggs. He stepped around the table quickly and took it from her. Setting the tray on the sideboard, he swung and pinned Avinelle with a look so severe her smile withered. Instantly, tears sprang to her eyes. He felt like a cad. This wasn't Avinelle's doing, he realized. He turned his glare on her mother, understanding at last who his true adversary was. They were treating Jodee as a servant. That had been their intention from the first.

"Do not look at me like that, Marshal Harlow," Widow Ashton snapped. "We are not mistreating your little charge. I have her sleeping in my guest room, after all, not on the back porch where serving girls belong. You have no idea the disruption her stay has imposed upon my routine. Getting her clean. Instructing her in the simplest of tasks. Constantly correcting her. Ever watchful lest she break something. Already she has dropped my best silver sugar." Shaking her head, she folded her napkin and laid it beside her plate. Her veined hands trembled.

"How are you feeling, Jodee?" he asked gently, trying to hide his frustration.

"I'm fine, really, Cor—Marshal. I don't know how to do none of—"

"Any," Widow Ashton corrected.

"Any of this work," Jodee said, scarcely noticing the woman's interjection. "I got to learn."

"Did the doctor give you permission to work already?"

"You know very well, Corbet Harlow," Widow Ashton interrupted in a shrill tone, "the doctor cannot call every day." She rose from her seat. "Perhaps we should have a private word." She started toward the door.

When he failed to follow, she gave a scarcely perceptible pause and continued on her way out of the room.

"I've got to pay for all I owe, Corbet," Jodee whispered.

At that, Avinelle stalked from the room as well.

Corbet felt torn three ways. "Are they treating you all right?"

Jodee leaned in close. "How much do I owe for the silver sugar? I didn't mean to drop it. It just slipped out of my hand."

He dismissed the question. He'd pay for it himself, if necessary. He took Jodee's elbow. She felt so thin. As he guided her into the kitchen, he struggled to conceal his concern.

Hanna was whipping cream with a bowl held against her bosom. "Well, hello there, Marshal," she exclaimed. "This here's an armed camp since we got your note Sunday. Who's that old man you got running errands for you? Better tell him to come to the back next time. Miz Ashton had a fit to think such like was seen on her front porch."

Corbet greeted Hanna and then fixed Jodee with a serious look. "I don't like seeing you work before the—don't give me that got-to-have-a-job argument, Jodee. Should I take you somewhere else? You're not getting any rest here."

"I don't know how to convince them I ain't going to rob them," Jodee cried. "I don't speak out of turn. I ain't touched a gull-darned thing. I'm not complaining, neither. I just can't figure out how to please them." She lifted her chin, her lips quivering. "I can't go around acting like a fool the rest of my life. They're willing to teach me. I got to learn."

Corbet studied the flush to Jodee's nose and

cheeks, the frustration pulling at the corners of her mouth. Just what were Avinelle and her mother trying to teach her, to do a job in order to earn a living? Or that she was second class?

"I need to talk to you this afternoon," he said, changing his tone to official rather than personal. "I'll call for you at two."

Jodee's eyes rounded. She looked pleased but suspicious. "Fine by me."

"Sorry about interrupting breakfast," he said to Hanna.

"No harm done, Marshal. All this food is going to waste anyhow. Them two eat dry toast and tea most mornings." She swept her arm around the kitchen. "All for show. Whipped cream in the morning. I'm glad you were here to see it. Things is just as hospitable around here as in a snake pit, all smiles and if-you-please. It's enough to make a body take to whiskey before noon." She clapped Corbet on the back. "Ask Jodee what she thought of church on Sunday. You'd think we had a medicine show going on the way folks trouped in and out of here all after-noon to pay calls, gawkin' and havin' their say. Now everybody thinks Miz Ashton is the most charitable lady in Wyoming Territory." She gave a chuckle in Jodee's direction. "Tell the marshal what fun we had, honey. A regular picnic."

As he headed down the hall, Corbet realized Avinelle and her mother waited in the drawing

166

room. No gang of outlaws ever looked more formidable. To Widow Ashton he called, "Sorry I missed dinner Sunday, Miz Ashton, but my deputy found a dead man in the mountains. I had to investigate. And bury the body." He opened the front door.

Widow Ashton hurried after him. "I had no idea. Your work must come first, of course. Our invitation stands, if you find time for us." She flashed a look in Avinelle's direction and then hurried up the stairs.

Something about that woman didn't ring true, Corbet told himself. He felt it now more than ever. Theia Ashton didn't like him, and yet she was shoving Avinelle at him with both fists. "Corbet, I assure you, Jodee gave us no indication she was in any sort of discomfort," Avinelle said. "Otherwise we would never have asked her to serve breakfast. She'll never make a satisfactory maid, cook, or governess if she can't stop asking questions when she should be working." Her lower lip quivered in a most attractive way. "We're doing our best, Corbet, truly we are, but she's so ill-bred. I fear you'll blame us when she doesn't find a job. Mother is at the end of her patience already."

Letting Jodee come to Avinelle's house had been the worst idea he'd ever had, Corbet realized. He squeezed his forehead, yearning to say something scathing, but Avinelle looked so brittle he couldn't bring himself to wound her further.

"I'll take Jodee to the hotel. That's what I should have—"

Avinelle rushed to him and caught his arm. "Corbet, no!"

Before she could press herself against him, perhaps even try to kiss him, Corbet held her off. "I'm calling for Jodee at two o'clock. I have something serious to discuss with her at the jail. Now let me go."

"But what about me, Corbet? Haven't you any time for me? After all I've done?"

He racked his brain. Did he owe Avinelle something? Did she think he was obligated to marry her because of the job of marshal she and her mother secured for him? If so, he'd quit on the spot. He felt worse than her puppet. He felt bought and paid for.

"Maybe a picnic," he blurted, feeling like an easy mark. "When it's warmer. You, your mother, Jodee, Maggie, and Hanna." He warmed to the idea, anything to get out the door, but Avinelle's appalled expression made him sorry he spoke.

She fled the room.

Swearing, Corbet slammed out of the house. He supposed Avinelle wanted him to court her in the parlor with posies in hand. She wanted Jodee serving tea on a silver tray, a servant, not a rival.

He wanted to deny that he was smitten with

Jodee, but he was more than smitten. He was in love with her. The realization struck him. By checking on her so often, he was revealing his attraction and feeding Avinelle's jealousy. He didn't belong in Avinelle's life. By accepting her invitations to dinner he prolonged a painful charade. The only way to free himself was to quit as marshal and leave town. But he couldn't leave. Not yet. He was not sure Burl Tangus was dead.

Jodee suffered through a cold breakfast, helped tidy the dining room, ate a distracted luncheon, and did various chores for Hanna before going to her room to brush her hair for Corbet's arrival at two o'clock. It was the longest morning in memory.

Jodee had just gotten her hair twisted and was attempting to get the first pins in place when Widow Ashton shouted, "Jodee, come downstairs this instant!"

Letting her hair fall free, Jodee hurried down the back stairs. She found the woman in the pantry, her face explosively red. The silverware box stood open with its gleaming contents arranged in perfect stacks.

"Yes, Ma'am?" Jodee said, hiding her hands behind her back. Having a hair comb in the pantry was surely wrong, somehow.

"Count the spoons, if you can."

Jodee's heart began to hammer. She took a step back. "Why?"

"Do not think you can run away from me. Count them. How many have you taken? Did you think I would not miss them? I have a mind to search your knapsack."

What could she say in her own defense? Jodee's breath came in short gasps. She had no idea how many spoons the old porcupine had started with, much less how many there were now.

As the front door's bell tinkled, Jodee stood with clenched teeth and her face afire with fury and fear. What good was silver except to make a body feel better than everybody else?

"You think I'm taking your scratched up old spoons? After all you and Avinelle have done for me?"

"Do not be so familiar with my daughter's name. She is Widow Babcock to the likes of you."

"I don't need no spoons! You can look in my knapsack if you haven't already, but I ain't taken nothing. Didn't I go out and trade for my own clothes? Ain't I done everything you asked of me?" Jodee's voice shook. She wished to Christmas she was stronger.

Maggie appeared in the shadows. "Caller for Miss Jodee. It's the marshal. He's in a buggy."

Jodee's heart leapt. How could she feel frightened, indignant, and overjoyed, all at the same time? The outing was spoiled, but she realized all at once that was Widow Ashton's intention . . . Were any spoons really missing? She took a deep breath. She had half a mind to slap the old she-devil, but she was decent now. Decent folks didn't slap their enemies. Without another word, Jodee stormed back to the front hall.

Corbet saw her and sobered. "What is it?"

"Widow Ashton was helping with my hair, but it don't take to pins."

Widow Ashton emerged from the shadows of the hall, her expression somewhat contrite. "Will you be long, Marshal? I do not like to be kept worrying."

He looked from one to the other, sensing something. "Not long, no. And you needn't worry. Jodee will be with me the whole time."

How could he know what women would do or say to make war with one another? Jodee wondered, tucking her comb into her pocket. She realized she'd forgotten her hand bag with the pistol in it. She almost went back upstairs. Then she decided if Widow Ashton wanted to search her things, let her find the pistol and know Jodee McQue was no fool she could bully.

Outside, Corbet handed Jodee up into his hired buggy. Jodee was reminded of afternoons when she sat alongside one creek or another, one hillside or another, dreaming of the life she would have when she and her father returned to

Arkansas. Buggy rides had been high on the list.

Feeling fidgety, Jodee forgot Widow Ashton and Avinelle Babcock and even her poor father lying dead in his grave. Corbet climbed into the buggy beside her. His shoulder brushed hers as he took up the lines. They started out with a lurch that jostled her hard against him. She felt so happy suddenly she was going to come apart.

"How do you feel, Jodee?"

"Just dandy." She grabbed the seat to keep balance.

Looking closely, Corbet seemed pleased. "And your shoulder?"

"It aches some, but doing chores keeps it limber. That ain't my problem, Corbet. I'm sorry, but I think Widow Ashton is addle-brained. Do all rich ladies act like her, watching and scolding and showing her true side when she's angry? She accused me just now of taking her ol' spoons. Why would I do that? She's got more spoons than Mr. Quimby in his store."

"She accused you?"

"It don't mean anything. I ain't taking things. What good would that do me? What would I do with them? Sell 'em to Quimby? He'd know they wasn't mine. She's just trying to make me feel bad."

Corbet sighed. "I don't know about rich folks, Jodee. I've never been rich. I worked all my life."

"Even when you was a boy?" she teased, forgetting the spoons.

"Even as a boy." He pulled to a stop in front of the jailhouse.

Why were they here? Jodee wondered suddenly. She kept smiling, but her stomach knotted. When Corbet helped her down from the buggy, momentarily something delicious flashed through her body at his touch. She wished he'd take hold of her. She wished—

They stood, looking at each other so long Jodee grew dizzy. She wanted to touch his cheek. She wanted so much more than just looks and polite talk.

"When I was ten," Corbet said, "I worked for a dairy farmer. He had a daughter who liked to hang around, pestering us boys. She was my first friend."

Jodee tried to understand what he was getting at. His gaze turned far away. Was he telling her this because she was like a friend to him? Just a friend? Her heart sank.

Abruptly he released her hand and led her into the jailhouse.

"What happened to your friend?"

"Diphtheria. She was ten when she died. You remind me of her. Her hair was always coming loose and getting in her mouth. I don't want you to relapse. That's why I don't want you doing chores just yet. I want you to take care of yourself." He offered her the chair. "Now I have something I have to show you."

She dropped onto the chair, frightened by his sudden serious tone and dulled eyes. Friend, she thought. Her chest ached with the pain of his revelation. Furtively, she glanced at the empty cell where she'd slept in such desolation.

Corbet disappeared into his sleeping room, reminding her of that night she laid in his bed burning with fever. Thinking she was dying, she had kissed him. What a fool thing. He never mentioned it. He probably didn't even remember it. Her throat got thick.

When she saw him bring a dirty coat and pistol from the sleeping room, her body filled with venom. She sprang to her feet.

"That there coat is mended on the back of the sleeve," she blurted before she realized how awful it might sound that she'd done mending for Burl Tangus. "He tore it in a fist fight with Lee Rike. They was always trying to best each other. Old man Rike never could make them stop."

Corbet let her take the coat, shake it out, and locate the place she had mended months before.

A sour taste came into her mouth. She was going to be sick. "I ain't no good with needle and thread, that's certain. And that's Burl's pistol. Many a time I watched him clean it." She met Corbet's eyes. What was he doing with these things?

"In the mountains on Sunday I took these things off a dead man."

"Burl's dead?" Jodee whispered. She looked long at the coat. Her hands felt dirty touching it. Something gave way inside. "I don't have to worry about him anymore?"

"I think so."

She didn't have to lie awake nights, listening for the varmint trying to climb through the window to get her like he used to threaten to do. She was free! She wanted to grab Corbet and shake him.

Corbet wasn't smiling.

"Did the dead man have long dark hair?" she asked, swallowing hard.

Corbet told her everything he had seen in the mountains.

Jodee's legs gave out. She sat down again. She pressed her hands to her mouth. "Then it might not be Burl. It might be somebody he killed and left with his coat and pistol to make it look like himself."

"Was he that clever?"

"Hell, yes, he was clever. He could sneak into a town, listen at windows, hang around saloons, find out things. Come back and make plans. One time he came back wearing some old lady's cape and a bonnet. Said he walked right down the street and nobody paid him no mind. Beard and all!"

"If he changed clothes with a dead man—a

175

man he murdered—why? Is he planning another holdup? You have to tell me!"

Jodee was afraid to look at Corbet. She didn't want to see doubt about her honesty in his eyes.

He shook her a little. "If Tangus is alive and hanging around town, we don't know what he's wearing, or if he has a horse, if he's clean shaven or bearded. He could look like anyone. I might have passed him on the street without knowing it."

Feeling sick, Jodee met his eyes. "I thought I saw him that first morning when I was in the cell. I was looking out the door . . . Remember how it snowed in the night? We saw tracks."

Corbet's eyes bored holes through her defenses. Her emotions began whirling out of control. If she said more, Corbet would never trust her again.

"I was so afraid of you," she whispered, desperate to make him understand. "I don't want to be with Burl Tangus! I don't know what he's planning! But if he's here, he's planning something. If he's here for me, I won't go."

Her mind whirled. Burl wasn't dead. Her fear of him filled the jailhouse as completely as if he were there holding a pistol on them right then.

"You claimed there was nothing between you."

"There ain't! Isn't! But he used to threaten me."

"Aw, Jodee, don't cry," Corbet said. He came to her quickly and pulled her into his embrace.

Jodee was so startled that she fought him. But he held her tenderly, snug against his chest, his arms strong across her back, the scent of starch in his shirt reminding her of home. She could hear his heart drumming. He felt so warm to her touch. Looking up, she saw his feelings for her naked in his eyes. He lowered his head slowly and his warm soft lips closed over her mouth.

An explosion of sensation went through Jodee's body like heat lightning.

Corbet kissed her. He was kissing her!

Jodee drew back, astonished, and peered deeply into Corbet's eyes as if trying to see the bottom of a well. Her body swirled with feelings she couldn't put into words. He kissed her again as if to convince her it was true what he was doing.

"I'm not going to let Burl get you, honey," he said against her mouth.

Honey? Now she couldn't breathe at all. She wasn't even certain she was in her own body. He released her. She staggered back, her chest so full the air didn't want to leave her.

Corbet looked so dear. She felt like leaping and spinning around. But she stood dumbstruck with joy.

Corbet's eyes went all around the room as if he wasn't quite sure where he was. His cheeks grew rosy. His forehead. His throat. Finally he met her gaze again. He looked abashed.

Don't say anything to spoil it, she thought.

Don't say the kiss was a mistake, or an accident or intended as a comfort. She wanted to hold tight to the moment, like a rock in her hand that she could take out of her knapsack later and remember.

Her first for-true kiss.

Corbet looked like he wanted to say more but didn't. He stepped back and made what sounded like a baffled chuckle to himself, like he couldn't believe what he'd just done. He swallowed hard and wiped his hand down the side of his face. A smile pulled at the corner of his mouth. He fought to keep it hidden.

He hadn't kissed like that many times in his life, Jodee guessed, watching him with wonder. Oh, he likely had his wild times in his youth. It wasn't his first kiss, certainly, but she was like that girl in his childhood who died young, only Jodee was alive, a woman grown, and ready to wrap her arms around his neck and show him what she had stored up inside.

The moment began to stretch into an awkward silence neither knew how to break. Finally Corbet gathered up the coat and pistol to get them out of sight in his sleeping room. When he came out, there was something new vibrating in the air between them that Jodee could feel like an invisible tether. Avinelle didn't have this with him, Jodee was certain, otherwise Avinelle wouldn't act like such a ninny when Corbet was around. Jodee felt like she was floating away. Corbet Harlow had kissed her. She had a beau!

For the first time in her life all Jodee's senses blazed with awareness. She knew exactly what Corbet was feeling. He wanted to kiss her again. And maybe more, although Jodee was not clear on the goings-on between men and women. She wanted it, too.

"I should be getting back," she said softly. She found her way to the door.

Corbet moved quickly to open it for her. She wanted to avoid his eyes and relish the feeling of that invisible tether she felt inside, but at the last moment she looked back. She saw Corbet's expression had hardened back to that of a marshal doing his job. It was stunning to see the transformation.

As she walked out into the wind and felt her unbound hair lift and snap, she sensed the invisible tether still. They rode back to Avinelle's in silence. *It took more than an impulsive kiss to bind a man and woman together,* Jodee thought. She wanted to sit easily beside Corbet and relish his company, but nothing felt quite right now. She felt as tense and foolish as Avinelle. She was in love and suddenly scared of losing Corbet, as a beau, but more importantly as a friend.

Ten

The moment Corbet and Jodee drove away at two o'clock, Avinelle turned from the parlor window. She wanted to put her fist through it. "When she's around, he doesn't even see me."

Her mother seized her arm and pushed her toward the staircase. "We do not have much time."

Avinelle stumbled up the stairs with her mother prodding her. "What're we doing up here?" She followed her mother into the guest room and watched her upend the contents of Jodee's knapsack onto the bed. Out fell a wad of tattered muslin, a blood-stained shirt, and several rocks.

She must be acting out a scene for the ever-watchful and imaginative Maggie, Avinelle thought. "Mother, what're you looking for?"

"My spoons!" her mother exclaimed, and convincingly, too. Then she drew three spoons from her pocket and threw them on the bed. "There," she cried. "Look. She *is* stealing from us."

As frustrated as she felt, Avinelle didn't think Jodee deserved this. "Mother, really. Isn't this beneath us?"

"If she robs us, Corbet will want to make it up to us, to you."

Avinelle felt ashamed to be part of such a

shabby trap. "I think you're wrong about that."

Was it necessary to trick Corbet? Avinelle wondered.

Spying Jodee's handbag lying on the chair, she sidled up to it. The bag was so cheap she wanted to laugh. Jodee was no rival, she told herself. Jodee was a mutt. She, herself, was quality. And playing helpless wasn't working on Corbet, either. Acting as if the holdup had scared her to death didn't attract his concern. She must try a different approach. She must act more like a lady. A courageous lady. By contrast, Jodee must be made to look like the ill-bred outlaw's daughter she was. Corbet would never prefer that.

Avinelle peered inside the bag. Coins, cartridges—"Mother, Jodee has a gun!"

"Perfect! We shall tell Corbet about the spoons and the gun and turn her out." She flashed Avinelle a wicked look of satisfaction.

"If Corbet doesn't love me, I don't want him. I don't want to marry again." Avinelle felt like crying suddenly and the feeling made her furious. If a mutt like Jodee McQue could stand up to her mother, why couldn't she?

Her mother got that hated wild look again. "You *must* marry. I am too old to find another man to support us. You have to do it. You have no idea how investors take advantage."

"Take the spoons back," Avinelle whispered.

"If Jodee sees what we've done, she'll come at us like a wildcat."

"Let her raise a hand," her mother hissed.

Avinelle didn't relish the idea of being attacked. "Just take back the spoons, please. This makes me feel cheap."

"All you need worry about, young lady, is getting Corbet Harlow to marry you." But after a moment she took back the spoons.

"Let's sell this hideous house and the damnable stage line and go home to New York," Avinelle cried. "I'm tired of going to Cheyenne to sell my things to make ends meet. I was meant for better than this."

Her mother seized her arm. "Let me tell you the truth then, you little twit. The stage line is not ours to sell. Nor the house. When Mr. Conroy came here the other day, he informed me that I inherited nothing. We have been living two years on a widow's stipend. Everything here was funded by investors. Out of respect for Harold's memory they have been waiting to liquidate. The investors want to sell before the railroad puts the stage line out of business."

"The nearest railroad is a hundred miles away. It'll be years—"

Avinelle gaped at her mother's crazed expression and wondered if the woman had lost her mind.

"Investors shall not dare to put us into the street

with a man like Corbet to defend us," her mother said. "I am done with settlements. I will not start over again."

When had they ever started over? For as long as Avinelle could remember they'd enjoyed the best of everything. "Does any of this have to do with my real father?"

Ignoring her, her mother stormed down the hall. Avinelle didn't remember her father. She happily went away to finishing school. At seventeen, she enjoyed a lavish coming out party where she met the very handsome Lambert Babcock. Her future had seemed assured

She ran down the hall. "Let's go home, Mother! Please!"

"You must go on that picnic," her mother said, searching for something in her room. "I will plead a headache. It will be just the two of you."

"I'm not going to entice Corbet Harlow over a hamper of tea sandwiches. Do you expect me to expose myself in broad daylight and cry rape?"

"You are right," her mother said, pausing, considering. "I will come along and make the accusation. He will marry you or be run out of town."

Avinelle wanted to shake her. "Explain to me how would that help?"

Her mother lunged at her, grabbing her arms hurtfully. "I have gone through too much to let you ruin everything. I will not be put into the street again. If there were a more suitable man for you, I would invite him for Sunday dinner. You owe me."

"If you want a businessman for me, Chester Clarkson is still in town. Philadelphia is almost New York. Why must we stay here? Why must I marry Corbet? You've lost your mind."

"Not Clarkson," her mother hissed. "He reminds me of—thank your lucky stars no man ever used you and refused to make good on his promises."

Avinelle stamped her foot. Why not just tell Corbet they were floundering financially? They were only two helpless widows after all, selling valuables to get along, at the mercy of outlaws and businessmen trying to take cruel advantage. Corbet might not desire her, but he had always enjoyed helping her.

Stalking into her room, Avinelle sank to the edge of her bed. A picnic. How very lovely. Road dust, blazing sun, and rattlesnakes. There were days in this awful town when she wished she were dead. There were days when she wished her mother was.

An icy wash went through her. An outlaw's daughter in the house . . . with a gun in her hand bag . . . Avinelle covered her face with trembling hands. At least she had her savings back. Why couldn't she just walk out the door? Was she a fool or a coward?

Floating as if in a fantasy, feeling as happy as ever in her life, Jodee pranced through the front door into Avinelle's entry hall. Corbet had kissed her. She had a beau!

Corbet followed Jodee inside.

The maid slipped into the shadows once the door was closed. The tantalizing aroma of supper filled the house. Jodee hoped Corbet was smiling inside just as she was. She longed to rise up on tiptoe and kiss him again just for the pure pleasure of it.

Widow Ashton appeared at the top of the stairs, her expression savage. Jodee's happiness vanished.

Freezing Widow Ashton with a hard stare, Corbet said, "I have a few questions, Widow Ashton, if you have a moment. About the holdup."

Widow Ashton clutched the handrail. "If you must, Marshal."

Jodee didn't like to think Corbet wanted to discuss the holdup so soon after kissing her. Wasn't his head in the clouds?

"I'll help Hanna with supper," she said, hurrying upstairs to tie back her hair. It was a mass of tangles after the buggy ride. She ran into Avinelle, who looked nearly as unpleasant as her mother.

With a toss of her head, Avinelle stomped down the stairs in a sulk. Seeing Corbet, she rallied.

"Dearest Corbet, are you sparing us a moment? How darling of you." Reaching the bottom of the stairs, she pulled him gently toward the parlor as if they were going to dance.

Jodee struggled to ignore them but saw how Corbet appraised Avinelle. He wasn't smiling, but he wasn't looking away, either. How long would she have to work to earn enough money for a dress like that? When would she ever be as beautiful?

Seconds later, in the guest room doorway, Jodee halted. Everything she owned lay scattered on the bed. The pistol had been removed from her bag and lay in plain sight. Her old bed dress was on the floor.

Damn their dirty hides, Jodee thought. She hadn't believed they'd really search her knapsack. Was it their right? She wanted to tear open their drawers and dump everything on the floor. She wanted to open the silver music box and let its music fill the house. She wanted to break every ugly knickknack in the drawing room and throw the last of Widow Ashton's silver spoons to hell and gone.

Instead, she smoothed her hair, gave it a vicious twist and began knotting it. Her hair pins were all over the bed. She picked up one after another and jabbed them into her hair until it stayed in place, if crookedly. Looking at herself in the mirror, she caught her breath. Her eyes were blistering blue fire. Her mouth was a slash of hurt. If she went to the parlor now, in this state of mind, she might end up back in jail. She had to do whatever was necessary to have her new life. That meant she had to control her rage.

Why the hell bother? Did Avinelle or her mother control theirs? Were they honest and decent? Jodee wanted to shriek.

The kiss had been a dream, she thought, disappointment crashing through her like a tide. It had been a kiss of compassion, not love. A moment ago she had seen Corbet gaze at Avinelle an instant too long. Taking the pistol, she stormed down the back stairs into the kitchen. The pistol was not loaded but two fools wouldn't know that.

No . . . No . . . take hold of yourself . . .

Jodee ignored herself.

Pots bubbled on the cook stove. Fresh rolls cooled on the pie table. Corbet's questions and the widows' soft replies could be heard coming from the parlor. Hanna came in from the rear porch, carrying two pails of water. Seeing Jodee's fiery expression, and the pistol, she set them down with care.

"They went through my things," Jodee growled. "It ain't right."

Hanna didn't look as concerned as Jodee expected she should. "Miz Ashton asked me to turn out my pockets this morning, too."

Jodee couldn't bear it. Were they going to turn

her only friend against her? "I swear, I ain't touched a—" She was losing control. Nobody trusted her. She was going to shoot something, anything, just like Burl used to do when he was rattled.

She marched into the front hall, heels thudding, heart pounding. If the parlor doors hadn't swept open at that moment she would've gone out the front door and never stopped. The urge to flee was all-consuming. How many times had she wanted to run when Burl pestered her, when it was cold and life seemed pointless. Like now. But always her father had been there to hold her with his love. She stayed with him because that's what her mother would've wanted. This was too much. She was done with them all!

Corbet caught her at the door. "Jodee? I'd like you to hear what Avinelle and her mother just told me about the holdup."

There stood Corbet with his handsome face and his coffee brown eyes filled with alarm like maybe he thought she'd gone crazy. The memory of their kiss confounded her. She loved Corbet. She wanted him to believe in her no matter what others might say. She yearned to leave, but finally she was able to turn. With all the dignity she could muster, she stalked into the parlor where her two hostesses sat, looking self-righteous and full of themselves. What did they have to be so smug about? They were just a couple of low-down snoops. She abandoned all respect for them.

Widow Ashton glared at Jodee, and Jodee glared back until, unbelievably, the widow dropped her gaze. Jodee couldn't believe it.

"I was just telling the marshal the holdup upset me so much I simply cannot talk about it. I prefer to forget everything." Widow Ashton clutched at her throat.

Corbet's lips thinned with impatience.

"Very well." Widow Ashton drew a deep breath. "The driver threw down the strong box and his rifle, but he had another gun hidden under his seat. The outlaws had trouble getting the safe to the ground—it was in the boot—then they couldn't open it. In a fit of temper, one of them shot it. Avinelle screamed. She thought he was shooting at her I suppose. I thought so, too. The driver drew the hidden gun. The one carrying on like a lunatic shot him and he fell . . . right next to me. Then two more shots." The widow covered her face with her hands.

"I thought I was killed," Avinelle cried.

Widow Ashton roused herself. "One of the outlaws dropped from his horse dead, too."

Jodee rubbed her forehead. She could picture her father lying on the ground.

"Listen, Jodee," Corbet said, touching her arm. "Tangus shot the driver. Then he shot your father. Accidently or on purpose, we can't know."

Burl said the driver killed her father. That

thieving snake Burl Tangus killed her father? She wrenched free of Corbet's hand. She looked at the women staring at her and her little pistol. "Burl Tangus must think he has some claim on me. That's why I need this." She brandished the pistol.

Corbet's hand shot out to caution her.

Trying to get out of the line of fire, Widow Ashton upset her chair. Amid the clatter of porcelain falling from a table, she shrieked, "Don't shoot!"

Avinelle hid behind Corbet.

"This damn thing ain't loaded. I've never even tried to fire it." Whirling, seeing Corbet recoil, Jodee continued to brandish the unloaded pistol. "While we were at the jailhouse, *Marshal,* these two *ladies* went through my knapsack. I ain't touched a thing of theirs. And don't think I didn't want to, plenty of times. No, I worked hard. I stood their nasty remarks. I held my tongue. I haven't done nothing to deserve my things being searched."

She swung on Widow Ashton. With a soft wail, the woman covered her face again.

"I tried to learn so's I can get out of this flea-bitten house." She handed Corbet the pistol. "If Burl comes for me, he can just shoot me dead. I don't care anymore."

Corbet's eyes snapped. "Simmer down, Jodee." He handed the pistol back to her. "Jodee needs this to defend herself," he said to Widow Ashton. To Jodee he said, "They told me Tangus shot your father. I thought you would want to know."

Jodee dashed away tears. She felt betrayed by her own emotions. "I reckon I'm sorry for acting like this, but I don't like folks going through my things no more than you would like it. I don't much appreciate the things I cherish being thrown on the floor. You try being poor some time and see how you like it."

Shaking, Widow Ashton edged away. "I was upset about the missing spoons." She didn't meet anyone's eyes.

"Did you find them among Jodee's things?" Corbet demanded.

"No, I did not."

"Did you take anything of Widow Ashton's, Jodee?" Corbet asked, more impersonally than she liked.

"Hell, no, and I'm tired of being accused all the day long. If I am to stay here, I want to be trusted."

"One cannot force another to trust," Widow Ashton intoned. "One earns trust."

"Tarnation! Would you tell me then what I can do to earn it?"

"Jodee," Avinelle said, moving to the center of the room, hands clasped in front of her as if ready to recite. "On behalf of my mother and myself, I apologize for invading your privacy."

She motioned to the maid peeking through the open doorway. "Maggie, fetch the dust pan and broom. We've had an accident." She indicated the broken porcelain on the floor. Attempting a valiant smile, Avinelle looked more beautiful than ever. "Forgive us, Corbet. Mother and I aren't used to hosting former prisoners in our home. I promise Jodee will be trusted from this moment on." She looked into Corbet's eyes in a way that made Jodee's blood dry up. Avinelle was offering much more than an apology.

But Corbet looked like he'd seen enough female foolishness for one day. "I'll make other arrangements—" He slashed his hand to silence Avinelle's bleat of protest. "Patsy might need help—"

"Patsy's visiting tomorrow. We have gifts for the baby. Come by while she's here and we'll ask. If Jodee doesn't feel safe here, perhaps—" Avinelle looked rather hopeful.

To hold back more blistering words, Jodee gnashed her teeth. Why was she waiting for Corbet to give her permission to go anyplace? Her wound was healed. She wasn't his prisoner. All she needed was money for a ticket out of town.

"I'll help Mrs. Robstart if she needs it," Jodee said, "but I won't work for free. So long as I have no money I'm stuck with folks who don't want me around." She turned as Maggie scuttled in with the dust pan and broom. "Let me do that."

"Forty-five cents a day plus board and meals," Widow Ashton said. "You'll move to the back porch." She flashed a challenging look at Corbet.

He said nothing.

Jodee scarcely knew what to think. The old nag was offering pay?

"Fifty cents, then."

"Done," Jodee said, pleased beyond all hope.

Corbet rubbed the back of his neck.

Feeling better, Jodee drew a deep breath and let it out. There. Given a few calculations, she'd soon know how many days she must work to earn her ticket out of town.

"Let me see you to the door, Corbet," Avinelle crooned, taking Corbet's elbow and steering him into the hall. "Leave Jodee to her work."

Before he went, Corbet caught Jodee's eye. She felt that invisible tether spring up between them. The memory of their kiss was in his eyes. Jodee puffed out her chest and felt like life had just taken a turn for the better.

It was chilly on the enclosed back porch where an array of trunks and packing crates were stacked. It reminded Jodee of the hovels she had lived in the past six years. Widow Ashton had failed to tell Corbet there was no bed on the porch, but Jodee didn't care. The space was clean and dry. At once it felt like her own.

One of the trunks she moved was so old its hinges were broken. As she pushed it aside, the lid slid off. She saw clothes and papers inside, and was naturally curious, but she ignored the temptation to snoop. Replacing the lid, she placed a folded carpet on the floor as her mattress, covered it with her old bed dress—it had served as a sheet before—and looked around for something to use as a blanket. She had Hanna's shawl. No matter. She had slept in the cold before.

From the back porch windows she could see a light in the carriage house where Bailey had his room. She wondered about the man, going about his daily chores with so little to say. Hanna paid him quiet attention, seeing that he got hot coffee of a morning and a good portion for his dinner each night.

What Maggie did at night, Jodee didn't know. Jodee hadn't ventured to the attic yet to visit her. She longed to talk to the woman, to ask questions about Widow Ashton and Avinelle, but in spite of Jodee's overtures of friendship, Maggie remained silent.

With Hanna gone for the night, the darkened house felt lonely. What did the widows do in the evening alone in their separate rooms? Her grandmother used to do mending in the parlor. When Jodee's mother was alive, they sat on the porch swing, or in the kitchen, talking. She remembered sitting at her mother's feet, playing with clothespin dolls. After her mother died, she sat near her grandmother, waiting for the woman to talk to her. The day never came.

Jodee and her father had enjoyed pleasant evenings together around a campfire or a hearth fire if they were lucky enough to be squatters in a shack. He always had a story to tell of his wild, youthful days. In the last few months he'd told the same stories again and again, but the sound of his voice and the rumble of his laughter had warmed Jodee. It was hard to believe those days were over. She'd never see him again in this life.

Growing drowsy, Jodee let her thoughts return to Corbet and his kiss. She relived it a dozen times, wondering when she would see him next, and if he would ever kiss her again.

Hearing a sound in the darkness behind the house, Jodee came instantly alert.

She heard footsteps near the house. With her heart suddenly racing, Jodee got up and looked through the porch's back window. Bailey's light was out. The rising mountainside behind the house was a shadowed hulk. The night air soaking through the thin porch walls smelled of pine and rock.

Was it Avinelle moving about in her room? Widow Ashton crossing from dressing table to bed? What might Maggie be doing in her attic room? Did she tiptoe through the house at night, listening at doors, opening drawers and ward-robes, watching people sleep?

Or was it Burl? He might have some small interest in her, but surely there was something more. The stagecoach holdup had been a bust. Nearly all the loot had been recovered. Burl probably had nothing left to live on. He was planning something. Jodee was sure of it. Something new.

Eleven

Turning up his coat collar, Corbet stood in the darkness near Avinelle's house. He hoped Jodee was comfortable on the back porch. It galled him to think of her relegated to such, but he must stop interfering.

He shouldn't have kissed her, either. That was an impulse he should've resisted. But she looked so hurt, so dear—

Out of the corner of his eye, Corbet saw a shadow move. Pulse leaping, he drew his gun and crept across the road. Eyes drilling into the darkness, ears straining, he came upon the shadowy figure and grabbed the intruder's collar. "Hands up."

Hobie cried, "Marshal, it's me!"

Corbet released the lad and spun him around. "What are you doing here? Let me guess.

Guarding Miss McQue. I ought to tan your hide."

"But Marshal—"

Corbet gave the lad a nudge forward and holstered his gun. "I might've shot you." He pushed Hobie toward the main road and hustled him back into town. The saloons were still open at that hour but the rest of the town was as dark as a bad dream. To put a good scare into the lad, Corbet nudged Hobie into the jailhouse.

"Don't arrest me, Marshal! I didn't do anything."

"Light the lamp."

Hobie struck a match with trembling hands. The lamp light cast the jailhouse into harsh brightness. "I was worried about her is all. All the day long I sit in the schoolhouse wondering about that dead man you found in the mountains. If you ask me, Marshal, it wasn't Tangus. He's here in Burdeen somewhere. She's in danger. You might not care—"

"I *know,* Hobie," Corbet said. "I was watching over her, wasn't I? I'll keep her safe."

Hobie wilted. "I guess you was at that, but now you got that old sot sweeping up for you instead of me, running errands that used to be mine. Tell Ma you need me back. I don't want to live with some uncle in the east and go to college next year. I've had enough of school. I want to be your deputy. I'll catch Tangus. I can almost smell him."

"No," Corbet said. Hobie didn't scare as easily as he expected. He took Hobie outside, pondering the fact that at the moment he wasn't guarding Jodee. At the gate to Hobie's cabin, Corbet chose his words with care. "You have a widowed mother, Hobart, five siblings, and an uncle willing to pay for college. You're duty-bound to go. Besides, according to city ordinance, you aren't old enough to be a deputy. I wouldn't swear in someone who hadn't finished school."

"Tell me Jimmy Hicks ever went to school."

Bad argument, Corbet had to admit. "You might get killed. Or Tangus might start robbing folks. How would you feel if you were helping me at the jail and your ma got robbed? There's more to life than doing what we want. When you have a degree, you can come back here and—"

"Don't you see, Marshal?" Hobie insisted. "I can't stop thinking about her. I ain't slept right in days."

Corbet understood only too well. He wasn't sleeping right, either. "At any rate, Jodee will leave town soon. She has to go home. Thanks to me, I don't think she'll ever find work in Burdeen."

Hobie twisted away, vaulted over the fence on his gangling legs, and disappeared through a back door. He didn't say good night.

After hearing Corbet haul Hobie away, Jodee couldn't sleep. It thrilled her to think Corbet had been watching over her, but afterwards she strained to hear every sound and went to sleep with her hand on her little pistol.

Hanna woke Jodee when she arrived for work at dawn. Jodee helped with morning chores, but the night air had left her aching all over. When Patsy arrived for her visit, Jodee heard the baby's shriek, and Hanna looked up and smiled.

"What's wrong with the baby?" Jodee whispered. "Is he sick?"

"Hungry, I'll wager." Hanna nodded toward the door. "Wait and listen."

In moments the shrieks stopped. Jodee whispered, "What happened?"

"You don't know nothing about babies, do you, honey?"

Jodee shook her head.

The parlor bell tinkled, signaling it was time for Jodee to carry in the tea tray. Hanna dried her hands. "I'll come with you. I love little ones."

Tiptoeing through the pantry where the silverware chest stood open as if to taunt her, Jodee pushed through the door into the dining room. Hanna held the door to the parlor so Jodee could walk through with the heavy tray, her shoulder aching. There sat Widow Ashton and Avinelle wearing elegant afternoon attire. There sat disheveled Patsy Robstart in her same brown calico dress. Jodee was startled to see her looking so haggard.

"Afternoon, Miz Robstart." Hanna curtseyed. "Might I see the little lad?"

Patsy moved the edge of a handmade blanket to reveal her son firmly attached to her left nipple. "How are your children, Hanna? How's the littlest?"

Hanna gazed fondly at the baby. "They're fine. What a handsome one he is."

After Hanna went back to the kitchen, Jodee placed the tray on the nearest table. She had seen foals nursing mares, calves with cows, and remembered kittens suckling in the barn back in Arkansas, but this was the first time she had seen a woman nursing a child. The sight left Jodee with a strong awareness of herself as a woman.

"For heaven's sake, Jodee, don't gawk," Avinelle muttered.

Widow Ashton cast Jodee a sharp look, too, but Jodee didn't know what she was doing wrong. "How long does it take to feed him?" she asked Patsy.

Patsy launched into a weary account of her child's feeding habits. Eventually she switched him to the other breast. It was just too amazing and wonderful. Had her mother nursed her like that, alone in that upstairs bedroom? Had she herself shrieked with hunger and been soothed?

With her eyes smarting, Jodee thought about all she should've learned as a girl. She didn't want to feel angry at her father for taking her away from all that, but now she acted like a ninny at the sight of a baby. If she were ever to marry and have a baby of her own, how would she know what to do? If she were to care for someone else's children, how would she know how to do it? All she knew how to do was shoot rabbits, saddle a horse, and start campfires.

"Are you all right, Jodee?" Avinelle asked, rising from her chair to look out the front window. Her face split with a smile. "Corbet's coming!" She hurried into the hall. "Go away," she hissed at Maggie. "You drive me crazy with your lurking. Mother, make her go away."

Jodee ached to hold the baby.

"Maggie has been with us such a long time," Widow Ashton said casually to Patsy. "So devoted—Avinelle wants to greet the marshal herself. He has been courting her, you know. It is only a matter of time before he proposes." She took on exaggerated seriousness. "I feel enough time has passed since Avinelle's husband was killed. Even though Corbet has no experience with business affairs, he will breathe life into our stage line. He—" She fell silent as Corbet came into the front hall.

Jodee couldn't breathe. As Corbet entered the parlor with Avinelle holding his elbow, Jodee couldn't meet his eyes. He greeted Widow Ashton and then Patsy who laid the baby's blanket over her shoulder. Her cheeks went red.

Corbet caught Jodee's eye and gave her a nod. As always he seemed to be asking if she was all right. Tarnation, no, she wasn't all right. He was almost bespoken. She wanted to hate him.

She scarcely heard a word of the pleasantries. Avinelle beamed. Her mother reigned over a stilted conversation. Why were rich folks so gull-darned proper? Jodee wanted to burst into a rant of cussing, but she recalled that was how Burl acted in a fit of temper. She wasn't going to act like him. Without a word, she poured tea and served little sandwiches with the crusts cut off.

When the baby drifted to sleep, Patsy struggled to right her clothes beneath the blanket. Corbet was only a few feet away. "I should get back," she said.

"Before you go, I'll bet Jodee would like to hold the baby," Corbet said.

Patsy looked torn. "Well certainly." She placed the baby in Jodee's outstretched arms.

He looked no bigger than a rabbit, Jodee thought. Her hands trembled as she closed her hands gingerly around him. His little body felt warm and firm and surprisingly heavy. She drew him close, her heart racing. He was wonderful! She managed to draw a ragged breath. Forgetting all about a proposal to Avinelle, Jodee lifted her eyes to Corbet. He drank in the sight of her.

"Henry Robstart, meet Jodee McQue," Patsy

said. "It feels like he needs changing. Thank you, ladies. I wish I could stay longer."

Everyone stared at Jodee's rapt expression.

"Changing?" Jodee said.

"His wet diaper drawers. Babies pee their drawers. It makes for loads of laundry." Patsy looked at Jodee as if she were simple-minded.

"Washing is one thing I know how to do," Jodee said, wondering if she'd be allowed to help.

Patsy glanced at Avinelle, hanging so contentedly on Corbet's elbow. "Want to hold him?"

"Not if he's wet," Avinelle said with an apologetic smile. "This is silk," she said, plucking at her skirt. "If Lamm and I had had any children, I would've had a nanny." She beamed at Corbet.

Corbet didn't see Avinelle. He watched Jodee hold a baby for the first time. Avinelle gave his elbow a tug. "Won't you please sit, Corbet?"

"If Patsy's ready to go, I'll see her home. I was headed there anyway."

"But we haven't begun our visit," Avinelle cried. "We have gifts."

The baby squirmed in Jodee's arms, startling her. Was he all right? Was she holding him correctly? He was so little, so indescribably beautiful. She studied his miniature fingers. "I could just look and look at him. It must be hard for you to put him down."

Patsy chuckled. "After a few nights with no

sleep it's easy enough. He sleeps good with Virgil."

"Is Virgil any better?" Corbet asked.

Patsy took the baby. "He's hanging on. Glad you're mending, Jodee. Come over anytime. I'll have washing ready." She started out of the room. "And thank you, ladies. I'm sorry. If Virgil should wake and need me, I want to be there. I'm too tired to be polite. Good day."

"I could come along and do up your washing before supper. No trouble," Jodee put in.

"*Any* trouble," Widow Ashton corrected.

"Nope, not *any* trouble at all," Jodee said. "I could meet your husband. He and the other posse men were brave to take out after the Rikes. I'm sorry somebody had to get wounded on their account. The Rikes weren't worth a plug nickel, the lot of them. I hope you don't hold it against me, my being in that cabin with them. My pa had just been killed. I didn't know what else to do with myself."

Patsy turned back. Her look was very direct. "If they weren't holding you by force, why were you with them?"

Jodee hung her head. "Burl said if I got caught I'd go to jail. I was afraid."

"Well, it'd help to have the washing done before bedtime." She patted Jodee's arm. "I would've been scared too if the marshal's posse was after me. Come along."

Jodee left her apron on a hall table—that was surely a breach of some household rule. "Can I carry him?"

Patsy bundled the baby and handed him over again. She accepted her gifts from a disappointed Avinelle, and they went out together.

"I'll be back in time to help with supper," Jodee called, hugging the baby close.

Corbet steadied her as she went down the steps. He took Patsy's gifts as they started away.

Jodee had missed so much, being with her father. Women things. Family things. How many cousins did she have now? Might she have been married by now with a family of her own? Had her father been selfish to take her and keep her? Jodee wasn't sure. Corbet walked beside her, watchful of their surroundings. Jodee felt safe with him near. "Do you ever think of getting a house, Corbet?"

"I have," he said, seemingly easy once again. "If you could have any house along here, Jodee, which would you choose?"

Jodee shook her head. "I couldn't tolerate a house in town. They've got me dusting and polishing, sweeping and scrubbing. A camp-site's easier. Just cold at night." She grinned as if making a joke.

"Were you comfortable on Avinelle's back porch last night?"

She had no intention of telling him she'd been

cold. "If I had my druthers, I'd have me a cabin with chickens in the yard or maybe a dugout in the woods. And a cow for milk and butter and such like. I used to churn for Grandmother. I'd have me a big washtub and a washboard. And an apron all the way to my feet. Good quality, like the kind I saw in Mr. Quimby's store. That first place Pa and me had, that was nice. We didn't have a cow or chickens, but we talked about having them. Pa was a dreamer of dreams that never came true. He told me the stagecoach holdup would be his last. After that we were going back to Arkansas. I didn't want to go, but he said they had no business keeping us away."

The memory of her father's words left her aching with sorrow. His life seemed so pointless. No more dreams of new boots or a hat. Such a waste that he died, lying in the road like some old buffalo. He hadn't deserved that.

"I guess it *was* his last."

Corbet gave her shoulder a hug.

At Patsy's cabin, Jodee shook off her sad thoughts. She had imagined Patsy in a big house like Avinelle, not a small and very humble cabin. She was even more surprised inside. The main room was cluttered, and the floor needed sweeping. Jodee let Patsy take the baby and watched as she removed the baby's damp clothes, leaving him squirming and pink as she hurried to tie fresh diaper drawers around him.

"His legs are bent," Jodee remarked softly, feeling concerned.

"He was wadded up inside of me," Patsy said, half smiling at Jodee. "He'll grow straight as he gets bigger, Doc says. You do know he grew inside me, don't you? You don't think I fetched him from a garden patch, I hope?"

Jodee gave a shy chuckle. "I guess I knew that much."

Patsy grinned. "I haven't wanted to like you, Jodee, but I appreciate your offer to help. I'm lucky Mother let me have yard goods on credit from the store to stitch him some clothes." As she dressed Henry, she went on, "As you can see, I'm not much good at sewing. My father owns Wilson's Mercantile. Him and Quimby are rivals. Your things came from Quimby's, didn't they? We don't have anything like that, blouses with pin tucks or skirts trimmed with a band at the hem."

"Is that why Avinelle and Widow Ashton stare at my clothes? Because they look nice? Half the time I wish I was back in britches."

Patsy chuckled. "There, he should sleep now. Avinelle stares because you're the prettiest girl in town. She's terrified you'll take Corbet from her. That, my friend, would not be difficult. He's sweet on you. Anyone with eyes can see that. And Widow Ashton? She has to feel better than everybody just to get through the day. If I had money, I wouldn't be like that."

Jodee couldn't believe it. Her clothes looked nice? Avinelle was jealous, and Corbet was for-true sweet on her? She stared at Patsy until the woman pointed her toward the laundry.

"Time's a-wasting, girl."

Jodee's face split with a grin. She wanted to throw her arms around the exhausted young mother and thank her. "Avinelle and Widow Ashton should have called on *you,*" she said. "It wouldn't have been far for them to come in their surrey."

Patsy wagged her head. "I didn't want them here. I can't keep up the place. Let's get a kettle on to heat—"

"Oh, I'm used to doing washing outside," Jodee said, hurrying to gather the mound of musty-smelling laundry. "I'll get a fire going. Do you have rope I can sling between the trees? I'll get it. You sit yourself down and rest."

Outside, Jodee dropped everything on the ground. There was no wind, just the refreshing scent of pine and sun-warmed dirt and bracing mountain air. It was like being at a campsite again. Jodee realized she missed the freedom of living outdoors. In no time, she gathered rocks to ring a fire and deadwood for kindling. Bringing an ember from the hearth fire inside—Patsy was already asleep in the rocker—she got a blaze going and water heating in Patsy's biggest kettle.

In time, Jodee was scrubbing just as she had

at her mother's side years before. How dear it was to recall her mother. As she draped diaper drawers and baby clothes over the rope line, Jodee paused to look at the cabin, the towering pines, and the looming mountains. She wondered if she might have a spread like this someday and Corbet Harlow waiting behind the hanging blanket.

Quickly she returned to the washtub. It didn't hurt to dream.

Perched on a flat rock on the mountainside overlooking Burdeen's road to Cheyenne City, Burl Tangus could just see the backyard of the Ashton Babcock house. Twice he'd seen a young woman moving around on the back porch who might've been Jodee, but he wasn't certain. In skirts, she looked different. Almost good.

He dribbled the last of his whiskey between his lips. His jaw was so swollen he couldn't open his mouth to eat or drink. Days and nights had become a blur. The damned barber was so busy all the time, with his chair in the front window where everybody in town could see, Burl was afraid to risk going to him for help.

Glaring at the house, he calculated how hard it'd be to climb up into that rear upstairs window. Not a hand or foot hold on the whole back side of the place. There was no chance of going in by way of the back porch, either. He snickered to think how Jodee always had slept like a rock. He'd watched her sleep more than once now, silent as death itself, but he didn't plan to open the door and step over her. If he did that he'd have to be ready to tangle with her. Nobody else believed it, but he knew she was a spitfire.

But sometime soon, even that old man who lived in the carriage house wouldn't stop him once he decided to get into that house. There was a certain little cash box in there, and he knew there was a lot of cash money in it.

Patting his green plaid vest's watch pocket, Burl made his way painstakingly down through the brush to wait for dark among the boulders. If he could've, he would've smiled. He wondered if that rich gal knew just how close he was, waiting with her little key.

Hanna and Bailey struggled to insert extra sections into the dining table. Fully extended, it sat sixteen. Rounding the tight space at each end would challenge Jodee when serving, but she was determined to manage. She helped Hanna prepare many elaborate dishes. The grocer's boy delivered twice. The butcher brought the roast by cart.

Patsy and Virgil Robstart declined their invitation to Sunday dinner. In their place, Avinelle suggested the barber, Walter Hamms, and his wife Sara. The banker, Ellis Sutton, and his wife

Arleta were coming. Burdeen City's mayor, Clay Winfield, and his wife Bertha would be there. Mayor Winfield also ran the livery barn where Jodee's pony, the old pack horse, and the Rikes' horses had been stabled. Hanna whispered that Burdeen's city officials were not a fancy bunch.

Patsy's parents declined due to family illness—Virgil's. Roy Trappe and Isaac Munjoy didn't respond. Hanna suspected the men didn't know to send regrets. Such a to-do, Jodee thought, wearily peeling potatoes and opening cans of peaches.

Artie Abernathy, Parson Caruthers, and his wife Patience, and the Reverend Boteller and his wife Clova sent word they could come. Hanna said the Botellers had nine children, ranging from one to fifteen. "They want to see inside this house," she whispered. "Otherwise, Clova wouldn't set foot in public. She's expecting next month. I think Miz Ashton invited every family needing a helper, cook, or nursemaid."

Jodee felt worried. "But I want to find work on my own."

"Ain't nothin' to be done about it, honey. Those two do as they like." Leaning close, Hanna whispered, "Wouldn't hurt you to show Abernathy some attention. Might make a certain other blockhead take notice. Wouldn't it be nice to go back to Arkansas on a wedding trip?"

Jodee stopped trimming the pie crust. "Who

would I marry? Mr. Abernathy don't interest me that way. And as far as I'm concerned, I'm never setting foot in Arkansas again."

"I meant the marshal, you ninny. Avinelle's had her eye on him since the day she took off her mourning black which wasn't very long after putting Mr. Babcock in the ground, let me tell you."

"Widow Ashton said Avinelle's expecting a proposal from Corbet."

"She might expect one. That don't mean she'll get one. The marshal needs prodding in your direction." Hanna winked.

Jodee laid the dining table with Widow Ashton's china, crystal goblets, and ornate silverware. There were plenty of spoons, she noted. Sixteen place settings. She counted the spoons twice. Two hostesses' spoons, fourteen guests. Eight spoons left in the chest. Two dozen spoons altogether.

After church the following morning Jodee tied on a clean apron she had starched and ironed herself with Hanna's flat irons heated on the stove. The house was fragrant with roast Baron of Beef and peach cobbler—Hanna had been at work since dawn and looked pale. The kitchen was hot, the wood box nearly empty. Bailey was in back, splitting kindling.

When the guests arrived, the babble of voices in the parlor and drawing room made the house come alive. Finally the silver bell tinkled, signaling everyone was seated and ready to eat. Jodee carried in the first course.

Remember, she told herself, steadying the heavy tray in trembling hands, *No hellos. No smiles. No talk. Just serve and vanish.*

The crowded dining room fell silent as she entered. With everyone in place and all the candles burning, the scene was a wonder to behold. Jodee felt proud to be a small part of it. As she squeezed past Widow Ashton seated at the head, she reminded herself not to spill soup down the woman's bejeweled neck.

Corbet sat at the foot of the table with Avinelle to his right. The gentlemen looked stiff in their dark coats and high collars. The ladies wore humble finery. With an uncharacteristic smile, Widow Ashton looked rather attractive in a burgundy gown and glinting garnet earbobs. Avinelle wore a champagne-colored gown displaying enough décolletage to draw the eye of every man. Her hair sported white silk flowers and dangly pearl strands.

Jodee edged around the table, passing Corbet, who looked dazzling in a high collar and dark brocade vest. She'd never seen him look more handsome. Flirt with Artie to make him take notice? She wouldn't do it.

He's going to propose to Avinelle, Jodee reminded herself. *He's here for her, not me.*

She felt so nervous she wanted to giggle.

Everything seemed so pretentious. Tiptoe just so. Place the plates on the table without making a sound. Keep her face soberly composed. As she passed Artie, she smelled fried fat back on his clothes. His handle-bar mustache was so stiff with mustache wax it looked false. She had to press her lips together to keep from grinning.

Then she heard Widow Ashton suck in her breath. *Oh no,* Jodee thought, *I looked at a guest. Throw me in jail.*

"You've done an excellent job with her, Widow Ashton," Mrs. Boteller said as Jodee went by. "Was it difficult, instructing her? Does she learn quickly?"

Jodee gawked at the woman. They were talking about her as if she wasn't there.

"The rolls," Avinelle hissed. "Jodee, fetch the rolls!" Avinelle gave everyone an apologetic look.

Jodee hurried back to the pantry. She hadn't forgotten the rolls. They were next. Hanna wore a stormy expression as she handed Jodee a woven silver basket filled with rolls covered in an embroidered cloth. Hanna shook her head. "Pay her no mind."

After Jodee finished serving the first course, it was time to clear plates and bring the next course. It went on like that for an hour. Corbet carved the beef, if awkwardly. Avinelle passed servings around as if handing each person a plate of gold. It did smell delicious.

One after another, Jodee brought in serving dishes brimming with savory creamed onions, colorful corn chowder, sweet and dilled pickles, then more golden rolls and a pitcher of fresh spring water. Finally Jodee cleared away everything in preparation for desert. By her own estimation, she'd done everything perfectly. Well, almost. Close enough.

The Botellers, Artie, and Corbet ate with gusto. Avinelle and Widow Ashton left most of their food on their plates. Jodee wondered what was wrong with them. Back in the kitchen, Hanna saved every scrap to take home to her children.

"Laced into their corsets too tight, is my guess," Hanna whispered.

Hanna had been working since dawn. By the time Jodee carried around the cobbler and silver coffee pot, her shoulder ached and she was hungry. She was tired of being watched and judged unworthy. It would've been a relief to drop something or let out a stray cuss word just to liven things up, but Jodee behaved herself. Catching her breath in the pantry, she heard Widow Ashton jingle her annoying silver bell. She wished the bell had disappeared instead of the spoons.

While Jodee took the tablecloth from the table the guests removed to the parlor. She was wondering how she would wash the gravy-stained lace when Widow Ashton appeared in the doorway. "Jodee, I *rang* for you."

Jodee's heart skipped. "Yes'm. I'll just wash my hands." What had she done wrong now? Hanna cast her a cautionary glance.

Entering the parlor, Jodee heard Widow Ashton say, "I did not want to distract Jodee while she was serving. She dropped my best sugar last week. You saw how she forgot to set my place with a soup spoon. Avinelle and I have to instruct her in the smallest of details—" Widow Ashton saw Jodee standing there. "Here she is at last. Step closer, Jodee."

None of those damned spoons had been missing, Jodee thought. The woman was lying. Why invite potential employers if only to— Jodee realized what Widow Ashton was really trying to do, humiliate her. They weren't trying to help. They wanted to ruin her. What had she ever done to them?

Corbet's voice rang with authority. "Miss McQue performed her tasks well, considering she is recovering a gunshot wound."

"Marshal, servants are not called miss," Widow Ashton corrected.

He looked hard at the woman. "She's 'miss' to me."

Hands clenched at her sides, Jodee summoned all her self-control. She'd show them. They wouldn't make her act like a ninny. She endured the scrutiny of every person in the room until she decided she'd had enough. "Will there be anything else, Ma'am?"

"Your work was satisfactory," Widow Ashton said, sounding anything but satisfied. "I have just informed everyone that Avinelle and I have concluded our mourning. We shall receive guests again on a regular basis."

Corbet started for the door with Avinelle attached to his elbow.

"Marshal Harlow, was your meal satisfactory?" Widow Ashton asked. "You, at least, had a soup spoon."

Corbet's eyes narrowed. "Sorry, Artie, but Hanna's the best cook in town. And Jodee is the best serving maid. Yes, Widow Ashton, my meal was satisfactory." He gave a formal nod. His dark eyes flashed. Patting Avinelle's hand, he extracted himself from her grasp and stepped away.

Jodee had never seen Corbet look so fearsome.

Widow Ashton continued. "Jodee, I believe you are acquainted with Mr. Artemis Abernathy, proprietor of The Hungry Bear Restaurant."

"Yes, Ma'am," Jodee said. "How do, Mr. Abernathy."

"You were most correct, Widow Ashton," Artie bellowed. "Jodee fits great in a dining room. Jodee, you got yourself a job at my place any time. You would get a penny or two, sometimes a nickel tip per customer, depending on the meal and the customer. I reckon you could make a dollar a day, easy."

Widow Ashton obviously hadn't expected the man to offer employment on the spot.

A dollar a day? Jodee might have the price of a ticket out of town in a matter of weeks. The promise of quick money tempted her to jump at the chance, but Corbet didn't smile. No matter how much she might like to accept Artie's offer, she wasn't going to do anything Corbet disapproved of. "Thanks, Mr. Abernathy. I'll think on it."

"You're most welcome, Miss—"

"And," Widow Ashton interrupted, "Reverend and Mrs. Boteller. This is the young woman I told you about."

The Reverend had long graying hair more untidy than Jodee would have expected of a church man. His suit needed brushing. He had smoldering eyes.

"I am enchanted to meet you, Jodee," his wife put in. "Let me take your hands."

Jodee went to the woman. Her touch felt damp and cold.

"Why, you're just as clean as you can be." The woman examined each fingernail. "I would welcome your help with my children."

Jodee pulled away. "It's nice to make your acquaintance, Ma'am," she said, "but I got no experience with children." She found the effect of bad grammar just what she hoped for. Reverend Boteller looked away.

Widow Ashton looked pleased. Jodee didn't care. She was relieved when the introductions were over. She didn't intend to keep house for the banker or the mayor. She wouldn't be sweeping the barbershop. Starting a new life suddenly felt impossible. That's how the widows wanted her to feel.

In the kitchen Hanna watched her. "Did somebody say something, honey?"

Jodee cast Hanna a sharp look. "Tarnation, and a double damn thrown in. I don't know how you stand it, working here."

"I worked as a girl. I worked after I was married. I'll work so long as I'm able."

"I know, but—" Jodee felt her throat tighten.

"Girl, you ain't had a mother since you was six. You ain't had a grandmother since you was twelve. Your pa got himself killed—it was his own fault—and you know it. He didn't have to turn outlaw. He didn't have to go on that holdup. He chose it. Now it's up to you to choose your future. I don't think you're stealing spoons. Or the diamond brooch or the gold scissors."

Jodee whirled. "Them, too? I ain't! Haven't! Didn't! I don't understand why they asked me to stay here but are all the time making me look bad. I'll do them dishes later, Hanna." She tore off her apron. "I got to get some air."

Twelve

Spring smelled wonderful in the mountains, Jodee thought, hurrying away from Avinelle's house through the backyard. Walking fast, she rounded the carriage house and started climbing toward the road to Cheyenne City.

Weeks had passed since she had been dragged into Burdeen on that travois. She felt amazed to think of all that had happened since. If she could hold out just a while longer, what more might happen? She was afraid to hope something good might come of all this.

Mindful of her skirt hem and new shoes, she followed a steep meandering trail up into some big rocks among the pines. Reaching a good vantage point, she dusted a rough ledge and sat primly as if preparing to receive guests in a parlor. It felt so good to be alone.

From her vantage point, she could just see the back of Avinelle's house. She was grateful to be there and all—

She heard scrambling footsteps coming up the trail. Oh, couldn't they just leave her be for a single moment?

When she saw Corbet emerge from the brush, panting and looking a bit worried, she let out her breath in surprise. Then she felt peeved with him. There he came, shattering her resolve and muddling her thinking. If he was courting Avinelle he ought to stay away.

Even so, she was secretly delighted to see him. Was it so terrible to want to be near him? Was it so terrible to love the way he looked, to love the sound of his voice and dream about him in the night? If she left town, she'd never see him again.

Lifting her chin, Jodee promised herself she wouldn't give in to childish fantasies of kisses anymore. Corbet was just a friend. He was almost ten years older and she was an outlaw's daughter not even yet twenty. They would never fit. He was just checking on her, she told herself sternly, making sure she didn't do something foolish. He didn't want her. And she didn't want him. She must not want him.

Of course she wanted him, she muttered tersely to herself. What woman wouldn't want such a man? He felt like life itself. He felt like her very own breathing. She filled up just knowing he was following her, whatever his reason. It was all she could do to keep from jumping to her feet and throwing herself into his arms. *Change me! Save me! Love me,* she wanted to whisper urgently into his ear. She clenched herself up inside, determined not to act like a ninny. She was a woman grown. She was going to act like it.

Seeing her, Corbet straightened and smiled with

relief. He took off his hat and ran his fingers through his hair. "Had enough of them all?"

"Just about." She didn't want to sound upset. She gave a slight laugh. She was glad to see him. And delighted they were alone. "All them fancy plates—I didn't break a one. All that silverware." With a toss of her head, she stood and turned out her skirt pockets. She grinned as if not stealing had been a victory. "All that polished crystal I might throw at somebody." She giggled. "All that food . . ." She threw out her arms and spun around.

Her stomach chose that moment to growl. Now he knew she hadn't yet eaten.

Composing herself, she flexed her shoulder and shrugged. Then she grinned in a false way. She cast Corbet a sidelong glance that was more provocative than a girl determined to leave a man alone should give. He was so handsome to look at that her mind went blank. A delicious sensation flooded her body. Oh, she wanted him so much. She stared into those dark eyes of his and felt exposed in a way she had never known before. He stared back. The touch of his searching eyes made her shiver with self-consciousness.

"All I need is a tin plate and a pot over a campfire," she said, sitting primly again, folding her hands. "That's what I'm used to. In a way I miss them days. Isn't that crazy?"

"Not really. May I sit with you a minute?" Corbet stepped closer.

"Just don't start kissing me," she said in a teasing tone. "It muddles my head."

He sat, leaving only inches between them. "The sun feels good." He breathed in. "It muddles my head, too. Kissing you."

"Don't worry," she put in before he could spoil the memory with an explanation. "It was a nice kiss, my first in case you had the wrong idea. But it can't *mean* anything. Not that I wouldn't want it to. But I can't . . ."

She couldn't explain how she felt, that she wanted him, but she didn't. She couldn't. She mustn't. She wasn't going to be the kind that men dallied with. Either Corbet wanted to pay her court or he didn't. And it was too soon, besides. She didn't feel up to figuring out a man's feelings when she didn't know her own. Corbet would never marry the likes of her anyway. She tossed her head to banish the thought.

His hand stole over hers where it lay knotted in her lap. She wanted to push its rough warmth away but instead, she sat very still, her thoughts riveted on the gentle touch of it, the warmth, marveling at what it felt like to be near him.

She reeled to remember how it felt, kissing him. Her body had known exactly where his kisses could lead. She found herself melting, wanting with every part of her being to fall back and pull him along with her. She ached for him to move closer now, to put his arm around her and turn her face to his. She felt herself spinning out of control at the thought of lying in the sun with him. She knew lovemaking had powerful magic. Her ma had known it with her pa. Her ma kept the magic alive a long time during those years she waited.

Jodee wanted the magic of lovemaking, too. She couldn't think clearly with Corbet touching her hand. She couldn't remember what she'd been so upset about moments ago that she would climb to this isolated place overlooking the houses below.

Corbet leaned closer. She watched his eyes travel her face tenderly. Stars burst all over inside her. She looked at his mouth, slightly open, curved and soft-looking. She filled up with something that got ready to—

They heard scuffling coming up the trail through the pines. Ever so casually Corbet edged back and removed his hand from hers. Slowly he reached for the gun he usually wore at his side. Today, however, he had not been wearing it at Avinelle's dinner. Jodee felt his body tense. If it were Burl approaching, Corbet wouldn't be able to defend himself. Corbet might be shot dead in seconds. Her, too. Jodee's heart seized up with fear.

Gasping and red-faced, Artie Abernathy broke from the trail like a bull, flailing against branches, struggling for balance. It was a steep trail, slippery with loose gravel and few handholds.

"Jodee—uh, oh, Marshal? I thought you went. I

was just getting ready to leave myself and wanted to say goodbye to Jodee, but we couldn't find you, Jodee. Everything all right?" His eyes seemed surprisingly sharp as he looked at the two of them seated on the same flat boulder. "Looks like the marshal caught you before you got far." He grinned as if he were joking, like she might be a pet, loose from her leash, but Jodee sensed he wasn't joking at all. He thought—he knew—she had been running away.

Corbet got to his feet. He wasn't smiling.

She stood, too. "Why, Mr. Abernathy." She sounded just like Avinelle. "I just needed a breath of fresh air. We were up at dawn, me and Hanna. You know how much work goes into puttin' on a good spread."

She took hold of her skirts. Mincing like a lady, she picked her way down the trail, skidding and scuffling, back to her new life, cussing silently the entire way. Artie plowed and stumbled down behind her, throwing up dust like a bull calf crashing through the pines. Even Corbet, in his silence, managed to look awkward coming down to the road to stand there and watch her with hooded eyes. What she wouldn't have given to have their moment of solitude back. Just one second more. Tarnation and a double damn thrown in!

She marched along the road, swishing her skirts, furious with Artie for interrupting her time with Corbet. *The oily-haired fool,* she thought, *and his silly waxed mustache.*

"Miss McQue . . . Jodee, wait," Artie called. "I need to talk to you." He lumbered after her.

"I can't be gone much longer," she called back to him in a sing-song. "Widow Ashton is real strict with me. I got all them dishes to scrub. All them pots and pans and *spoons.* Good afternoon, Mr. Abernathy. Nice seeing you again, Marshal." She sashayed away, thinking that if she hadn't been such a ninny and filled up their private moment with talk, Corbet might have kissed her.

Artic caught her right elbow and spun her around. "Miss McQue, I'd like permission . . ." Gasping for breath, he glanced back at Corbet.

"You can talk to Jodee in front of me," Corbet said, strolling after them. "I just wanted to make sure Jodee was safe."

"May I call on you sometime, Miss McQue?" Artie gushed.

She pulled her elbow free of his hold and rubbed her aching shoulder. This was the last thing she needed, an unwelcome beau.

"Oh, sorry," Artie added with his face turning red, realizing he'd hurt her.

"I'm not accepting callers, Mr. Abernathy," Jodee said, meeting his eyes and making herself clear. "Thanks all the same."

"Please call me Artie."

"No, I can't do that, Mr. Abernathy, and I can't work for you."

She dashed toward Avinelle's backyard. Her new life seemed a heap more complicated than she imagined it would be while fantasizing around a campfire. How was she going to get out of this town? Where was she going to go? How about Cheyenne City? She needed, first off, to find her father's resting place. She had to stop dilly-dallying over the marshal.

Before Jodee went inside the back door, she dawdled still, wondering if Corbet would see her to the door and give her a kiss after all. She watched him stand in the road, looking so grand in his vest, watching her. He took off his hat, hit the side of his leg with it, and then put it back on, settling it low in front. Abruptly he came erect in a watchful manner that Jodee found electrifying.

Presently she saw what he was looking at, a man approaching from the direction of Cheyenne City on horseback. She felt frightened. When the man drew abreast of Corbet, he dismounted. They shook hands and talked several moments. Then they walked on together toward town. Corbet didn't look back.

Jodee felt crestfallen. What was she going to do? She was in love with a lawman.

Whirling, she was startled to find Widow Ashton standing in the shadows of the back porch, watching her. Going inside, Jodee noticed that her pallet looked mussed. Had the woman searched her things again? Glaring at her, Jodee clenched her teeth. What would she be accused of this time?

When Widow Ashton said nothing, Jodee found courage she hadn't known she possessed. "I'm grateful for all you've done for me, Widow Ashton. My shoulder's back to near normal, so I'll be leaving as soon as I have the price of a ticket. Thanks for helping me earn it."

Widow Ashton's jaw sagged. It was obvious she hadn't expected thanks. She clearly didn't know what to say.

"I'll be getting to the dishes now. Mr. Abernathy went back to town. Marshal Harlow, too. Do you happen to know how much it *costs* for a stagecoach ticket to . . . Cheyenne City? Or Denver? I reckon with all you've taught me so far, I could get work most anywhere."

Widow Ashton looked like she was struggling to reclaim her air of superiority. "Surely you will want to go home to your people."

Jodee shook her head. "They didn't want me. No, I got to move on. I got to see to my pa's headstone. I'll work in a nice house like yours, or in a restaurant. Some place."

"You would need a good deal of money to set out on your own," the widow said as if she knew about being a woman alone. "Proper clothing. Travel fare. Hotels. Meals. Did you accept Mr.

228

Abernathy's offer of a job? Fifty dollars might do well to start you out."

Fifty dollars? Jodee's heart sank. She'd have to work months to earn so much. What was she thinking, wanting to set out on her own? What was the first thing she had done when she learned her father was dead? Like a dumb ignorant fool she followed Burl. She got herself shot. She ended up here.

Jodee's voice came out small. "I didn't want to work for him." That was probably a mistake, she realized. What made her think another proprietor in another restaurant in Cheyenne City or Denver wouldn't look at her just as Artie did? "Easy as the money sounded," she said, "the work didn't sound decent for a lone girl. Maybe some places would be all right, but not Artie's place, not with him around."

Widow Ashton raised her brows. "Well, there are certainly great difficulties ahead. You have a good deal more to learn if you intend to be a proper domestic in a respectable household like mine. I am willing to teach you so long as you are still willing to learn."

"I am," Jodee said in earnest. Hadn't she proven that, she thought, wondering just what more she needed to know.

"Then let us say you may work here two more weeks. I can afford to pay you that much. If you have no further prospects for employment after that, we will discuss it again. If I may be allowed to retire now, I would like to do so. I am tired." After a pause, the widow added, "You did quite well today."

Strangely, Jodee didn't relish the praise.

Widow Ashton turned and mounted the back stairs in a forceful manner that belied her claim of fatigue.

For the rest of the day Jodee threw herself into her chores and was done in time to take leftovers to Patsy. Hanna had gone home early. By the time Jodee got back, it was well past supper. She'd been so busy she never thought to sit down and taste all that she and Hanna had taken the weekend to cook. Alone in the kitchen, Jodee nibbled leftovers while pondering her future.

When she curled up to sleep on the back porch that night, she realized the small chest with the broken hinges was gone. Although she was glad to have more room to lie down, she wondered why Widow Ashton removed it.

Corbet sat at his desk facing Ed Brucker, his new deputy from Cheyenne City. He looked to be a lawman of the first order.

"But I can't draw worth a damn," Brucker said, holding up a scarred right hand crippled by a bullet wound. His pale blue eyes were direct. "I can still aim and fire, but I'm not fast anymore."

It had to be humiliating, Corbet thought, for a

man of Brucker's experience to admit limitations. He suspected Brucker had been a formidable lawman in his prime. He didn't like imagining where he might end up if wounded in the course of his duties. "I'd be proud to work with you, Brucker. Welcome to Burdeen."

After giving the man his instructions, Corbet asked if he wanted to live at the jailhouse and Brucker agreed.

They discussed the holdup at Ship Creek Crossing. Brucker studied the wanted circular on Tangus. "Reminds me of a jake I tangled with years back goin' by the name of Beryl Tanner." He thumped the circular with his stiffened hand. "This rendering looks like him. And now you mention it, I do recall the boys bringing in McQue's body after the stage came back to town. A good man, Willis Burstead." He shook his head.

"Where's McQue buried?" Corbet asked. "Jodee will want to know."

"City of Cheyenne don't waste much on outlaws. There's a ledger noting the spot." He squinted at Corbet, his eyes flashing. "What's she like?"

"She's staying with two widows who claim she's stripping the house of valuables, but where she might hide so much plunder I haven't been able to figure out." Corbet felt disloyal, speaking of Jodee like that.

"I'll look forward to meeting her."

There was a twinkle in Brucker's eye that Corbet didn't appreciate. "The widows offered to take her in. I was impressed, at first. They're good at drawing me in like that. I realized too late I was supposed to think Avinelle Babcock the perfect female and fit myself for her harness."

Brucker grinned. "More than a few times I seen that widow lady parading between Cheyenne's mercantile stores with her cash box in hand for all to see. She never bought much, you know. More often than not, I saw her at pawn brokers. Good idea, though, using Miss McQue as bait. Any sign of Tangus?"

Corbet bristled. It was the first remark Brucker had made that put Corbet off. "I haven't been doing that."

" 'Course not. And she ain't stealing from those widow ladies." Brucker detected Corbet's change of attitude and softened his tone. "She's just taking notice of where everything is for Tangus."

"She wouldn't do that," Corbet said, holding Brucker's challenging gaze. "She hasn't left town because she doesn't have the price of a ticket."

Brucker's eyes turned crafty and he winked. "If you wanted her gone, Marshal Harlow, I expect the town council would've voted her onto the stage free and gratis. Tangus is laying low, watching and waiting. You can bet money on it. I'd say she's got herself a shopping list. I'd wager my first month's pay on it. Yep, I'd like to meet T. T. McQue's little girl. I'll bet she's a regular spitfire when she ain't charming the socks off folks."

Corbet reined in his temper. Without Brucker's help, he was stuck in Burdeen, so he didn't send him back to Cheyenne City as he wanted to suddenly. Jodee was not keeping a list, and he wasn't using her as bait to lure Tangus into jail. He dreaded the day Jodee had enough money to buy her ticket.

Standing, Corbet felt in sour spirits without warning. "I'll clear out my things from the sleeping room."

Brucker tipped the chair back like he already owned the jailhouse. "It's going to rain." He flexed his hand. "Wet weather makes old wounds like this ache like a son of a bitch."

The rain began later that night. Brucker got soaked making rounds and getting acquainted with storekeepers and town officials. The man might as well get used to it, Corbet thought, packing his saddlebags and heading out of town without a word to anybody. Let them get used to the possibility that he might not be around much longer.

Making his first camp under a rock overhang and suffering the cold, Corbet spent a troubled night alone in the mountains with his thoughts.

He should've told Jodee where he was going, but he no longer trusted himself where she was concerned.

Early the next morning Hanna's eldest daughter Bonnie tapped at Avinelle's back door. "Miss Jodee? Are you awake? Ma's staying home sick today. You'll have to do the cooking. Will you tell Miz Ashton, or you want me to? I ain't a-scared of her."

Scrambling up from her clammy pallet on the back porch, Jodee shook sleep from her eyes. "Is Hanna all right?" She pushed open the back door to the dripping dawn gloom. "Come inside for coffee."

"I can't dawdle, thanks all the same. Ma'll mend. She always does." Bonnie was a fifteen year old version of her mother, heavily freckled and plain as a post. "Ma was sure you could manage. Feed 'em dry toast and weak tea. Ma says they're getting fat as ticks."

Chuckling, Jodee was sorry to see the girl disappear into the rain with nothing more than a shawl over her head. In minutes she had the cook stove lit and the kettle on. She fixed coffee for herself and Bailey, pulled on her old boots to spare her good shoes the mud, and hurried out to tell him about Hanna before the ladies were out of bed. The carriage house smelled of horse and hay.

"Could we take Hanna something later?" she asked the man when he answered his door. "I want to check on her."

With his hair sleep-mussed and his suspenders down, Bailey looked alarmed in an endearingly befuddled way. "It's not like her to stay home," he said, revealing a slight accent. He sounded like Mr. Quimby. "I'll take you. Tell Miz Ashton the horse needs exercise."

Jodee bustled around the kitchen, thinking of all she must do in Hanna's place. She laid the table and counted the spoons—all twenty-four stacked in the chest—and gave a start when Maggie appeared as silently as ever to catch her staring at the ornate finery.

Maggie looked pale as she noticed Jodee's boots peeping from beneath her rain-damp hem. Jodee's heart sank. She had tracked muddy footprints all over the dining room floor. She'd have to tend to that later. While Jodee readied a basket of food for Hanna, she braced herself to ask permission. The moment she heard Widow Ashton seat herself in the dining room, she hurried in, her heart in her throat. The woman's hair was still in curling ribbons, a startling sight compared to her usual impeccable appearance.

Jodee dipped a curtsy. "Morning, Miz Ashton. Hanna sent word she's staying home sick today. I think she wore herself out yesterday. Do you mind if I take her some leftovers—to keep her strength up? Here's what I have put by, slices of beef and cobbler. It shouldn't go to waste. Bailey said the horse needs airing, too. He'll drive me. If you don't mind. Please."

Widow Ashton held Jodee with a hard eye. "Can I hope for hot tea before you leave?" If she noticed the footprints on the floor, she didn't complain.

Jodee found herself scurrying back to the kitchen like Maggie. Forcing herself to return at a calm pace with the tea steaming fragrantly in the silver pot, she poured and then stood at attention, waiting.

"Finish your chores first," Widow Ashton snapped. "Take a loaf of bread and a jar of jam." She selected a key from a ring of keys hanging from a cord at her waist. "You may go into the cellar with Maggie. She will know what to pick. Let me see everything you take."

Jodee took the key. "Thank you, Ma'am."

Across from the sewing room was a wall covered with floor to ceiling cupboards. Maggie took the key from Jodee and unlocked a narrow door revealing a steep set of stairs leading down. "Fetch a candle," Maggie whispered, squirming with anticipation.

She crept down the stairs, holding the candle high, searching the shadows with wide eyes. Jodee followed, surprised to learn of this storage area under the house. The stone-walled cellar was lined with wooden shelves stocked with enough food to feed a family for months. Jodee had never seen the like. Across the room stood crates in stacks, and several large trunks.

Maggie plucked a quart mason jar from a shelf and held it close to read the hand-printed label. Then suddenly she whirled. Her eyes were quick all around the space. Thrusting the jar of home-made apple butter into Jodee's hands, Maggie dashed to stone steps on the right of the cellar. Above the steps slanted double doors leading outside. Maggie pushed on them. They appeared loose to Jodee but didn't open.

"I smelled fresh air," Maggie whispered. "Bailey's been in here. He robbing us."

Jodee shook her head. "He wouldn't." Was Maggie as addle-headed as Widow Ashton? Was Maggie feeding lies to her? *The woman seemed crazy,* Jodee thought, watching her look around, eyes stopping at each open space on the shelves where items had been removed. Jodee supposed they'd used a good many supplies for their Sunday dinner just past.

"Is anything missing?" Jodee asked.

Maggie looked frightened but excited by the prospect of a confrontation. "My—Miz Theia will be so upset. She'll scold him terrible. She might fire him! She'd fire me if I wasn't so stupid."

Jodee shivered. She noticed footprints in the hard-packed dirt floor, hers and Maggie's. And scuff marks. Drag marks suggesting a sack of something had been moved and then shoved back into place. Was she going to be blamed for something?

Grabbing a small brown bottle of cod liver oil and a loaf of bread which Jodee recalled wrapping in a cloth for Hanna only days before, Maggie ran up the stairs to the kitchen. "Hurry! She'll want the key back."

Upstairs, Jodee watched Maggie lock the narrow door and tug on it to make sure it was secure. Jodee had never seen her look so lively. With reluctance, Maggie turned over the key and waved Jodee toward the dining room. Why, even Maggie found her suspect, Jodee thought, furious to think the little old lady of a maid assumed she was a thief, too.

Setting her teeth, Jodee placed the apple butter and cod liver oil in the basket. She carried it and the cellar key into the dining room. Avinelle had joined her mother by then and sat at her usual place, looking sullen.

"My tea, if you please, Jodee," Avinelle snapped.

"Yes, Ma'am." Jodee stood, waiting for Widow Ashton to look at the contents of the basket. She placed the cellar key on the tablecloth without making a sound.

Widow Ashton glanced at Avinelle, then Maggie lurking in the pantry doorway. Then she stared hard at Jodee. Her lips bunched together. Would the old harpy consider this food part of Hanna's pay?

"Oh, Mother, let her take the stuff," Avinelle snapped. "We've got enough put by to survive a siege. Go on, Jodee. I'll get my tea myself." She hitched back her chair and stood, glaring at her mother.

Jodee retreated with the basket and nearly collided with Avinelle when fetching back the kettle to refill the teapot.

"I'll take that." Avinelle snatched the kettle from Jodee's hands and returned to the dining room.

Trying not to feel affronted, Jodee hurried out to the carriage house to climb aboard the surrey with Bailey. It was a relief to be outside, away from whatever was transpiring in the dining room between Avinelle and her mother.

Thirteen

Hanna lived south of town more than a mile, just off the road to Cheyenne City. It was surely a long walk each day at dawn and dusk, Jodee thought, worried and impatient to see her friend as she rode alongside Bailey in the surrey. Rain fell steadily as they arrived. Bonnie appeared in the doorway of the cabin and welcomed them with a smile.

"Look who's here, Ma!" she called as Jodee climbed down from the surrey and dashed inside.

Bailey followed with the basket, doffing his dripping cap the moment he ducked through the doorway. He looked relieved to see Hanna seated in front of a modest hearth fire. She wore the shawl Jodee had given her. Her graying hair was down, hanging in a long braid. In spite of her red nose and eyes she looked years younger.

The place smelled deliciously of coffee and cinnamon. Grinning, Jodee presented the basket.

"Would you look at all this! Think she could spare it?" Hanna winked, her voice hoarse. "You're one for giving presents, aren't you, Jodee?" She fell into a fit of coughing. "Hello, Cedric," she said to Bailey, smiling in a way Jodee hadn't seen before. "Sit yourselves down. There's plenty of coffee. My young'uns are at school, except for Bonnie here who quit and does mending for local ladies. She'll probably get herself married soon. Then I'll have grand-children." Hanna laughed and sputtered into another coughing fit. "I—I—imagine me, a g—g—grandmother!"

Bailey remained by the door. When it was time to leave, Hanna promised to be back at work the next day. "Say hello to our favorite ladies for me."

As Jodee and Bailey arrived back at Avinelle's house a while later, Jodee whispered, "Would you

240

mind showing me the outside door to the cellar? This morning Maggie thought it was unlocked."

Bailey's eyes sprang wide. With a tremendous frown, he slopped through the mud to the slanting doors set in the foundation of the house on the north side. The sturdy padlock seemed secure, but he studied the house and the stone foundation and the surrey's tracks already filled with rainwater. "If anybody's been coming around, their tracks are washed out."

"She smelled fresh air, she said. Would she toy with me? You know how folks like to say I done things I haven't."

Bailey slogged to the dining room window and hooked his fingers on the sill as if judging whether someone could climb in. Squinting, he prowled all the way to the front porch.

"Could somebody get in through these doors?" she asked. Like Burl, she thought. "I'd be blamed for anything taken."

"I keep a close watch every night, Miss. Won't nobody get in that I don't hear 'em. Get yourself dried off now, before you catch your death." He gave her a rare smile that folded his face into charming lines.

Worried nevertheless, Jodee supposed there was no use going to the Robstarts' that afternoon. She couldn't do laundry in the rain. Glancing at the pallet where she slept on the porch, she supposed it looked undisturbed, for once. Sometimes she felt more at risk of being robbed than ol' Widow Ashton or Avinelle.

In the kitchen she built up the fire in preparation for making luncheon. Knowing there was another way into the house left her uneasy. Bailey might keep watch, but he was no match for Burl Tangus. Burl wouldn't hesitate to shoot that padlock, or Bailey for that matter. If he got inside the widows' house, he'd pick the place clean.

When the rain let up later in the week, Jodee was so busy she didn't have a moment to worry. Widow Ashton had Jodee, Maggie, and Hanna, barely recovered from her cold, turning the house upside down with spring cleaning. Each lower room was aired, dusted, and swept from the ceiling to the farthest corner under the heaviest furniture. Rug beating was the worst.

On Saturday all chores associated with bathing and preparing for Sunday occupied Jodee's time. Corbet hadn't called all week, so Avinelle looked worried, too. Her attitude toward Jodee became unbearably harsh.

When a knock came at the front door Saturday afternoon, Avinelle, who was seated in the kitchen near the cook stove drying her hair, broke into a huge smile. It had to be Corbet, Jodee thought with a pang of excitement. She listened in the rear hall as Maggie answered the door.

The voice they heard was not Corbet's but that of a gruff stranger. Jodee felt let down. And anxious all the more.

Maggie rushed back into the kitchen. "It's a deputy, Miz Avinelle!"

"Well, for pity's sake, Maggie, I can't receive, looking like this. You go, Jodee. Get him off Mother's porch. Deputy, indeed. He could be anyone. Even your former associate," she snapped at Jodee. "What was his name? Turner? Tangle?"

Jodee's stomach rolled over. Burl would never come to the front door. He wasn't that brash. She smoothed her apron and soon faced a stocky stranger. He looked her over with no effort toward decent manners.

"Miss McQue, is it?" His voice had a harshness she didn't like.

Jodee's mouth went dry. Now there was a lawman. How did he know who she was? "The widows' ain't receiving," she said. *Aren't,* she thought.

"Truth be told, I came to see you, Miss McQue. Ed Brucker's the name. I'm the new deputy up from Cheyenne City. The marshal wanted me to tell you, next time you're in Cheyenne that the sheriff has a ledger. He can tell you where your pa's buried at."

Jodee was so surprised she could scarcely speak. "My—how come Marshal Harlow didn't tell me himself?"

243

"He's out of town. Don't know when he'll be back."

Corbet was gone? Jodee felt bereft.

The deputy took a step closer. Jodee edged back. "Anything else?"

"Want to walk out with me some evening, Miss McQue?"

He was asking to *call* on her? She couldn't think. "I . . . uh . . ."

Blessedly, Widow Ashton's voice stabbed from the far side of the parlor door. Jodee had never been so glad to hear that severe tone. "Who is it, Jodee?"

Coming into the entry hall, the widow jerked the front door wide open. The deputy's grin vanished, replaced by an expression every bit as forbidding as Corbet's most unyielding stare. "Afternoon, Ma'am," Brucker said, touching the brim of his hat but not removing it. He flashed the deputy's badge pinned to his vest. "Paying a call on Miss McQue. Nothing's the matter. It's personal."

Shaking her head, Jodee brushed against Widow Ashton in her haste to get back from the doorway. "I don't want to," she whispered. "Tell him I don't go nowhere with no stranger." She was about to run back to the kitchen when Widow Ashton's hand closed bitingly around her arm.

Regarding the deputy with her most contemptuous expression, Widow Ashton said, "Get off my porch," and slammed the door.

Jodee was stunned, but grateful.

Whirling, the woman glared at Jodee, her face purpled with fury. "Back to the kitchen at once. You shall not open this door again."

Jodee opened her mouth to protest. Maggie had answered the door, she wanted to say. Avinelle instructed her to speak to the stranger. Hanna and Maggie sprang out of the way as she burst back into the kitchen, curses about to erupt.

Hairbrush in midair, Avinelle exclaimed, "Whatever have you done now?"

Jodee's breath came in gasps. "I ain't done *nothing!*"

The desire to flee was so intense that Jodee had to go out to the back porch and stand stock still for five minutes to regain control of herself. It wouldn't be enough to climb the trail up the mountainside this time and sit a spell on a boulder. She needed to get away. For good.

When she could think again, Jodee marched to the parlor where she found Widow Ashton watching the street from behind the curtain lace. Hearing Jodee, the woman stiffened but didn't turn.

"I don't know that man," Jodee blurted out in a tone she'd never used on anybody before. "I don't know anything about him. Thank you for sending him away. I was just wondering if you would let me take a few hours to go shopping. I need a work shirt. I'm getting smudges on my blouse. Then I should stop by Mrs. Robstart's. I ain't done up her wash since the rain let up."

"Go, if you must," the widow snapped. When she turned, her face was as severe as Jodee had ever seen it. "If you are slipping away to meet that man and I find out, I will discharge you and not let you back into this house. Be warned."

"I ain't meeting him! I ain't never seen him before this day. You don't believe nothing I say, do you? Will you ever take me for who I am?"

"I know precisely who you are, young woman, and this is the last time you will back-talk me. Buy two yards of the cheapest calico. I will teach you to make an apron. You are a servant in my employ, not some urchin wearing whatever you can find. When seen in my household you must dress appropriately. Now get out of my sight. You have brought nothing but turmoil to this household."

At the end of her tether, Jodee dipped a curtsey and ground out, "Thank you, Ma'am." She left the parlor with all the dignity she could muster.

Within a half hour, wearing her boots and britches beneath her skirts because it made her feel more secure, Jodee marched toward town. She hadn't brought turmoil to Widow Ashton's household. Turmoil followed that woman like a shadow.

• • •

Burdeen's main street was crowded with Saturday afternoon wagon traffic. Watching for trouble in every direction, Jodee headed straight to Quimby's for the calico. Signs of spring were everywhere—weeds springing up in muddy alleyways, buds thick on bushes, upstairs windows open to fresh air. She never reached the store.

Hobie called to her. "Where you headed, Miss McQue?" Hobie trotted toward her, clutching a broom. "I sweep up at Wilson's now. It's better work for a college-bound boy," he said with sarcasm. "I'll get me a degree in sweeping while I'm back east."

Still upset by her encounter with the Widow Ashton, Jodee stepped up to Quimby's boardwalk. "If you don't start calling me Jodee, I'm going to stop speaking to you!" It had been more than a week since she'd seen Hobie. She marveled at how his crooked teeth made him look so charming. "I don't know nothing about college, but I'm glad to see you." In an instant, she forgot the deputy and Widow Ashton's harsh words.

"I been thinking about you, Jodee," Hobie said, ducking his head and blushing. "You sure do look pretty in them new clothes. Will you be going to the May Day dance? Girls dance around the May pole. My sisters make fancy baskets to leave on the doorsteps of whatever fellas they like. Did you ever do that?"

Jodee recalled, ever so dimly, the spring when she was eleven, hearing about May baskets at school. "Does anyone leave a May basket on your doorstep?" she asked in a teasing tone. Taking note of passersby staring at them, she edged away. Hobie shouldn't be seen talking to her, she thought. Then she felt bitter, realizing she felt tainted and inferior.

Hobie blushed. "*Two* last year." A sheepish grin tugged at his mouth.

She nodded with a smile but felt suddenly old. She adored the way his ears reddened. "Who left them for you?"

"Girls don't leave names. Will you leave me a May basket, Jodee? I'll ask you to dance. I don't care what anybody says."

Jodee sobered. "I don't reckon it would be proper, me being older and all."

"We're friends, aren't we? Leastways, I'm your friend."

She looked into Hobie's clear blue eyes and felt a rush of affection for him. He was all she could have wished for in a brother. "Yes, I'm your friend," she said in her most sincere tone. "You and the marshal were the first to do me a kindness. I won't never forget."

He looked as if she had given him a rare gift.

She couldn't stop herself from reaching out to touch his arm. "I just heard the marshal isn't in town. Do you know where he went?"

"He hasn't been around in days. There's letters at the post office, piling up. That new deputy, he don't have nobody running errands for him. He does everything himself. The jailhouse floor's covered with mud. I . . ." Hobie looked around, giving Mr. Wilson standing in the mercantile's open doorway a defiant nod. "I hear tell Brucker got his hand shot up in a gunfight. Makes up for it by scaring the beans out of everybody. He's got drunks locked up in both cells every night. He's handing out fines for the least thing. I guess a lawman's got to be hard, but he's not as good as Marshal Harlow. Marshal Harlow cared about this town. Brucker's just doing a job."

Jodee felt relieved to know her first impression of the deputy had been correct.

"Brucker claims the marshal's goin' to quit. I thought he was going to buy land north of here where he took me fishing one time. I went out there Wednesday. I thought sure he'd be there. He wasn't. He's trailing Tangus. I'm sure of it."

"So he's not gone for good?" Dizzy with relief, Jodee stepped down to the street.

"I think he went back to that cabin where the shootout happened. That's where I'd start if I was hunting a desperate outlaw like Burl Tangus."

Her relief vanished. What if Burl had waylaid Corbet and he was already days dead? Jodee felt beside herself.

"Don't worry," Hobie said, "Marshal Harlow

can take care of himself. I don't have to be home for an hour. Maybe he's back by now. We could go out there and see. I got money. We could rent a couple horses."

After a moment Jodee nodded.

Throwing his broom aside, Hobie grabbed Jodee's hand and they raced down Main Street, laughing. Jodee felt ten years old again.

Jodee's better judgment screamed, *Get the calico and go back,* but she could no more stop herself from heeling her rented mount and racing after Hobie than she could have stopped herself from loving Corbet. Thundering past Hobie, she rode with abandon. Her hair came loose and lifted into the wind like a banner. It had been weeks since she'd ridden on horseback, not since after the holdup. Her muscles felt feeble, but for a few blessed moments she was free.

Hobie called to her. Not wishing to worry him, she reined finally at a twist in the trail and became aware suddenly of how alone they were so far from town. The way ahead looked desolate. Her pistol was in her knapsack on Avinelle's back porch. Hobie probably carried nothing more than a whittling knife.

Jodee's joy fell away. The mountain loomed like a shadow. The wind rushed in the pine tops. The roaring creek ahead and a hawk wheeling in the afternoon sky reminded her of her father and her heart broke afresh. She could almost picture her father riding toward her from around the bend. It felt as if the holdup had never happened and he was still alive.

Hobie galloped in behind her. "You win," he yelled, reining beside her and panting as if he had done all the galloping himself. His blue eyes searched her face with fretful yearning.

Jodee tried to smile, but she couldn't shake sad thoughts of her father. She wondered if she'd ever get used to the fact that he was gone. "How much farther?"

"Yonder there." Hobie pointed.

She walked the horse alongside Hobie's, unable to think of anything to say. What did folks talk about if they weren't discussing holdups and loot?

"That new deputy came by a couple days ago, asking if I wanted to sweep up at the jailhouse for him," Hobie said as if the idea disgusted him. "Ma lit into him—she told me later he had the smile of a snake. I've never seen a snake smile, have you?" Hobie grinned. He was flirting.

Hobie, she wanted to say, *I seen smiling snakes near every day for the last two years,* but she remained silent.

"Out of its banks with snowmelt," Hobie said, pointing to the raging creek as they walked the horses. There, on a wedge of level ground out of the creek's tumbling reach huddled a canvas field tent. There stood Corbet's big horse tethered to a stake. His campfire gushed smoke.

"He's here!" Hobie yelled with a grin.

At the sound of their approach, Corbet ducked out from the tent's front flap. He had his gun in one hand and an oily rag in the other. Jodee's heart filled at the sight of him. Before she knew what she was doing, she threw herself out of her saddle, hit the ground hard, and ran full speed at Corbet. She had her arms around his neck—his hands were too full to return her embrace—and hugged him with all her strength.

"I thought you was gone," she cried. She marveled at the tall, solid warmth of him. It was all she could do to keep from kissing him full on the mouth.

She realized then what she was doing in front of Hobie and released Corbet. But she couldn't worry about Hobie. Corbet's eyes carressed her face, although he was aware of Hobie's presence, too.

"What are you both doing here?"

"You went off without a word!" Jodee scolded. Oh, now she sounded like Avinelle. "I've heard no end of it from Avinelle. Where'd you go?"

"Whoa," Corbet said, chuckling. He laid his gun aside.

Hobie dismounted. He tethered the rented horses to a nearby pine. When he met Jodee's eyes, his expression had turned dark with hurt.

"Marshal," he said with an air of formality. He stepped forward to shake hands like a man. "You've got letters and telegraph messages waiting. Brucker's filling the jail with drunks. Walter Hamm got himself a hard knock on the head early this morning in his shop. He was pulling a tooth, but the man apparently didn't appreciate the effort. Or pay. Hamm claims the same man was in his shop weeks back, and none too friendly then, either. You think Brucker could find him? Hell, no. I don't think he even tried."

"All right, Hobie. I'm headed back," Corbet said, his smile worn down. "Can you both stay and help me finish this coffee? You think Brucker's wrong for the job?"

At being asked his opinion, Hobie seemed mollified. "I guess he'll do so long as you're around to keep him in line, but you can't just up and leave whenever you want, Marshal. We need to know where to find you. I have to get home to my chores now. Jodee probably has things she was planning to do, too. I got her off track."

Jodee had forgotten all about buying calico for an apron. "I had to get out of that house. Things ain't healthy when Avinelle's in a snit. Aren't," she corrected herself. "And that deputy asked me to walk out with him. Widow Ashton was ready to throw me in the street. I hadn't done nothing! Not nothing! Anything. If I was all she

253

claims I am, I would've cleaned her out days ago and been gone, but no, I keep taking her guff and working the best I know how. What ails you, Corbet? Say something."

"I would if you two would let me get in a word. Sit down. There's little to be done at the moment."

While Jodee poked at and improved the draw of Corbet's poorly built campfire, Corbet poured coffee from a pot that looked new. "I went back to that cabin, found the hole in the floor. That place is about to fall in. I found tracks under the cabin. All up and down the creek. Weather erased all trace of Tangus beyond that."

"Tangus?" Hobie put in excitedly.

"I waited two days, but saw no one. I hiked up-creek a ways. If he got away by that route, he's a mountain goat. I returned along the route we took to Kirkstone."

As she sat, relishing the sound of Corbet's voice and the last of the afternoon sun, Jodee watched from the corners of her eyes. If Burl were near, wouldn't she sense it? Wouldn't she smell him? Something had the hairs standing up on her arms.

When the sun went below the ridge, casting the valley in twilight, Corbet tossed the dregs of his coffee into the fire, kicked dirt over the flames and went for his horse. Leaving his tent standing because he intended to return, they were back in town within ten minutes. Returning their rented horses at the livery, Hobie scarcely looked at Jodee as he bid her a hasty goodbye.

"Thanks for the horseback ride," she called after him.

He didn't answer.

Hating to start back for Avinelle's after being gone so long, Jodee sighed. She cast Corbet a longing look. "I'd best be going, too. I'm in for a scolding."

She saw Brucker leaning against the jail-house porch post. He tipped his hat to her, but she gave no indication she'd seen him. A dozen things to say raced through her mind, all unladylike.

Corbet looked like he wanted to say something, too, but he saw Brucker as well.

The deputy forced himself upright as if it were an effort and sauntered closer. His very walk irritated Jodee. Didn't Corbet see the man was trouble?

"Find anything?" Brucker asked.

Corbet turned a casual eye on the man. "Nothing to speak of. I'll see Miss McQue home. Then I'll want a report from you."

"Yes, sir," Brucker said, winking at Jodee.

Offering his elbow to Jodee, Corbet launched at once into what Jodee sensed was a lot of empty conversation. She tripped alongside him, scarcely able to follow his long stride. When

Brucker was out of sight, Corbet slowed. "Sorry, Jodee. I didn't mean to make you run. From now on I want you to be extra careful. I might have flushed Tangus."

She looked around at the buildings with upstairs windows overlooking the street and shadowed alleyways where Burl might be hiding, watching them. She saw nothing unusual but felt uneasy nonetheless. "I can't figure why Burl would stay around. Are you expecting a big shipment of gold for that new safe at the depot?"

Corbet studied her face. "Gold doesn't ship to a town this size, Jodee. It ships away from places like this to bigger places like Cheyenne City and Denver. If I didn't know better I'd think you were fishing for information."

Abruptly, Jodee drew away, stung to the core by his insinuation.

"Just saying, Jodee," he said, catching her arm. "I didn't mean anything by that."

"Then what's the safe for, if not gold?" she snapped. "It looked heavy. I saw it from your window."

"This town's growing. The depot needed something better than a strong box behind the agent's chair. If that's what Tangus was after, if that's why he robbed the stage, he would've been in for a big surprise when he got it open. The safe was shipped here empty."

Jodee clapped her hands over her mouth. For a

few seconds she wanted to laugh. Then a wash of horror went through her. Her father died for an empty safe.

"That's all Burl talked about," she cried. "That safe. He came here before the holdup, talked to people probably, found out things. I told you that's how he decided what he wanted to rob. Big safe, he told Pa and old man Rike. Full of gold, he said."

"Does he think it's still full of gold?" Corbet asked. "It's heavy, sure. It's the latest thing. Fireproof. Double walls of plate iron."

Jodee longed to sit down.

"It's either the safe, or you, Jodee," Corbet said. "Why come for you after all this time? It's all right to admit it. Did you ever lead him to believe you'd accept him?"

"Never," she bit out. "I told you, I hated him, and he knew it."

"Aw, Jodee, when you look at me like that, all I want is to kiss you. I can't kiss you here."

She glared at him, but what was the use? She couldn't stay angry with him. "If he's still hanging around, I don't know why. There's a May Day celebration next week. Will you dance with me?" She fought the urge to move closer.

With a gentle nudge, Corbet headed her on toward Avinelle's. "There's a parade down Main Street in the morning. A picnic in the afternoon, a dance that night. Of course I'll dance with you.

And every other woman in town. I can't play favorites, much as I might like to."

Why couldn't he play favorites if she was, indeed, his favorite? Corbet had no intention of settling down, Jodee thought. She could tell just by looking at him. This town was his responsibility and his life. He'd never give that up. She marched on, feeling tired and dejected.

When they arrived at Avinelle's, the front door opened as if Maggie had been on watch. Corbet followed Jodee into the silent house. Hanna appeared in the rear doorway long enough to make Jodee think she'd been waiting, too. Taking one last look at Corbet, drinking in his face as if for the last time, Jodee set her jaw.

Widow Ashton appeared in the parlor doorway. She tried to look as if she had only just been passing that way. Jodee knew she was acting a part. "To what do I owe this newest unexpected visit?" She tried to make it sound as if Corbet's visits were a trial. Jodee was certain that was only because his visits were not to see Avinelle.

"Just escorting Jodee home," Corbet said with an air of casualness that seemed expert. "There was an assault in town. Make sure Bailey keeps the place locked up tight."

"No trouble with Jodee, I trust," the widow said. "You told me you were going to town for calico."

Jodee marveled at how Miss Ashton always

258

managed to make her feel on the defensive. "It must be time to serve supper. Evening, Marshal. Thanks for seeing me back safe from all the thieving renegades and outlaws lurking hereabouts."

He gave her the slightest of bows.

Jodee found Maggie and Hanna huddled against the door, listening. She took a place beside them. "Where's Avinelle?"

"She and the old cat have been fighting all afternoon," Hanna whispered.

"Because I was late?"

"Do they need a reason?"

Burl sat on a crate of wine bottles, nibbling cheese and picking at a loaf of bread, leaving holes like a mouse. His jaw ached, but with the molar out he felt some better. He itched to know what those harpies had been shouting about all the day long. He heard footsteps pacing back and forth in the room overhead. The kitchen, he supposed. He smelled cooking. His belly clenched with hunger but it was too soon to chew.

With a sliver of late afternoon sunlight coming in around the slanted doors, he plucked a whiskey bottle from his pocket and took a deep pull. He held the burning liquid on the side of his mouth where the crater in his gum throbbed.

Burl hoped the barber's head hurt equal to his own. He should've hit him again, but someone came along. He lit out the back. He was done

259

with this town, he thought. The moment the pain was bearable, he'd strip this place clean.

Hearing a man's voice coming from the front of the house, Burl swallowed, hunched low, and listened hard. The marshal. Burl aimed his pistol at the cellar ceiling and went "pop" with his lips. His mouth responded with a deep stab of pain. Moaning, cussing under his breath, he crept to the top of the narrow stairs and pressed his ear to the door that was locked from the other side. Like that would stop him the moment he decided he was going through it . . .

Faintly, he heard the marshal's bootsteps cross the front porch.

"Bye-bye, Marshal," he whispered, draining the bottle and wishing he could throw it. He heard voices and footsteps in the kitchen. Easing silently down the stairs, Burl curled up on the dirt floor, pistol loaded and cocked. In moments he was asleep.

Fourteen

Widow Ashton's orders were to clean the upstairs rooms. Jodee and Maggie dusted, polished and rearranged everything. Maggie pointed out fascinating details from the crystal-fringed lamp on the side table to Widow Ashton's silver dressing set, a matching comb, brush, hand mirror, plus a complete set of silver-topped glass jars. Jodee stared, wondering how much such finery cost. By comparison, her own belongings seemed tawdry indeed.

In the guest room Jodee noticed the music box missing. Her heart did an anxious patter when she showed Maggie.

Maggie nodded, "I make them doilies," she said, pointing to where the music box had been. "It's called tatting. I'll show you." She took Jodee into the hallway. Going up the narrow back stairs, she unlocked a plank door. The attic room smelled fresh because Maggie's dormer windows were open to the mountain air.

Jodee ran her hand over Maggie's bright bed quilt. The pillow slip had the most elegant embroidery Jodee had ever seen. On the night-stand lay her handkerchief which she had given Maggie. There was a chair close to a window. Beside it stood a table with a lamp and basket of thread on top of mounds of white frills. Maggie lifted a handful, unfurling yards of tatted lace.

"What do you do with all of this?" Jodee took some in her hand.

"We trim Miss Avinelle's things," Maggie said as if Jodee should have known.

"I wonder what Mr. Quimby would give you for this." There was a camel-back trunk in a far corner and a flat-topped chest near the door. "You sit here night after night, making all this?

I've never seen you go to the store for thread."
Jodee had never seen Maggie set foot outside
the house.

"Miz Theia brings what I need from Cheyenne
City. She takes care of me."

"Well," Jodee said with a sigh. "She don't like
me, that's certain. If I knew how to do this I'd
make a mile of it and sell it for a ticket out of
this town. Do you ever think of working for
somebody else?"

Maggie looked baffled.

That's when Jodee spied the music box on the
floor on the far side of the chair. With an impish
smile Maggie snatched it up and handed it to
Jodee.

So, Maggie had the music box. Almost loath
to touch it, Jodee turned it over and saw an
engraved name on the bottom. She expected it to
be Widow Ashton's name, but elegant swirls
spelled some-thing different.

"Do you read? Books, I mean," Jodee asked. "I
don't read much. I ain't been to school in a long
time."

Maggie's expression was lively, but she said
nothing.

"Did you live back east with Widow Ashton and
Avinelle?"

Maggie nodded.

"Does this belong to Widow Ashton or
Avinelle?" She ran her finger across the name.

"E—lee—a—nor Holl—ee—worth," she read aloud. "New . . . York."

With a look of horror, Maggie scrambled backward. "I won't tell!" she cried. "You can't make me!"

"Maggie, sh—h—h." Trying to calm the woman, Jodee put the music box down. "I'm thirsty. Are you thirsty? Would you like a taste of coffee with lots of cream and sugar?"

Maggie pushed Jodee out of the room, locked the door, and flew down the stairs. Back in the kitchen, Jodee edged close to Hanna and explained what had just happened. "Who's Eleanor Hollingsworth?"

"Nobody around here by that name, honey. New York, you say? That's back east. A real big town."

"You don't suppose the music box is stolen."

"More like Miz Theia bought it in a second-hand shop. I told you she ain't as well fixed as she'd like everybody to believe." She explained what a secondhand shop was.

Jodee returned to her chores, but for the remainder of the day she took note of all the beautiful handiwork all over the house. Just where did Widow Ashton and Avinelle come by their finery? She didn't see Maggie again.

In spite of Widow Ashton's announcement that she and Avinelle were ready to receive, no one called on them. With the coming of spring, the house seemed less chilly. Jodee went to Patsy's each afternoon to do laundry and visit with Baby Henry who was thriving. Virgil sat in the rocker, frail and thin. Patsy looked happier.

At night, Jodee was certain she heard stealthy footsteps outside the house but never saw anything. Sometimes she heard strange noises inside the house she couldn't account for. Maggie avoided her.

"Do you know anyone named Eleanor Hollingsworth?" she asked Bailey one afternoon.

"Some wealthy socialite back east," he said, turning a flower bed. "Saw her name in a newspaper one time. Married a financier, I believe. A money man, lassie." Then he smiled one of his rare smiles. "I wasn't one for reading the society column." He had to explain what a newspaper society column was. *Were Widow Ashton and Avinelle pretenders?* Jodee wondered. Was she dipping curtseys to a thief and a liar?

Early Thursday morning, preparations for the May Day celebration began. Hanna prepared extra dishes for the picnic. "You watch," Hanna said with a smirk. "Avinelle will change her clothes three times."

"I wish I had something special to wear to the dance," Jodee said. "These clothes are decent enough, but they're showing wear already. Someday I'm going to have me a real nice lady's dress with a bustle. And a parasol. Me and my

264

ma, we used to play-act we was ladies at a tea party. We'd be scrubbing clothes in the wash tub, blistering in the summer sun, and we'd laugh. Or me and my pa would pretend we had us a nice house with a porch. Pa would say he'd have a different rocking chair for each day of the week. And a silk top hat that he'd tip to neighbors as they passed, admiring our place." She chuckled with a pang of heartache.

"Your people were fine dreamers," Hanna said. "Me and my husband, we used to dream of having a ranch with a thousand head of cattle. You reckon Corbet will ask you to dance tonight?" She slipped that question in with a sly smile.

"He said he couldn't play favorites. I just have to accept he likes me well enough, but it don't go no farther than that. All he thinks about is finding Burl. To tell the truth, that's about all I think about, too."

"I'm not a gambling person," Hanna said, laughing, "but I'm placing my bet on who J. Corbet Harlow dances with first tonight. The whole town will be watching. There's nothing to be done about your clothes, Jodee, but we can brush out your hair 'til it shines. You'll be the prettiest woman there."

Jodee's heart skipped with anticipation. Hanna's words gave her confidence. She spent the next hour trying to imagine Corbet walking up to her in front of everybody and asking her to dance. She couldn't quite believe it would happen.

At nine-thirty that morning, as Bailey was bringing around the surrey for the ride into town for the parade, Avinelle descended the front stairs and called to Jodee. She wore a walking suit of pale green taffeta with a snug bodice and a skirt with a complicated bustle. Her matching hat perched on her elaborate curls. She had a ruffled lace parasol that made Jodee stare.

"I wanted to wear this blouse to the picnic," Avinelle said, thrusting a wad of something white and delicate into Jodee's hands. "Press it for me and have it ready when we get back from the parade. Hurry now, and take care. That came all the way from Paris. It was part of my trousseau." Avinelle tugged on bone-colored kid gloves, fussing a long time getting the fingers just right.

Trousseau. Another word Jodee didn't know. Avinelle looked so beautiful she couldn't help but feel admiration. "You look wonderful."

"Oh, Jodee, when will you remember you mustn't make personal remarks about your employer?" Avinelle wandered into the parlor, shaking her head. Looking out the front window, she called in an unladylike caterwaul, "Mother! Bailey's waiting. Are you ready?"

Feeling foolish for having spoken, Jodee clutched the item Avinelle had given her and wondered what it was made of. The fabric didn't feel like her own clothes or like anything she had washed or ironed so far.

Starting down the staircase, Widow Ashton looked dignified in a dusky rose walking suit. She moved like a queen. Dipping a curtsy, Jodee hurried back to the kitchen before she said something more she shouldn't. If she was to have the blouse pressed by the time Avinelle returned from the parade, she wouldn't be able to go to the parade herself. That had surely been Avinelle's purpose.

"Look at this," Jodee muttered, thrusting the blouse toward Hanna.

Hanna's hands were wet. She refused to touch it.

Jodee didn't have the slightest idea how to press it. Before going into the sewing room to get the flat irons on the stove to heat, she stood a long moment frowning at the blouse. "I wanted to see the parade. Didn't you, Hanna?"

"If I'm lucky I'll get to see Bonnie dance around the May Pole this afternoon." Her expression was troubled.

They heard Widow Ashton and Avinelle go out. Moments later the surrey rolled away. Jodee felt as much relief as disappointment.

"If you hurry," Hanna said, "you might see part of the parade and be back in time to press this. Get your boots on."

Throwing off her apron, Jodee was out the rear

door in seconds, trotting around to the side street. The road was busy with wagons and buck-boards and buggies. She waved to everyone. Not knowing who she was, people waved back, women in sunbonnets and children staring from the backs of wagons.

By the time Jodee reached the first boardwalk in town she could hear the thumping of a drum and some kind of brass horn honking. At the head of the parade came the mayor and his family in their carriage. Behind him rolled the town's pumper fire wagon drawn by a matched team.

Along with children set free from school for the day, Jodee scampered from boardwalk to boardwalk, past Quimby's and the photographers and the newspaper office. She saw the surrey ahead of the banker's buggy and a hay rake carrying the May Day girls in their white dresses. That was why Avinelle and Widow Ashton left the house early. They hadn't wanted Jodee in the parade with them.

Trying not to feel slighted, Jodee resigned herself to the fact that she would miss most of the day's activities. She ran back to Avinelle's house and presented herself in the kitchen, ready to tackle the ironing.

"We get to go to the picnic, don't we?" Jodee asked, setting up the cloth-covered board. She laid out the first sleeve to press and tried to smooth it flat. The blouse was so wrinkled it looked as if it had been stuffed in a trunk for years.

"We have to serve, so don't plan on having too much fun today. Then you won't be disappointed." Hanna winked. "Tonight at the dance is when you'll outshine Avinelle."

"I can't hope to do that," Jodee said softly. "One dance with Corbet is all I hope for, to remember after I'm gone."

"Oh, honey, you won't never leave Burdeen. I seen how you pine for Corbet. You want to marry him."

"I don't know what being married is like. And . . ." Jodee licked her fingertip and tapped the first flat iron to make sure it wasn't too hot, just as Hanna had taught her to do. Wrapping a rag around the handle to protect her hand from the hot metal, she deftly touched the tip of the heavy iron and moved it quickly along the seam. She watched in horror as the fabric vanished beneath the tip.

Snatching the iron away, Jodee smelled a peculiar odor and gave a cry. "Oh, Hanna!"

Three inches of the seam was gone, burned away in an instant.

Grabbing up the blouse, Hanna held up the sleeve to look at the damage. "We can mend this. She'll never know."

Jodee's heart felt as if it were leaping around in her chest like a snared rabbit. She felt wild with anguish. "I've ruined it."

"It's all right. Fetch the needle and thread. She should've known this shouldn't be ironed. I should've known."

Jodee felt panic. It was all she could do to keep from running out the back door. She didn't want to face Avinelle and confess she'd ruined her expensive Paris trousseau blouse. She owed so much for the things she'd damaged already she had lost count. She'd never get out of debt.

The front door closed loudly as if Maggie were warning that the widows had returned.

Hanna whispered, "Don't say a word."

Widow Ashton and Avinelle entered the kitchen as if expecting something was amiss. Jodee shrank back, feeling sick.

"The hampers are packed, Miz Ashton," Hanna said loudly. "Bailey can load the surrey while you change into your picnic clothes. We're still trying to get the stain out of this blouse."

"Stain?" Avinelle exclaimed with exaggeration.

Widow Ashton looked where Hanna was pointing. She regarded Avinelle as if shocked. Snatching it from Hanna, the widow shook the blouse in her daughter's face. Looking as if she remembered she was not alone, she faltered. "You cannot wear this, Avinelle. You will have to select something else. Now we will be late." Dropping the blouse on the ironing board, she sailed out of the kitchen.

Avinelle stared at Hanna. Finally she said, "It

270

didn't have a stain when I gave it to you," She remembered something. "And don't think you weren't seen in town, Jodee, when I told you to stay here."

Did they think they owned her? Jodee wondered.

Hanna picked up the blouse in a way that hid the damaged sleeve.

Avinelle snatched the blouse from her hand so forcefully it tore. She glared at Hanna with blazing eyes. Jodee realized the smell of scorched fabric was still in the air, too. When Avinelle held up the blouse, the damaged underarm seam became visible.

"My best blouse! Mother, look at what Jodee did."

Jodee realized Avinelle purposely waited until the last minute to ask her to press the blouse. And she chose the blouse because it could so easily be damaged.

"We'll wash—"

"Stay out of this, Hanna, if you know what's good for you." Avinelle advanced on Jodee. "Don't you think you'll get away with this. Mother will dock your pay. I have half a mind not to give you a letter of recommendation. You're a worthless, dumb, ignorant little harlot, and I'm sorry I ever laid eyes on you."

"What has happened now?" Widow Ashton said returning to the kitchen as if greatly wearied of all the trouble.

"It's not enough we take her in and give her our best, she has to ruin every single thing she touches. This can't be fixed."

"A patch," Hanna offered, her face flushed with anger.

"I wouldn't wear a patched—"

"All right," Jodee snapped. "You could have told me that there fabric would melt. I don't know how I'm supposed to press something you don't care enough about to pack away clean and folded. If I owned something that nice, I'd take care of it. No, you got to keep me from having any kind of fun today, like seeing my first parade, and there you both are, heading it like you own the town. Now I got to buy you a new Paris trousseau blouse because you can't wear something patched. Well, all right, I will, but I ain't no harlot. And don't you go saying nothing against my pa. He paid his debt to the world. He's dead. You want me to clear out, I will."

Slamming the back door, Jodee stood on the porch glaring down at her meager belongings. She waited to see if they were going to call her back. Hearing nothing, she went out into the backyard and wondered what it would feel like to slap Avinelle's face hard enough to leave a mark.

As Corbet made his usual circuit of town, he wanted to feel optimistic, but his heart was heavy.

It seemed like half the county had come to town this day. The weather was fine. Traffic was heavy, the stores were crowded, and a throng of folks were setting up for the picnic in the open field outside town.

All he could think about was the letter he just received. At his own request, T. T. McQue's horse, saddle, and the gun he had been carrying when he was killed during the holdup at Ship Creek Crossing had been sold at a private auction in Cheyenne City. In his shirt pocket Corbet had the proceeds, a bank draft for two hundred thirty-seven dollars and forty-one cents.

Jodee was as good as gone.

Folks tipped their hats to him as he passed. He was gratified to see it, but he had decided to recommend Ed Brucker as sheriff. This was his last day on the job.

Seeing Avinelle's surrey at the jailhouse, Corbet turned abruptly into an alley, surprising two youths trying to light a stogie. Chasing them off with a scowl, he thought about the telegraph message that arrived from Wisconsin days ago. Old man Harlow was dead. That in itself was enough to fill Corbet with complex emotions. He had sometimes hated the man for working orphaned boys so hard, but the gruff dairy farmer had turned those boys into men. He'd been the closest Corbet had to a father. Now it was too late to make amends for leaving as he had done.

Inexplicably, Corbet had been named in the will. Old man Harlow left him the farm.

As Corbet returned back to the street and saw the surrey moving on toward the picnic grounds, he watched for Jodee. He hadn't told her he had bought his little spread by the creek, but now he needed to see the farm where he'd spent his lonely youth. He wanted to tell her there'd be a delay in starting the cabin he wanted to build. He wanted to visit little Jenny's grave, too. He wanted to be sure he was doing the right thing settling in Burdeen.

The smell of wood smoke and roasting beef in barbeque pits filled the spring air with a pleasant tang. He wandered into the picnic area, a scrubby field dotted with spread quilts, food-laden hampers, and noisy people. Children ran wild around him. He knew them all by name. There was Hobie with his mother and siblings. The only notable family missing was the Botellers.

There had been talk of turning the area into a city park. In another five years, Burdeen would be a real town with a railroad, a stone courthouse, and a bank. The stage line would be history. Avinelle and her mother would have to move on. That made their relentless pursuit of him all the more puzzling. Did Avinelle expect him to follow her to New York like a well-trained parlor dog?

Corbet saw a large tent set up with a long red

pennant snapping from the center pole. Thinking it the community refreshment stand, he barged in expecting to find Artie Abernathy inside serving sarsaparilla and lemonade. At the sight of Avinelle decked out like a princess, his heart shriveled.

"Corbet!" she exclaimed, gliding toward him. "I've been hoping you'd join us. Isn't this lovely? Rented, of course. Bailey set it up early this morning. No wind. No smoke." She gave him a sly smile. "Privacy."

Hanna and Jodee stood at the ready behind a long table draped with a white cloth. The table was heaped with enough food for the entire town. Hanna wore her usual patient smirk, an expression that told the world just what she thought of such pretensions. It was Jodee's surly expression that captured Corbet's concern. He had seen her look like that before. Something was wrong.

He started for her, but Avinelle seized his arm. "Corbet, I have something I must discuss with you. It's urgent." She gave his arm a meaningful squeeze. "Hanna? Jodee? See if there's something more you need to carry in from the surrey. Bailey may want to let the horse graze." She smiled up at Corbet as if to say she had the afternoon well in hand.

To see Hanna and Jodee dip a curtsey and obediently leave the tent set Corbet's teeth on edge. Jodee didn't even cast him a glance.

"Jodee doesn't look well," Corbet said, letting Avinelle know where his interest lay.

She shook her head. "I've tried my best, Corbet, but she's hopeless. She'll never make a suitable domestic. Too coarse. And she's rude. Not just back-talk, but threats. I'm not certain we're safe. She needs to be on her way."

Corbet studied Avinelle's upturned face. He couldn't figure out how she could look so beautiful and sound so heartless. "You're right."

Avinelle beamed. When she looked like that it was easy for a man to forget everything. One last time Corbet asked himself if he felt anything for her. Any normal man would find her irresistible, and she wanted him so. He felt nothing but impatience and irritation. He pulled his elbow free. He was done with this foolishness.

She had to see how he felt, he thought. She caught hold of him again and pressed herself against his chest with her arms entwined around his neck like a noose. She went up on tiptoe. She was going to kiss him.

"No, Avinelle," he said, catching hold of her arms and pulling them from around his neck. He held her away and stared fiercely into her eyes. He watched for hurt or disappointment or the pain of unrequited love in her eyes, but he saw only frustration. He saw fury. He saw fear.

"You're beautiful," he said. "You know that. You could have any man in town, any man in the territory. I'm sorry," he said, trying to be gentle, "but I don't love you."

With her bosom rising and falling, she struggled, as if trying to embrace him again and kiss him.

He held her fast. "No."

Her jaw hardened. Her eyes turned to glass. It was disconcerting to see the change. One cry and it might look to some as if he were trying to assault her. He might find himself arrested, or worse, married to her. He'd been foolish to allow himself a single moment alone with her.

"If need be, Avinelle," he said, "I'll turn in my badge today and leave town." He reached for the badge on his vest, then hesitated. A lot could happen in a town overrun with strangers.

"Don't be foolish, Corbet," Avinelle said with a sneer.

"I'll turn in my resignation to the mayor tomorrow."

Before Avinelle could think of something more to say, Corbet made for the tent's doorway. He'd see Jodee safely on her way to Arkansas, and then he, too, would leave. Emerging from the tent into eye-stinging sunlight, Corbet headed blindly for Hobie and his family. Distractedly, he talked with them a while, but Hobie was distant. Corbet wished there was something he could say to mend the rift between them.

Noticing Patsy's arrival, Corbet laid his hand on Hobie's shoulder and gave his young friend a farewell nod. To see Virgil climbing with care from a buggy borrowed from Patsy's parents filled Corbet with satisfaction.

"Virge!" he called, hailing his friend. "Look at you, all healed up and out and about again." It was an exaggeration. Thin and pale, Virgil was a shadow of his former self, but he had a genuine smile for Corbet. Gone was the wild impatience that had once characterized his crooked grin.

"Thought I'd help you out today." Virgil gave Patsy a wink.

They watched the May Pole being erected with its trailing ribbons. The girls in their white dresses soon danced around it, singing. Corbet hardly heard them. He longed to sit and talk with Virgil but it took all his friend's strength to sit in the sunshine and cradle his son.

Corbet drifted away, wandering the crowded picnic area like a ghost. With the sound of gun shots in the distance, he forgot his melancholy and set out at a trot. By the time he arrived, Brucker already had a brawl between cowhands in hand. No one was hurt. By suppertime Corbet's jail was full.

While making rounds after dark, Corbet wondered how Avinelle was treating Jodee now that he'd rejected her advances. He needed to give Jodee her money. She might be on the stagecoach by morning.

Tomorrow, he thought, pausing, struggling with

what he knew would happen with what he wished could happen. Too much was happening too fast. He stormed along the boardwalk. Folks gave him plenty of room to pass.

Hungry, dusty from the day's exertions, and feeling disheartened, Corbet decided he needed to wash up and change his shirt before going to the dance. He might be duty-bound to let Jodee go, but tonight he would allow himself what his heart longed for, a dance and one last very sincere kiss.

An hour later, Corbet stood in the back of the crowded Winfield livery barn talking with Mayor Winfield and the town councilmen. The place had been swept clean and the floor covered with fresh hay. Lanterns hung from the rafters, spreading golden light over the dancing townspeople.

Quickly he was cornered by the town's councilmen.

"It can't be true that you're thinking of leaving us," the mayor said.

"Brucker's an experienced man, more than I ever was," Corbet said, disconcerted by the anxious expressions on the men crowded around him.

"You're the best marshal this town's ever had. We hardly know this man. Where would you go? What would you do?"

Patsy Robstart's father cut in. "If it's a matter of money . . ."

Flattered, Corbet chuckled. "You'll get used to him. He's rough, trying to prove himself. I was a stranger when I started out."

He wondered if they had all accepted him on Widow Ashton's word.

Worried that he hadn't seen Jodee yet, he noticed an excited hush spread across the barn. Excusing himself, he turned to see whose arrival was causing such a stir.

Beaming her famous smile, Avinelle appeared between the livery barn's double doors. She wore something that reminded Corbet of a wedding cake. It set off her narrow waist and décolletage. She belonged some place grander than Burdeen, for sure, but he didn't change his mind about her. He'd had enough of her pouts and manipulations.

Wondering what was keeping Jodee, he made another circuit of the barn. All eyes were on Avinelle as she sashayed into the throng, greeting everyone like a visiting princess. She positively glittered with charm, but whispers followed her. Avinelle wasn't liked, Corbet knew. He felt sorry for her. Behind her by several steps came her mother, who caught the eye of several older ranchers and businessmen. Corbet watched Quimby approach but go unnoticed. The man bore his snub gracefully and drifted away.

Before Avinelle could turn and capture Corbet with her hawk-like gaze, he slipped out the side door into the darkness. There were a lot of people milling around in the street, many mere shadows, quickening his senses. He smelled whiskey and cigar smoke. He heard low talk and laughter. A mental picture of saturnine Burl Tangus plundering the stage office or robbing a store . . . or worse yet, carrying Jodee away into the mountains, made his stomach knot. He had no business mooning over who was dancing with whom when this night was ripe for trouble.

What if he sent Jodee away on the stagecoach in the morning and Tangus held it up and took her?

Fifteen

A short time before the dance began, Avinelle had been rushing around, readying herself. Jodee watched her storm back and forth between her room and her mother's, fretting over her hair, snapping and snarling like a wolverine, and hissing comments Jodee was glad she couldn't hear.

When Avinelle and her mother were finally ready, they came down the stairs wearing their glorious gowns, their faces like warriors approaching a battlefield.

Widow Ashton spied Jodee waiting near the door. Momentarily she looked flustered. "I suppose you must accompany us," she said, "but you cannot go inside until Avinelle has led the Grand

March with Marshal Harlow. Remember, you are a servant, Jodee, not a young lady of this town. You have no male protector, no father, and no brother. Stay in the background. Speak only when spoken to. Under no circumstances should you make a spectacle of yourself. I advise you not to dance. If you associate with strangers you will be thought a loose woman. You must guard your reputation every moment or be ruined before the night ends."

Jodee hadn't known what to say to that. Avinelle had no male protector and she was going to the dance. She scolded herself for forgetting the woman enjoyed crushing her hopes.

Widow Ashton went out to the waiting surrey. Avinelle swept past, leaving Jodee standing in the entry, wondering if she could stomach a ride into town with them when she hated them both so. She considered staying behind just to bedevil them. Let the woman worry she was looting every room.

Wanting to cuss and break things, Jodee caught sight of herself in the hall mirror. Her hair looked wonderful, hanging down her back in a pale cascade. Her blouse and skirt still pleased her. What would everyone think if she showed up at the dance in britches and boots, wearing her pa's gun and that slouchy hat she lost back at the cabin? Widow Ashton and Avinelle didn't realize who they were insulting, Jodee thought, burning to best them somehow. Avinelle didn't know how to twirl a pistol and shoot a jackrabbit at a hundred paces like a shootist.

Jodee smirked at herself. Fighting disappointment and fury, she pointed her finger at the mirror and said, "Bang," softly to her reflection. Startled to see a change in her expression, Jodee hid her hand behind her back. For an instant she had looked like Burl. Fear flashed through her. How much longer could she hold out? Wasn't she exactly what everyone believed her to be? An outlaw? For true?

Plodding out the door, Jodee felt suddenly as if she didn't dare go to the dance. When she climbed into the rear seat of the surrey she understood that she would never be on the same social level as Avinelle and her mother. She was only weeks out of jail, after all, still living down her father's bad reputation. She *was not* a lady, and never would be. Some days she didn't really care to be a lady, but she was still a human being. Didn't she deserve a chance?

Heart-sore, Jodee feared she'd been expecting too much too soon. She understood now how her pa had felt all those years, frustrated and impatient. He dreamed of better things but was never able to make a go of his ranches or dirt farms. He gave in to Burl's wild schemes for fast money and an easy life. Even if no one else did, she forgave him his weaknesses.

She felt impatient, too. She wanted the past to vanish and be forgotten, but she must work, perhaps years, to earn cash money for things half as nice as what Widow Ashton and Avinelle tossed aside as nothing. Whatever made her think she could build her new life in a month?

She mustn't make the mistakes her impatient father had made. Or her defiant mother. As Bailey drove, Jodee hardly noticed the brightly lit, noisy livery barn at the end of the street where the townspeople had gathered. The atmosphere was festive, but she didn't move when Bailey helped Avinelle to the ground. Looking spectacular in her gown, Avinelle sashayed through the barn's double doors like she owned the town.

Bailey came to help Jodee down, but she remained in her seat, hands clenched in her lap.

"Miss Jodee?" Bailey looked concerned.

Jodee shook her head. "I don't feel much like dancing after all," she said, her voice small. "I think I'll just sit here. I should've stayed at the house, but I didn't want anyone thinking I was there, fixin' to rob the place while everyone was here, having a good time."

The street outside the livery barn was choked with wagons and teams, horses tied up in long lines, folks milling about like cattle. Corbet wound his way between them, watching shadows. His gut told him Tangus was in the crowd, picking pockets or listening to talk, planning something, ready to strike. The sound of laughter and dancing faded as Corbet prowled. If he didn't find Jodee soon he'd have to return to his rounds. There were too many drunken cowhands and suspicious looking strangers in town for the marshal to be lollygagging at a dance.

Then he saw Avinelle's surrey and Bailey standing nearby as if on watch himself. He saw Jodee seated on the surrey's rear seat, head down, facing away from the light.

Bailey straightened. "Good evening, Marshal."

Corbet tipped his hat. Bailey escaped into the darkness. Reaching up, Corbet touched Jodee's elbow. Startled from her thoughts, she shrank from him as she had done when he first brought her to town.

"I thought you'd be dancing with Avinelle by now," she said with a catch in her voice. "All she talked about today was being next to you in the Grand March."

He shook his head. Jodee looked so hurt, so sweet, so dear with her hair down like that. His heart went out to her. "Let me help you down. I have something to tell you."

She let him hand her down but she quickly edged away. "You should go inside, Corbet. She's waiting for you. Go ahead. It's all right. I don't belong in there. I know that now."

"Of course you belong in there. What's wrong, Jodee? Where's your fire tonight?"

Like a child, she shrugged.

"How's your shoulder feeling?"

She shook her head like it didn't matter.

Corbet gnashed his teeth. He'd put her in jail, damaging her reputation beyond repair. She'd done all right, facing Avinelle's dinner guests, but now she was afraid to face the judgment of an entire town at the dance. He leaned in quickly to give Jodee a kiss. Her lips felt damp. She dashed her palm across her cheeks.

The farewell kiss would have to come later, he decided, when she felt better. He brushed his lips against hers a second time and felt a jolt flash through his body. He might not want his feelings for her to grow, but something was inside him, strong and persistent.

To hell with everything. He was about to kiss her like he meant business when he heard a rider galloping hell for leather in from the darkness.

In a hail of gravel and dust Reverend Boteller's oldest boy reined alongside him. "Have you seen Doc? It's Ma's time."

"On the bandstand," Corbet said, pointing, "playing the fiddle."

The horse reared and pawed the air. The boy tumbled to the ground, found his feet, and raced inside.

Corbet rubbed the back of his neck. "You'd

think after eight siblings, he'd be used to his mother having babies."

Jodee said nothing. Seconds later the boy emerged from the barn with the doctor.

"Bailey," Corbet called. "Can you give Doc a ride? It'd take too long to get his buggy."

After Bailey appeared, and with the doctor aboard the surrey and on his way, the Boteller boy galloped after him. In moments all was quiet again. Corbet swallowed hard and looked around at the people crowding the livery barn's open doors. He shouldn't be here, he thought. He should be somewhere else, but where? From where would the trouble come?

He turned back to Jodee. "It's time for us to go inside." With an encouraging smile, he offered his elbow. He hadn't intended to enter the dance with Jodee on his arm, but it seemed all at once the only thing he could do, the only thing he wanted to do. It might have to be a quick dance, but by God, he was going to show this town he wasn't some damned puppet, nose-ringed bull, or well-trained and obedient parlor dog.

After feeling so certain she had lost her chance to dance with Corbet, Jodee could scarcely believe she was slipping her chilled fingers into the warm crook of his elbow. Her worries vanished. There was no telling what she might be doing come morning, she thought, but for

287

tonight a dream was coming true. She walked into the dance on the arm of her beau. Corbet was her beau because, in spite of all her protests, he had just touched his lips to hers.

As Corbet led her inside, folks loitering near the doors straightened and moved aside. Heads turned. Whispers followed. Jodee couldn't get her breath to go out. The musicians played something that sounded like a Tennessee reel. Couples swirled in laughing, whooping circles. Jodee had never seen anything like it. The excitement was around her like smoke, making her dizzy and giddy. She didn't have time to explain that she had no idea how to dance like that.

The reel came to an uncertain conclusion. A cheer went up. Jodee felt like folks were cheering for her and Corbet. She almost couldn't bear it, she felt so happy. Not only were they going to dance together, they were the talk of the town. Her throat began to swell with joyous tears that she battled with all her strength to control.

For the first time in her life something seemed to be going right. An hour ago she might have run away and cheated herself of this. She didn't have time to think of how dearly her mother had wished for a moment like this for herself, to be seen in public with her love, T. T. McQue, and dance with him in front of her family and the town. This was Jodee's moment to relish in her mother's place.

Marshal J. Corbet Harlow led her to the center of the barn floor where dancing feet had crushed scattered hay to a fine powder. Golden lantern light lit their faces as they smiled at each other with rapt attention. A gentle tune began on a mouth harp. Jodee's ears roared so loudly she could scarcely hear it. Her cheeks felt hot. She didn't know what to do.

Corbet put one hand on the small of her back and lifted her right hand in his. She felt a slight ache in her shoulder that reminded her of the doctor's words—that she would dance someday. Holding her breath, she looked up into Corbet's handsome face and thought she was going to die of happiness. Tarnation, it felt good to be decent.

They began moving together, their feet somehow finding the rhythm of the tune and their hearts drumming as one. Corbet looked tender as he guided her in slow circles. Jodee didn't notice that no one else was dancing. They were turning and turning around the gritty floor, oblivious to the watching faces and stunned expressions.

When the song ended and another began, they went on dancing. Eventually other couples joined them until once again the center of the barn was crowded with dancing couples. Ranchers and their wives, cowboys and young ranch cooks, lads in long pants and the May Day maidens in white, all waltzing as if the simple music were perfect.

From his chair on the sidelines, Virgil Robstart climbed slowly to his feet and led his wife in a few exquisitely slow turns before the two headed quietly out the doors. More than a few gossips took note of Avinelle Babcock standing near the mayor and his wife. She smiled a brilliantly brittle smile as if she didn't notice that no man had asked her to dance.

Jodee looked ethereal with her pale hair streaming down her back and her young face upturned, her eyes fixed on Corbet's beaming face. She might not be a girl of the town, more than a few were thinking, but there was no doubt she was Queen of the May. Corbet looked tender—folks would say later they had not realized their marshal was such a handsome man.

Everybody watched Marshal Harlow and the McQue girl dance as if in a rapturous daze, eyes locked, bodies moving gracefully together until a young lad with crooked teeth stepped forward to tap the marshal on his shoulder.

"Excuse me, sir," he said.

Jodee stumbled as Corbet broke the rhythm of the waltz steps and looked down into the darkly serious eyes of Hobie Fenton. Without a word he relinquished his hold on Jodee. When Hobie took Jodee in his arms, she could feel him trembling. His fingers felt cold and thin in hers. His cheeks sported two blotches of nervous color. Jodee's heart melted with affection. "How-do, Hobie."

"Miss McQue," Hobie began, looking directly into her eyes. "Jodee," he corrected himself. "I promised you a dance. Here I am." He relaxed his chilling hold and forced a sheepish smile.

"I want to thank you for treating me decent when I first got to town," she said to Hobie. "You were my first friend. I hope you find all you hope for in life. Back east. In college."

"Oh, I won't be leaving just yet. I go in the fall, but when I get back," he said, beginning to grin with all his crooked teeth showing, "you won't recognize me, all duded up in eastern clothes and talking law."

She grinned. "You'll look fine, but I won't be here. I'm going away soon. I don't know where I belong, but I'm going to try fresh someplace else."

"Some folks around here think real high of you," he said. "I'm proud to know you."

Artie Abernathy cut in next. Jodee felt disoriented, not getting a chance to tell Hobie goodbye.

For a husky man Artie moved surprisingly light on his feet. He danced Jodee away from Hobie, talking non-stop. Jodee didn't hear a word he said. Then a handsome young cowhand cut in. Jodee felt like the belle of the ball, swirling in circles, smiling until her cheeks ached . . . but then in the shadows she saw Widow Ashton's frowning face and remembered her warning. Was dancing with this stranger ruining her reputation? Was she making a spectacle of herself? How could she extract herself from this young man's eager grip without seeming unkind?

Looking around, Jodee saw the woman rise to her feet, outrage purpling her face. A stab of fear went through Jodee until she realized the woman was watching Avinelle refuse the invitation of broadly grinning Deputy Brucker. Jodee stumbled. Then, blessedly, there was Corbet again, tapping the shoulder of the cowhand and taking Jodee back into his arms. Her heart shivered with happiness. Oh, if only she could go on like this forever.

"Having fun?" Corbet asked.

"I don't know."

Corbet laughed. It was such a wonderful sound. "Of course you are."

They went on dancing several more slow dances. Then they stood aside, watching couples attempt the faster, more complicated reels and quadrilles. When Deputy Malone, who had been manning the jail approached, he looked winded.

"It's all right, Marshal. Brucker just now took over at the jail," he explained. "Said he wasn't having any luck here. Where's the food?" He dragged off his hat and bowed to Jodee. "Evening, Miss McQue. You look real nice. Are folks heading home already?"

Corbet looked around. His brow knit. He was looking for Avinelle, Jodee thought. He hadn't danced with her yet. She didn't see her or her mother. "I should check on something, Jodee," he said. "Charlie, would you mind looking after Jodee a moment?"

Deputy Malone blushed. "I can't dance a step, Ma'am."

Jodee watched Corbet stride out of the barn into the darkness. She guided the deputy toward the refreshment table. Shoving pie into his mouth, Deputy Malone said, "It's been a helluva day. 'Scuse my language, Ma'am. Jail's full. We was trying to track down a whiskey thief who's been breaking into the Bail 'O Hay Saloon in the wee hours." He swallowed hard.

Jodee sagged with relief when Corbet came back. He drew her aside.

"Theia and Avinelle weren't very happy that I sent Doc to the Botellers' in their surrey. Bailey just got back and he's taking them home now. We should go, too."

Jodee felt uneasy. "Is that all that's worrying you, Corbet?"

He offered his arm. Feeling the tension in his body, she followed him into the darkness.

Where would she go if Widow Ashton refused to let her back into the house? After all, she had done precisely what the woman told her not to do. She had danced. With a stranger, too.

Corbet patted her hand where it lay in the crook of his arm. They moved quickly along the dark road no longer so crowded with wagons. "I have important things to talk to you about, but now isn't the time. There won't be any trouble when you get home tonight because I spoke to Theia and Avinelle just now," Corbet went on. "Theia wants you gone—you already know that."

Jodee nodded. She couldn't speak. Tears stung her eyes.

"I released her from her obligation to take care of you, as she put it. It was never an obligation as far as I was concerned. I thought it was an invitation. I thought they wanted to help you, but I'm an idiot. Avinelle just wanted to make me beholden to her. You don't have to work for them anymore. Consider your debts paid in full. All of them. Don't argue, honey," he said when she began to protest. He remained quiet a moment. His grip tightened.

The desire to weep subsided as Jodee chuckled. This was all so silly.

Abruptly he pulled her close and hugged her. The more he tried to cushion the blow of what he was going to say next, Jodee thought, the more frightened she became.

"I'll see to it that Theia and Avinelle don't exclude you from going to the funeral."

"What funeral?" Jodee whispered, pulling away so she could see Corbet's face.

"Mrs. Boteller died about an hour ago. Bailey got Doc Trafford to the house in time to save the baby, but she was gone. While I was making heartless remarks about her having so many children, the woman was drawing her last breath. She'll be buried Saturday."

Jodee went still inside. The woman with the cold hands? The end was coming for her, too. She couldn't prevent it.

Corbet released her and cupped her upturned face. "I don't want you to worry, Jodee. Trust me on this. Everything will be all right. I'll talk to you in a couple of days and help you plan what to do." Then he lowered his head and pressed his warm soft lips to hers.

Taken utterly by surprise, Jodee's body blossomed with fire. She closed her eyes and fell headlong into the delicious sensations coursing through her body. His strong arms enfolded her. She went up tight against him, too surprised by the suddenness of the kiss to have her arms free to encircle his neck. She stood deliciously restrained, feeling the urgency of his mouth against hers until her hands clutched his waist.

When Corbet pulled free, he buried his face in her hair. He held her and held her as if he never intended to let her go. They stood like that in the darkness as one, safe together. She tightened her hold on him in a way she had never imagined before. This big strong man with his formidable eyes and the gun on his hip clung to her as if she were his pillar of strength.

When at last the moment passed, they released each other. Corbet captured her hand in his and they walked slowly, without speaking, through the darkened town. The night air felt cool against Jodee's burning cheeks. She couldn't capture a single thought. All she knew was the sound of their footsteps and the quiet rush of the night wind high in the pines.

Sixteen

Hanna's shawl wasn't enough to keep Jodee warm as she stood among the mourners at the cemetery that Saturday morning. Reverend Boteller stood at the head of the coffin balanced on two lengths of lumber over an open grave. Alongside him were nine stair-step children from the oldest boy to the newborn in the eldest girl's arms. The newborn's white blanket stood in stark contrast to the children's mourning black. His cry was feeble, filling everyone with sorrow.

Before the funeral that morning, Jodee had served Widow Ashton tea even though she was no longer in the woman's employ. Without asking permission, Jodee prepared a basket for the bereaved family, filling it with sweet rolls, leftover chicken, and tea cakes that Hanna had made for the May Day picnic. Widow Ashton didn't object.

Now they were gathered on the windswept hill. Corbet stood alongside the doctor, who looked downcast for having lost his patient. As Jodee listened to words spoken by Reverend Boteller, her weeks in Burdeen seemed like a dream. Jodee suspected Corbet wanted to buy her ticket out of town, and she intended to accept. When the coffin was lowered into the ground, and the mourners started moving away, Jodee laid the hamper at Avinelle's feet and turned away, too.

"Miss McQue," came the widower's deep voice.

Jodee discovered Reverend Boteller staring at her. She felt startled and embarrassed that he was speaking to her, of all the people there, drawing everyone's attention to her. She'd been beneath his notice at Widow Ashton's dinner party.

"I'm sorry for your loss, sir," she said, unsure if she should've spoken to him before the funeral. They were strangers, after all. Widow Ashton gave no indication what Jodee should do. Avinelle's eyes remained averted. Maggie stood behind them, sniffling.

"I have need of a housekeeper and caretaker for my children," the reverend said.

Jodee's cheeks flamed. She spoke without thinking. "You're willing to have me in your house now?" Oh, that sounded unkind.

"Yes."

Jodee tried not to scoff. "I'm sorry, but you need somebody with experience." She was thinking of Hanna or some other woman who had raised children. She couldn't imagine cooking, cleaning, and caring for eight children and a newborn while trying to please an employer as exacting as that preacher would surely be.

"Fifteen dollars a month, plus room and board," he said as if someone had coached him. "Space in the attic to sleep."

The same wage Widow Ashton offered. Nine times the work. "I'm sorry," Jodee said, trying to soften her tone as she shook her head.

She felt awful, refusing, but as Hanna had whispered earlier, he kept a wife over forty years of age still bearing children although she'd clearly been worn out. Besides, caring for so many wasn't the new life Jodee imagined. Frantic to escape the dismal scene, she pushed through the cemetery gate and broke into a trot.

Deputy Brucker leaned against a fence post, drawing cigar smoke deep into his lungs. Watch the Ashton Babcock house during the funeral, the marshal told him. Fine and dandy. There he was, sizing up the place, watching for Burl Tangus with no idea what the renegade looked like. Whatever name the outlaw was going by these days, Brucker intended to be the one bringing him in. It'd seal his position in this town. He'd be appointed marshal and Harlow could go build himself a cabin or whatever it was he intended to do with his time.

He tossed his stogie aside. This was the part he liked anyway, the waiting, the watching. He picked up a brown button from the dirt. Harlow claimed Tangus had disguised himself as a button drummer. Brucker smirked, imagining Tangus loitering in this same shadow, watching the house, waiting for his chance to break in. With sample case in hand? Hardly. Brucker sauntered along the fence. No tracks. Nothing to indicate Tangus passed that way—

A faint sound caught Brucker's attention. He straightened, eyes moving quickly from shadows between pines to dark windows lined with lace. He heard muffled thumping, either an echo from town or something going on inside the house. Sometimes mountains made it difficult to distinguish where sounds came from.

Dropping to a crouch, Brucker drew his gun, his hand damnably stiff. All the womenfolk were at the funeral, and the driver as well. The place was supposed to be empty. More thumping. Brucker dashed to the gate. By damn, somebody was in there. How had anybody gotten past him? Trotting around to the side street, he slipped past the carriage house up close to the stone foundation near the front porch.

He heard a faint crash inside. The hair rose on the back of his neck

Once on the porch with his ear pressed to the front door, Brucker listened to bootsteps inside, slow-moving, pausing, prowling. Almost smiling, Brucker cocked his gun. He might not be able to outdraw Tangus, but he'd hit what he aimed at. With all his strength he took aim and landed his boot sole squarely into the center of the front door. It went flying inward, splintering the frame and slamming against the inside wall in a tremendous crash.

Not knowing the lay of the rooms inside, Brucker stepped cautiously inside, gun at the ready. For damn certain, whoever was inside knew he was there now. He whirled, saw a figure and fired without thought, shattering a mirror in a hailstorm of glass shards.

Ducking, feeling stupid for shooting his own reflection, Brucker was caught by surprise when he heard something move behind him. He heard the explosion of a gunshot and was struck hard. He hit the wall and slumped. Son of a bitch. Not certain where he'd been shot, he let himself topple to the floor. Fire flooded his left arm. Cussing in two languages, he saw someone slip into one of the side rooms. He dragged himself through the doorway into a cluttered parlor. Then, playacting that he was losing strength, dying, dead, he lay motionless, finger on the trigger, to wait.

Panting, Jodee hurried down the hill from the cemetery. She'd raised a blister on one heel and began limping. Hearing a loud pop ahead, she stopped and cocked her head. Was that a gunshot? Heart leaping, she heard another. Quickly she moved to the side of the road and huddled alongside a fence. The shots seemed to have come from up ahead in the direction of Avinelle's house.

Waiting, listening, growing anxious, Jodee crept closer. She was imagining things. It was a hunter far off. She shook off impossible fears that Burl had chosen this moment to come for her and went on with her plans to fetch her knapsack and change into her britches for the long walk to Cheyenne City. It would take days—

At the gate to Avinelle's house, she saw the front door hanging open. They hadn't left it like that!

Someone had broken in! It wasn't safe to go inside. For a long moment Jodee couldn't think what to do. Corbet was back at the cemetery. She should run back to get him, but if it was Burl— how could he be in Avinelle's house? How could he know where she was?—she'd be blamed. She knew it as surely as she'd ever known anything in her life.

With a shudder, she tiptoed up the walk and saw the splintered door frame. Feeling sick to her stomach, she dropped down beside the front steps. She had to be sure. Silently, she climbed the front steps and crossed the porch to peek into the entry hall. She saw the floor covered in shards of broken mirror and a bullet hole in the back of the mirror's frame. There was blood on the floor.

The silence inside the house was interrupted only by the ominous ticking of the tall case clock and the thunder of Jodee's drumming heart in her ears. When she saw the silver dish for calling cards missing from the hall table she knew all her fears had come true. But if she fled without trying to stop Burl, it'd be the same as helping him.

Darting across the crunching shards she skidded down the hall into the kitchen. A loaf of bread lay on the table half eaten. The butter crock was open. Burl had taken time to eat? How long had he been there? She clutched her hair. This didn't make sense!

The cellar door hung off its hinges. The center panel lay smashed on the hall floor—he'd been in the cellar? Her stomach lurched. Turning in circles, she was about to race up the back stairs to get her pistol when she saw the silverware chest lying empty in the pantry. A single spoon lay on the floor. Damn that worthless varmint of a man. And damn them snake-bit spoons. She'd shoot Burl dead just for touching them.

In the dining room she found the silver sugar

missing from the sideboard. The creamer, too. The silver coffee server stood on the table, too heavy to tote away. Thinking Burl might be gone already, she bolted up the back stairs and pounded down the hallway to the guest room. Her belongings were strewn on the bed and her pistol was gone. The knapsack, too. She doubled over, wanting to scream.

Heartsick, she tiptoed down the hall, afraid of all she'd find missing wherever she looked. She heard what sounded like silverware being dragged in a bag along the floor and froze. Burl was still in the house! In Widow Ashton's room. With her damnable snake-bit spoons and her knapsack full of loot.

Like a mountain cat stalking prey, Jodee paused in a crouch outside Widow Ashton's doorway. "Burl?" she croaked, unable to see him. "I know you're in there, you dirty son of a bitch. I got Pa's gun and it's aimed at what you don't want me to shoot off."

She heard paper rustle and the scrape of a boot against floorboards. Her heart slammed in her chest. Edging around the door frame, she saw nothing amiss. The widow's bed looked tidy. The crystal drop lamp glinted in a shaft of sunlight coming in the side window. When she heard the dragging clank of silver again, she realized Burl was on the far side of the bed, on the floor. She couldn't draw a breath.

Burl lifted his tousled dark head.

Jodee ducked down, but he'd seen her. He swung his gun over the edge of the bed, cocked and ready. She'd never stared down a gun barrel before. The sight sent her into full panic. She flattened herself against the hallway wall, gasping, unable to think. At a mad scramble, Burl burst through the doorway and hauled her up by the scruff of her neck, hair included. Her collar cut into her throat, choking her.

"Why, girlie-girl, what're you doin' back so soon? Where'd you steal them clothes from?"

Desperately she tore at the hand clutching her hair. "Get out of here before they come back." She waved her arm toward the front stairway. "They're right behind me."

"You never was a good liar."

He threw her down. She crashed to the floor, landing hard on her hip and gave a sharp cry. He slammed his boot onto her right shoulder to keep her in place. She howled.

"Let up! That's where he shot me!"

"Where? Here?" He dug his boot in harder.

Glaring up at him, shaking with terror, dizzy with pain, Jodee thought, there he was. Ugly weasel face. Dark dirty hair cut short. Beard growing in, sparse on his chin, bristly under his nose.

"Where's the cash box, girlie-girl?"

"What cash box?" She kicked at him.

He yanked hard on her hair.

Yelping, sick with fear, she gave a sneering laugh. "And what's that getup you're wearing? Green britches. You look like some kind of scarecrow."

Burl kicked her. "Got 'em off a stupid little man in the mountains. Offered me a ride in his buggy. Gave me a lecture on buttons and sundries enough I had to shoot him just to shut him up. I drove his buggy and horse into a ravine. If you want to know, I been all over town in this outfit. Tipped my hat to the marshal himself. Sold buttons to the best ladies in town and a store-keep who paid in advance. I been livin' high, girlie-girl." He nudged her with the toe of his boot. He spoke with his mouth twisted dangerously tight. It looked swollen on one side. "Tell me where the goddamned cash box is. You know the one I mean. You seen it at the cabin."

Jodee remembered Avinelle clutching a cash box in the marshal's office. That had been Avinelle's cash box at the cabin? She choked back fear. "You went through that hole in the floor like a rat," she said, desperate to think. "Get out of this house 'for the marshal gets here. He'll shoot you dead. I'll dance a jig on your grave."

"Tough words, girlie-girl." Burl jerked her to her feet as if she were made of rags.

She threw herself against him, hoping to push him off balance and make him fall down the stairs.

"Don't think so!" He grabbed her right arm.

It felt like he was pulling her arm out by the roots.

"That hurt?" He twisted harder. "I want that cash box, and I want it now."

With all her strength Jodee screamed, startling him. Maybe somebody outside would hear. Screaming her throat raw, she threw herself toward the staircase, half afraid she'd fall to her death. Burl wasn't much taller than herself, but he was stronger. She grabbed his sleeve and tried to heave him against the railing. Shrugging off the knapsack's strap handle, he cuffed her head with his gun. She saw stars. In a raucous clatter, the knapsack tumbled down the stairs, spewing spoons and silverware all the way to the entry floor.

"This way," Burl said, dragging her back toward the widow's room. "Show me."

"No—"

He threw her across the room. She landed by the bed. He dragged her around to the far side where he had the trunk with the broken hinges open, contents scattered. Still clutching her hair, he crouched. He looked under the bed. He aimed his gun at the bureau of drawers where every-thing was falling out from his frantic search earlier. He shot the crystal drop lamp, shattering it.

"Where is it?" He aimed at her.

Jodee squeezed her eyes closed. "I don't know what you're talking about."

He threw her down. She hit the floor hard. Bracing herself, trying to decide what to do next, she stared down at a yellowed certificate laying on the floor beneath her hand. The name Fanny Healy was written across the top in a bold script. Jodee tried to make out more words, but Burl pushed her backwards. She fell into a small table covered in whatnots that toppled over with a crash. He rummaged in the drawer.

"You been here long enough to know every bit of this place," he said, pulling fistfuls of little medicine bottles from the drawer and throwing them at her. "I been here a while, too, girlie-girl. Listening. Heard all that boo-hooing over the dead lady. Saw my chance when you all traipsed off to the funeral. Mighty short funeral, you ask me. They treat you like one of their own, don't they now? Gave me an idea. We could do this other places. You set yourself up working someplace. Find out where all the loot is. I come along. . . . We could live high." He grinned at her, then sobered and leveled the gun at her again. "So now you tell me where the goddamned cash box is."

Biding her time, Jodee lolled on her side. There had to be something—

Home and Industrial School for Girls—

Burl grabbed the certificate. "What's this? Stocks and bonds? They's like paper money, I hear." He threw the papers onto the bed.

"Turn loose of me," Jodee whispered. "I don't know nothing about bonds."

Struggling to sit up, she picked up another certificate. *Eleanore Hollingsworth Home and Industrial School for Girls, New York State, 1847.* It stated Fanny Healy, aged fifteen years, was certified as a seamstress.

Burl yanked the drawer from the dressing table and upended the contents into Jodee's knapsack. Rings and brooches rained to the floor.

"Don't use my knapsack!" She kicked Burl squarely in his shin.

As he hobbled out of range, she saw another certificate. Maggie Healy, aged fourteen years, certified as a lace maker. Underneath was a tintype likeness of two little girls in ragged smocks. The younger was barefoot. By her timid posture it had to be Maggie as a child of eight or nine. On the back was written in pencil, Fanny and Maggie Healy, 1842.

Jodee picked up another paper. Theia Hollingsworth's marriage certificate to Harold Ashton, June of 1858 in New York. Another likeness—Widow Ashton in an elaborate wedding suit beside a grinning gentleman. Another of a beautiful child wearing foot-long corkscrew curls. Young Avinelle and her famous smile.

Widow Ashton was Fanny Healy. She and Maggie were sisters, and Burl had stopped ransacking the dressing table to watch her study the photographs.

He leaned in, trailing the muzzle of his gun alongside Jodee's face. "What're them things you're looking at, girlie-girl? You find something valuable?"

Jodee narrowed her eyes. "All this time," she crooned, trying to look at him, "all this time I never guessed how stupid you are. You can't read a word, can you, Burlie-burl? You couldn't even open an empty safe." At his gasp, she slapped the gun aside and leapt to her feet. She went at him, claws spread, her mind crazy with rage. "You killed my pa! I wouldn't tell you where Avinelle keeps her cash box if you kissed my feet."

He fought hard and slammed her against the wall. He knew just where to put his hands, too. She forced herself to laugh.

"You wouldn't know what to do with me if I gave you half a chance."

He howled. They battled into the hall again. She glanced at Avinelle's room across the hall, thinking she had to keep Burl from going in there, realizing too late, she'd given away the very place he wanted to ransack.

Letting her go, Burl shoved her into Avinelle's room. She landed on hands and knees beside Avinelle's unmade bed.

"You'll be sorry you ever set foot in this house," Jodee growled. "Marshal Harlow will shoot your rotten gizzard." Avinelle's room

309

would be easy to pillage, she thought. She took no trouble to put away her valuables. Her clothes were strewn over furniture and floor. Set squarely in the middle of her dressing table lay a plain grey metal cash box.

Jodee's heart sank.

Burl seized the cash box and shook it.

Drained of hope, Jodee watched him drop to the floor. Laying his gun aside, Burl placed the cash box on the floor between his outstretched legs. Grinning like Christmas, making certain she was paying attention, he dug a wrinkled ribbon from his green plaid button drummer's vest watch pocket. At the end dangled a small key.

Jodee went limp with disbelief. She watched in horror as Burl waved the key at her, making nasty little triumphant faces at her, letting his tongue hang out and laughing. Then, with great ceremony, he inserted the key in the lock and twisted. Without making a sound, he lifted the lid and stared inside.

Wondering if she might dash past him, and kick him senseless in the process, Jodee watched him grab a few greenbacks from the cash box. Instantly his expression soured. "What the hell?"

Clutching handfuls of her skirts, Jodee leapt to her feet, kicked, missed, and vaulted through the doorway, landing hard at the top of the stairs. She slid halfway down, nearly falling out of control when she saw Avinelle venture through the shattered front doorway below, her round eyes taking in the shards covering the entry floor.

Not now! Oh, dear God, not now!

Grabbing a baluster, Jodee stopped herself from pitching the rest of the way down. This couldn't be happening. This just could not be happening to her!

Widow Ashton pushed in beside Avinelle. Maggie crept in close behind. The three saw Jodee hanging twisted on the stairs with Burl coming down behind her in a mad scramble. Burl took aim. Maggie gave a hair-raising shriek.

Pushing past screaming Maggie, Corbet lunged, drew, and fired.

A thrill of fear and hope mixed with dread crashed through Jodee's body as Burl slammed hard against her back, falling, arms, legs flailing. She felt his blood spread warm on her back. Twisting, jabbing wildly with her elbow, she tried to make him fall the rest of the way down. His shot went wild. The blast was deafening. Catching himself, struggling to remain on the step where he landed, Burl threw an arm around Jodee's neck and yanked her close in a strangle-hold.

He dug the gun's barrel into Jodee's bleeding temple.

"Where the hell's the money that was in the cash box?" Burl yelled, his voice cracking. "*All* the money. Thousands—" Clutching Jodee in front of himself like a shield, he picked his way down the remaining steps. "Tell me or I kill her."

Avinelle's mouth hung open. She looked for all the world as if she were smiling just a little, as if her baited trap to catch a thief had worked better than she could ever have dreamed.

With a savage tightening of his arm across Jodee's throat, Burl took another step but slipped on a spoon. His boot shot forward. He wrenched back hard, sliding, lost his hold on Jodee and cartwheeled sideways down onto the broken glass below. Jodee tumbled after him, landing on top of him with a wail of revulsion. Nearly in her face, her knapsack lay open on the first step, the silver creamer visible within.

Burl tried to fire again but another deafening gunshot rang out from the direction of the drawing room. Thinking she was being shot at, Jodee twisted away. Burl arched up behind her. Another shot above her, and he hit the wall and slid down until he lay still.

Maggie screamed.

All Jodee saw was Corbet's face.

He wasn't looking at her. His gun wasn't smoking. He hadn't fired. He gawked at the gaping knapsack, at the scattered silverware. When he lifted his eyes to hers, she saw no hint of recognition in his eyes. He looked as if she were a stranger. His eyes went cold with disbelief.

He saw her for a thief.

Seeing her pistol deep in the knapsack, Jodee lunged and grabbed it. Days ago, on the back porch, she'd loaded it. Taking aim at Burl she pulled the trigger. Nothing happened. The pistol was too old to fire.

Corbet tore it from her grasp and threw it aside.

Widow Ashton slapped Maggie into silence.

Panting with heartbreak, Jodee struggled to get as far from Burl as possible. For several seconds there was blessed silence. *It was over,* Jodee thought, wilting. Her life—her new life— was over.

Burl's hand flexed.

He flung up his arm and pulled off one more shot that hit the tall case clock. Another gunshot hit the ceiling. A rain of plaster came down. Maggie went flying toward the kitchen, howling.

Avinelle cringed behind Corbet, but he pushed her away. Teeth bared, he advanced on Burl, who leveled his gun one last time at Jodee. Grabbing Jodee, Corbet flung her across the floor. She slid headlong into the doorway to the drawing room. Another shot whizzed by so close she recoiled and cracked the back of her head against the door frame. A few feet away, Deputy Brucker lay on the drawing room floor, a smoking gun in his hand. He fired again, and Burl fell dead.

Brucker winked.

Slack-jawed, Corbet glared at Brucker. Then he

turned his dark gaze on Jodee. He might as well have killed her with his eyes.

As if a gun battle took place in her entry hall every morning, Widow Ashton asked, "Is the man dead, Marshal?"

Numb, Jodee watched Corbet level molten eyes on the woman. She shrank away from him. Corbet watched Avinelle dissolve into tears. He grabbed the knapsack and dumped the last of the plunder onto the floor. Silver calling card tray. Golden scissors. Spoons.

"Burl was here when I—"

Jodee didn't have enough strength to say another word. There was no use. Corbet believed what he saw. She knew what she had seen, too. He thought she left the funeral early to help Burl. She felt disillusioned beyond words.

Breathing hard, Corbet flung down the empty knapsack. A war began behind his eyes. His lips pressed hard against his teeth.

Taking a ragged breath, Jodee let her acid gaze travel from Corbet to Widow Ashton and finally to Avinelle. Dripping blood, Brucker struggled to his feet. His spurs caught on the fringe of the Turkish carpet. He gave Jodee an insolent smirk she didn't understand. Nothing she'd done in the past weeks made any difference. They believed what they wanted.

Well, they could all go straight to perdition. She was done with Theia Ashton and Avinelle

Babcock and poor sobbing Maggie the lace maker. She got to her feet, pushed back her disheveled hair, and dashed tears from her face.

She didn't bother to look at Corbet.

She hoped never to see his face again. He thought her capable of robbing her benefactors. Well, she was done with him, too. She knew she'd never be able to prove herself to any so-called decent folk. She knew what she was. She was decent, and that was all that mattered.

She edged past Corbet and started up the stairs. She got all the way up to the guest room before she heard talk begin downstairs. Brucker and Corbet, their voices deep and harsh. Widow Ashton and Avinelle, their voices shrill.

Jodee tore off her skirt and petticoat. She pulled on her old britches over her long white drawers. Dreaming of lace trimming—fool girl, she thought. No more nonsense. She stuffed her feet into her boots.

There lay Corbet's blue shirt she'd worn in the jailhouse. She couldn't bring herself to touch it. She wished she could say goodbye to Hanna, but maybe it was better not to see the woman again. She might not be able to bear the condemnation in her eyes.

Seventeen

Wearing her pin-tucked blouse tucked into her old britches, Jodee headed down the stairs of Avinelle's house, wondering if her locket and gun were still at Quimby's store. She could hold up the place and get them back.

Damn fool notion, she thought, disgusted with herself. She wasn't going to hold up no damned store. Her heart hurt so bad she thought it might be nice to get good and drunk like her father used to do when he couldn't bear another moment of missing her dead mother. She shook her head. She hated whiskey.

"Jodee?" came Corbet's voice. "Are you all right? Did Tangus hurt you? There's blood all over your back."

Jodee went still. Corbet was talking to her? Asking damn fool questions like he hadn't just shattered her heart? She dashed across the glass-strewn entry but Corbet was ready. He captured her in his arms and pulled her tight as she fought him.

"Let me go!"

"Wait. Stop it, Jodee. Listen to me."

"Varmint!" she screamed. "I didn't do nothing wrong. I didn't help him. As God is my witness, I did not help Burl Tangus rob this house."

She lunged for the door, but Brucker was there, leaning against the splintered frame, holding his bleeding arm. She saw Avinelle and her mother huddled in the parlor with a hiccupping Maggie between them. Hardening her heart, Jodee shoved past the deputy.

"Hold on," Brucker said, grinning. "Didn't you notice I was on the floor, waiting to help you? You didn't see me? I heard every word you said, you know. You might try being a little friendlier to me now. I can vouch for your innocence."

She didn't know what vouch meant. She didn't trust him an inch, either. Heard all she said? What did that matter? She couldn't remember what all she said, good or bad.

Corbet touched her elbow. "Brucker says you risked your life to stop Tangus."

Brucker flexed his wounded arm. "When you came in I knew by the way you moved you weren't with that fleabag." More blood dripped. He cussed softly. "One more place to ache when it rains." He gave her a wink. "Where you going in that bloody shirt and old britches? You look half ridiculous. I say you would've died before letting Tangus take that loot." To Widow Ashton, he said, "You ladies better get upstairs. Tangus tore up the place. Said he was sick of sleeping in your cellar, drinking peach brandy."

Widow Ashton hiked her skirts and stomped upstairs to investigate.

"You'd better go with her," Jodee said to Avinelle. "There's papers you might find interesting."

Brushing past Corbet without a glance, Avinelle followed her mother up the stairs.

Jodee went into the parlor where Maggie sat abandoned. "The bad man's dead," she said to Maggie. "He won't bother us again. You don't have to be scared no more."

Maggie just looked at the floor, shivering.

"Jodee, I have to talk to you," Corbet said, interrupting. "Brucker, can you make it to Doc's or do you need help?"

"I'll send someone for the body." Brucker started out the door.

Jodee wandered out onto the porch after him and watched him walk, head down, toward town. She supposed she couldn't dislike him anymore. Deputy Brucker had saved her life. She heard Corbet come out and stand nearby.

She didn't want to listen to anything he might have to say. Trembling all over, her knees went suddenly weak. She made her way to the swing and sank down, leaning forward a little to get her bearings. Where had her fury gone? She felt exhausted.

After a moment Corbet crouched in front of her and looked into her eyes. Gone was the savage, mindless rage. His gaze was as open as she had ever seen it. She stared at him, feeling empty.

She wanted to hate him. He'd let her down. When he moved to sit beside her, she tried not to notice how wonderful it felt to have him near.

Varmint.

He put his arm around her and sat quietly. *Oh, that felt so good,* she thought, longing to lean against him. She felt heart-sore, but he'd wounded her. She didn't want or intend to ever forgive him. Loving him had made her foolish. It made her believe in wild hopes and impossible futures.

"I don't know what to say," Corbet began. "To see you with Tangus made me think I might accidentally shoot you again, or he would. And I felt like an idiot when I realized I'd seen him weeks ago."

"You aren't fooling me, Corbet. You thought I was *helping* him. You thought I was *with* him. I'll always be an outlaw's daughter. To you. To everybody. That's because I *am* an outlaw's daughter. And the daughter of a troublemaker. I did everything I could to prove I was better than that, but it wasn't good enough. Not for this town leastwise. So go on. Leave me be."

Corbet went still. He took his arm from around her shoulder. He sat for a long time staring at his hands.

Jodee shivered. Was she wrong to condemn him for his moment of doubt? She doubted him now, and she still loved him. Would he condemn her for that and walk away forever? She wished he'd put his arm back around her. She might end up alone if she sat so stiff like her grandmother used to do.

He reached into his breast pocket and withdrew a thick fold of bank notes. "This money is yours."

She'd never seen so much.

"I got it yesterday at the bank. I planned to tell you about it at the dance but—"

"I don't want your money!"

"It isn't mine, Jodee. Thursday morning I received a bank draft in the mail from Cheyenne City. A bank draft is a way of sending money in a letter. I cashed it for you. This is your money. You can do whatever you want with it, buy whatever you want. Go wherever you want. This is your new start."

She didn't believe it. It was a trick.

"They sold your father's horse and his gun— the horse he was riding during the holdup. And his boots, his saddle—I'm sorry, Jodee, I know those things would've meant a lot to you, but you needed money for your new start. Your father would've wanted this for you."

"Pa was buried in his stocking feet?" She fought tears, but they overwhelmed her. She shrugged off Corbet's comforting hand when he tried to touch her.

Placing the money in Jodee's lap, Corbet stood. She refused to look at him. All she could see was the money. He trudged back inside the house.

She wanted to lie down someplace and sleep a long time. Instead, she rocked in the porch swing until Deputy Malone and the undertaker arrived with a buckboard to take away Burl's body.

The cash money lay in her lap, taunting her, tantalizing her. It was all that was left of the father she loved. She was afraid to count it. It looked like enough to live on for a year. Maybe more. And Corbet, damn him, was right. Her father would've wanted her to make a new start with it. "Oh, Pa," she whispered. "You damn fool."

Scrubbing away tears, Jodee stood and straightened her back. She felt old. Going back into the house, she picked up her knapsack. Burl's blood was all over the stairs, the floor, and on a corner of the knapsack's flap. She saw his dried blood on her hand and felt it stiffening the back of her blouse.

Upstairs she changed back into her skirt and button shoes. After scrubbing the blood from the blouse in the wash basin, she put it on, still wet. She didn't need the primer or the tattered bed dress. She turned her back on the torn, blood-stained shirt she had been wearing when she got shot at the cabin. She didn't need her britches or boots. In fact, without those things she didn't need her knapsack. She looked around the guest room. She felt blank as a new school slate.

Twenty minutes later Jodee checked into Burdeen's Congress Hotel, empty-handed except for a handful of greenbacks, unconcerned that decent women didn't stay in hotels alone. She asked for a room with a bath and paid two dollars for the privilege.

"Send a message to Mr. Quimby, if you please," she said to the desk clerk. "I need a traveling outfit and carpetbag. No trade this time. I'll be paying cash money."

Where was Jodee? Corbet realized she was nowhere in Avinelle's house. Outside, he circled to where Bailey, his expression stormy, showed him the missing hinge pins in the cellar door. That was how Tangus gained access.

Worried, Corbet scrambled up the trail behind the house where he found Jodee that day after Sunday dinner—she wasn't there. Back on the road, he looked for tracks. Nothing. Was she that angry with him? He couldn't help how he looked, seeing her half falling down the stairs, fighting for her life, and Tangus with his bloody arm around her neck, all the house valuables spilling out of her knapsack. He knew she hadn't been helping Tangus. Why fight him if she were?

Had she left town? If she hitched a ride with some passing wagon he'd never know where she went. Taking off his hat, he stood in the middle of the road, looking toward town and back, remembering dragging her to jail on that travois. In spite of everything he'd done, he'd failed her.

He ran all the way to the jailhouse. It felt like a lifetime since he'd carried Jodee into that cell and questioned her. Now Tangus was dead, and Jodee was free. She had money, and she could go anywhere she wanted. She wasn't his little desperado any longer.

His heart hurt, his face hurt, and he couldn't seem to breathe right. He didn't want it to be over. He wanted to see Jodee, to say goodbye at least. He was a grown man who had marshaled an entire town and gunned down outlaws without a thought. Why should he want or need one scrappy female with a quirky grin? He stepped out onto the jailhouse porch, twitchy and miserable.

The hotel desk clerk loped across the street. "That girl outlaw, Marshal . . . she just checked into my best room! And she's got cash money. Is it from the holdup?"

Corbet went weak with relief. Clapping the man on the shoulder, he forced a wry grin. Through his teeth he said, "Give her whatever she wants. It's her money. She had nothing to do with that stagecoach holdup. Jodee McQue is innocent."

The desk clerk frowned. "Then somebody ought'a tell her to keep that money out of sight. She could get robbed."

At a knock at her hotel room door the next morning, Jodee paused in her efforts to do up her hair.

"Visitor to see you, Miss McQue," called the morning desk clerk through the closed door. Thanks to the night clerk, the entire town knew she was at the hotel. In spite of trying to sleep in the big hotel bed, she felt tired. Over and over, she relived the battle with Burl. She still couldn't believe he was dead for good and all.

"Yes? Come in." She swallowed hard.

The door swung wide. There stood Avinelle holding her knapsack. Sighing, Jodee turned to face the young widow one last time. How would the woman think to bedevil her now? Thanks to Mr. Quimby, however, Jodee had on a pretty new blouse with a lace frill at the throat—no stains, no blood. And a seven-gore skirt—all the rage back east, he said. She looked presentable. She looked better than presentable. She looked decent. She met Avinelle's eyes and didn't flinch.

"I'm probably the last person you want to see," Avinelle said, stepping into the room. "I brought this." She put the knapsack on the floor by the door and handed Jodee an envelope. "My letter of reference. With it, you should be able to gain employment anywhere. What are your plans?"

Jodee wasn't so sure she wanted to say what she intended to do. Avinelle's voice was softer, deeper. Her hair was tied back. Her dress was plain.

"I'm leaving town," Jodee said.

"I wish you well then. And thank you for telling

me about Mother's papers. They explained a lot. She would've gone on with her ridiculous charade forever if I hadn't walked in. She denied everything, of course, but it seems she was a seamstress when she was young. Can you imagine?"

Jodee wondered if she should invite Avinelle to sit.

"And apparently Mother seduced someone's nephew who refused to marry her. And here I am." She smiled, but she looked tired, too. "Not high-born after all."

Jodee didn't know what to say.

"I was going to offer you something to wear, but you look well set. I thought about offering you a reward, as well. Thanks to you, that outlaw didn't get my savings a second time." Avinelle gave an inquiring look.

Jodee shook her head. "Burl was after your cash box?"

"I've wanted to escape this town since the day I arrived. Mother wouldn't go, so I saved in secret. When she and I went to Cheyenne City this last time, I was planning to leave her but at the last minute I lacked the courage to step out on my own. My entire savings was in that cash box. When the stagecoach was held up and that outlaw got my key—I thought I was trapped here."

"I'd pay all I owe you and your mother right now," Jodee said, "but I don't know how much I'll need where I'm going."

Avinelle waved her hand. "You owe nothing, truly. We were horrid to you. It was Mother's idea, but I went along. I never loved Corbet. He's nice, but . . . I thought you should know that. I'm sorry, Jodee. Really, I am."

Jodee scowled. That was a damn fool lie. It was impossible not to love Corbet Harlow.

"Goodbye then." Avinelle stepped back into the hotel's hallway.

Following her to the door, Jodee watched the woman disappear down the hall. She felt oddly as if she were losing a friend.

An hour later Jodee waited for the morning stagecoach on the hotel's porch. Her new hat was pinned in place. Hanna had stopped by earlier. She showed Jodee how to pull the hat's veil to her chin. "This'll keep dust off your face, honey."

"I won't forget you, Hanna," Jodee said, hugging her. She could scarcely let go. "Say my goodbyes to Patsy, Bailey, and Maggie."

"Maggie took tea in the dining room with Miz Theia this morning," Hanna said. "Imagine that, a sister, all this time. She sent this." Hanna produced a handkerchief trimmed in tatted lace. "Be happy in your new life, Jodee."

The morning sunshine poured from a wide clear sky. Jodee breathed in fresh mountain air as deeply as her corset would allow and felt a nervous fluttering in her stomach. Did she have the courage to set out on her own? It was a fearsome thing, facing the open road alone. She planned to stay in Cheyenne City as long as it took to find her father's grave and buy a marker. From there . . .

As she had weeks before from her jail cell, Jodee heard the stagecoach's rattling approach. This time she was going, and paying her own way. As the coach thundered to a stop, a cloud of dust boiled up. She looked around one last time. She'd done a good a job of rejecting Corbet, she thought, sick at heart. He wasn't there to see her off.

"I'll change out the team and be back in a few minutes," the driver called down to Jodee, his only waiting passenger. He pitched dusty traveling cases to the ground and endured the annoyed glances of weary passengers debarking the coach.

To leave without seeing Corbet—Jodee wasn't sure she could do it.

Everything that might have been with him was over. She closed her eyes. She wasn't going to pull at Corbet's sleeve for the rest of her life. There'd always be the past standing between them. She was done crawling.

The stagecoach rolled slowly away toward the corrals at the end of the street where the spent team was taken away to rest and a fresh team was hitched up. Jodee watched the coach make a wide turn and start back toward her. This must've been what it looked like for her father as he and the gang hid behind the rocks at Ship Creek Crossing to watch the approach of that Ashton Babcock stagecoach. She imagined Lee Rike riding into the coach's path and Old man Rike and Mose shooting into the air. Witt probably rode around, crazy as he was. And Burl would've ordered everybody out. She could imagine the passengers' frightened cries. Avinelle in her billowing cloak and Widow Ashton in her black hat. She imagined the driver throwing down his rifle and the strong box with Avinelle's cash box tucked inside. She could just picture the struggle over the heavy new safe in the boot and the exchange of gunfire. Avinelle's scream. The driver falling to the ground. Her father toppling from his horse and left for dead in the road.

Now they were all gone, and here she stood alone, as the Ashton Babcock stagecoach rolled to a stop in front of her. The driver set his long wooden brake, looped the team's lines, and climbed down to help her board. Swallowing hard, Jodee savored the fresh morning breeze one last time. She felt the man's hand cup her left elbow.

But she couldn't move.

"Don't be frightened, Miss," the driver said in a kindly tone. "Didn't you hear? They kilt every last one of them thieving outlaws. You'll be safe. No more holdups on this stage line."

She took a step, and then another, down from the hotel porch to the dusty street. She placed her foot on the ornate metal step of the coach. She grabbed the edges of the door frame and dragged herself up into the coach that smelled of tobacco and leather and road dust. She sat herself on the thinly padded seat facing forward and remembered to arrange the back of her skirt to avoid wrinkles. Avinelle would be proud of her ladylike demeanor.

"You want your carpetbag inside or up top, Miss?"

She hardly heard the driver speak. She gasped for air. Tarnation, she was going to faint. She couldn't do this. It was too hard.

Then she heard the thunder of hoofbeats coming up the street and the scrabbling halt of a horse nearby. Boots hit the ground. She held her breath.

Corbet grabbed the door frame and thrust his face inside the window.

Oh, that grand face, those wonderful dark eyes, those rosy lips—Jodee's heart exploded with hope.

"Jodee!" Corbet panted. He took a deep breath. His cheeks were red. His hair was standing on end. He had lost his hat. He wasn't exactly smiling. "I thought I missed you."

She drank in his face. Her eyes burned with unshed tears.

"Give us a moment, would you, Daniel?" Corbet called to the driver, who was settling himself on his high seat.

Tearing the door open, Corbet climbed into the coach and sat opposite Jodee. He grabbed her gloved hands. She couldn't feel his warmth through the thin leather. He seemed to be memorizing her, from the veiled hat she wore to the snug bodice of her new traveling suit.

Tell me not to go!

"I've been at my campsite. There's so much I want to say. And now there's no time. You're going, and I'm not going to stop you. You need to go back to your people and set things straight. We both know you need that. You must know that I wish you weren't going. We're not done getting to know each other. We need time to talk."

"Ain't no use in talk," Jodee said, her voice husky. "I'm bound to go."

Make me stay!

She wanted Corbet to propose. They'd get married that afternoon—she let the thought slip away. They were strangers really. If she stayed and they didn't marry, she'd have to live somewhere. She'd have to work at something. She'd have to endure the questioning of her character for years—perhaps the rest of her life. If she left now, she was making a clean break.

She made a brave, unhappy smile. Finding her voice, she said softly, "I'll come back someday, Corbet. I owe you and Artie and the doc." She nodded with determination. "I feel beholden. You tell them I'll be back. They didn't have to help me. You didn't have to, either, but you did. I won't forget it." She began to tremble.

Corbet's grip on her hands tightened.

She willed him to say what she wanted to hear.

"I want you to listen to me. This is the last time I'm going to say this. I did *not* think you were with Tangus or helping him. You were fighting him. We all saw that." He spoke emphatically. "I was upset leaving Brucker to guard the house when I should've done it myself. When I saw him on the floor, bleeding, I thought, there's another man, wounded on my account. Can't you understand, Jodee? Can't you forgive me? I was thinking only of my own damn self."

Jodee didn't understand, but she nodded anyway if only to ease the anguish on Corbet's face.

"Is Brucker all right?"

Corbet nodded. He looked so unhappy. Jodee's heart overflowed with love for him. She pushed the annoying veil off her face, up over the top of her hat. "I love you," she said softly.

Corbet blinked.

Oh, he did have the most wonderful coffee brown eyes, she thought, gazing into them. Corbet wasn't going to stop her.

"It's time for me to go," she said. She sounded like a woman grown. Doc Trafford would be proud of her. She was proud of herself.

Looking into her eyes one last time, Corbet finally leaned forward and pressed a very chaste kiss to her cheek. He released her gloved hands and climbed out of the coach. He took hold of the door and closed it firmly, pulling on it to make sure the latch was secure.

Kiss me one more time!

The window opening was uncovered, affording Jodee one last look at Corbet's tortured face. She grabbed the window ledge and stuck her face out. *Kiss me, Corbet Harlow, damn you,* she said with her brimming eyes.

And he did finally. His mouth closed over her trembling lips. Stars went off in her head. Lightning flooded her body. It was like she was one with him, locked to him, drinking him in while pouring herself into him at the same time. The kiss lasted so long she felt like she was pitching into space, spinning.

Tears spilled down her cheeks. She was scarcely able to see as Corbet stooped and straightened. He was smiling now, really smiling, but his brows were tilted up in anguish, making him look boyish and dear. He reached through the open window to hand her a stone he had grabbed up from the street. It was nothing special, just a mottled tan rock with a vein of white quartz running through it. It was the most commonplace rock in all the west. She might find countless millions of them alongside any roadway.

When he handed it to her, she curled her gloved fingers around it. She squeezed until its hardness felt imprinted into her palm. She looked into Corbet Harlow's eyes and basked in his love for her. He loved her. She could see it! She hoped he could feel her love for him.

But Corbet didn't say he loved her, and he didn't say he'd wait for her return. As he stepped back he waved to the driver. "Take care of my best girl, Daniel."

Then Corbet stepped out of the way of the stagecoach's big wheels. He grinned that fabulous grin, all his teeth showing. His eyes squeezed up, as if he was having trouble seeing. As the driver gave a yell and snapped his whip, Corbet lifted his hand, half wave, half salute.

Jodee held up her trembling fist with the rock clenched hard against the thin leather covering her palm. She had no thoughts in that last moment. All she knew was the look on Corbet's face. He loved her, and he was letting her go.

The stagecoach began rolling forward, slowly at first, then faster and faster, past Ellis Brothers, Boots, Shoes, and Leather Findings; Stanley Holt, Seller of Whiskey and Cigars; and Munjoy's Fine Furniture and Coffins—Jodee still had trouble reading the signboards. The stagecoach rolled out of Burdeen City to the road headed south toward Cheyenne City.

Jodee sank back stiffly in the seat, heart drumming so fast she couldn't think. She was leaving, she thought, rocking uncomfortably in her hard seat. She sat like that a long time, stiff and numb and baffled that she had the courage to do what she was doing. Corbet's smile was etched in her vision, blurring everything. She listened for him, but he didn't follow.

In time, she turned her eyes to the piney vista passing outside the stagecoach windows. In time, she grew thirsty. In time, the driver halted at a stage stop for another change of horses. The stage stop was not too far from Ship Creek Crossing. Jodee got out to stretch her legs, not knowing if she was anywhere near the spot where her father died. She could still taste Corbet Harlow's kiss.

That fifth of May, Ed Brucker took over as town marshal of Burdeen City. Some claimed Corbet Harlow was seen sitting in the Bale 'O Hay Saloon, staring at an untouched shot of whiskey. Then he was gone.

Corbet spent the summer building a cabin on the land he'd bought. All he thought about was laying foundation stones in a perfect square, felling the straightest pines he could find, and raising straight log walls. He ate in the open air, got sunburned, and his arms and shoulders swelled with aching new muscles. He began to think about the years he'd worked on the dairy farm in Wisconsin, milking, pitching hay, laughing with little Jenny.

When the weather turned bad that fall, before the cabin's roof was on, Corbet slept in his tent. When the roof was done, and a porch stood across the front, wide enough for two rocking chairs to sit in shelter, Corbet realized the place reminded him of that cabin in the mountains where he'd first seen Jodee . . . after he shot her. He sat on the edge of his porch every night, remembering that fateful day. Jodee was in Arkansas now, he told himself. She'd gone back to her family. She was home and happy at last.

She hadn't written. She'd never come back. He was certain of it.

One morning in late October, Corbet packed his saddlebags and headed into town. He rode slowly, taking note of the changes since Jodee left. Hobie had gone east. Several new stores were under construction. The place seemed colorless and devoid of spirit. He felt like a ghost.

He saw a man in a dark suit and bowler hat entering Avinelle's house, so he kept going. Avinelle didn't miss him. He didn't miss her. His face itched beneath a summer's growth of whiskers. Folks probably didn't even recognize him. As he turned south toward Cheyenne City, Corbet retraced the route he and the posse took months before. He thought of Jodee and how she had looked that day in May, sitting in that stagecoach in her veiled hat and traveling suit. She'd looked older—except in her eyes. Those wide, wide wonderful blue eyes full of fire and hope.

Jodee was gone, and he had let her go, his girl with the outlaw heart.

Epilogue

Jodee felt as if she'd left Burdeen City only days before. In two years, she could see that much had changed. The Ashton Babcock Stage Line was no more. The depot had been turned into a bank.

From Cheyenne City she'd traveled to Burdeen in a railroad coach car named Spirit of the Rockies on the newly opened Denver and Cheyenne spur. Where cattle pens once spread now stood a new train station. Wagon sheds, warehouses, and a lumberyard had taken over the area where the livery barn used to be and where she had danced one magical night.

Main Street had grown two blocks longer, sporting new stores all along the way. The ugly little jailhouse was gone, replaced by a brick courthouse with two officious white pillars in front. New streets had sprouted, lined with houses, cabins, and bungalows.

As Jodee hurried along the train station's platform, her heart filled with anticipation. *What was left of Corbet's feelings toward her?* she wondered. Two years was a long time to be away. He might've forgotten her. From her pocket she pulled out the rock he'd given her that last day in the stagecoach and held it tightly. Not a day had passed in two years that she hadn't yearned to see his face and hear his voice again.

"Send my trunks to the hotel," she instructed the baggage man, tipping him.

It was a brilliant midsummer day, the sky as clear as she remembered. Wagon traffic was heavy. Dust hung in the air. More than ever, Burdeen looked to be a prospering place.

Hurrying along board walkways, Jodee paused in front of Wilson's Mercantile, her gaze fixed on a plump, red-haired woman inside. Pasty Robstart stood behind the counter, waiting on a rancher's wife. She was as pregnant as any woman could be and still show herself in public. Behind her trailed a two year old with wonderful red ringlets. Was that little Henry?

Two years, Jodee thought, marveling that she had been able to stay away so long.

All those years, living with her father in shacks and rough camps seemed to have happened to someone else. That month recovering from her gunshot wound here in Burdeen was a dim memory, too. The scar on her shoulder only ached when it rained. The Rikes and Burl Tangus rarely crossed her mind. In the end she did go home, and she was happy enough there, but that, too, now seemed like a dream.

Unready to face Patsy, Jodee stuck to her purpose. At the hotel she met a desk clerk who looked astonishingly similar to Hobie. "Is room 8 available?"

"Yes, Ma'am," he said, grinning with a mouthful of crooked teeth.

She signed the register Jodeen McQuerin. That was her father's true and legal name, spelled out on her parents' marriage certificate. She found that, just as her mother said she would, stored in a trunk filled with her belongings.

Upstairs, the hotel room looked just as it had the day Avinelle had bid her goodbye. "Have my things brought up when they arrive from the depot, please."

Jodee wondered if she'd see Avinelle and her mother, but she hadn't come all this way to think about them just yet, or see them. She had come *home* to find Corbet.

Home, Jodee thought. *Burdeen felt like home.*

Outside again, holding her hat as wind gusted, she wondered where the new jailhouse was. Would she encounter Corbet making his rounds? Wouldn't it be fun to simply walk up to him on a board walkway and say a casual hello? For a thousand miles she'd lived on the fantasy that he would see her coming toward him but not recog-nize her at first. Then she'd see the blossoming of his smile and she'd know . . . she'd know he still loved her.

Passersby tipped their hats, but no one recognized her. For two years no other man had captured her interest. There'd been former schoolmates ready to court her, but she hadn't liked any of them.

After several minutes of walking, Jodee began to worry. When she came to the restaurant once called "The Hungry Bear," she saw a hand-lettered signboard in the window that read, "Hanna's Home Cooking."

Without hesitation, she rushed inside. There, bustling between tables, was Hanna's daughter Bonnie in a long apron, sporting a wedding band and looking as if she was expecting, too. Hanna came into the dining area to serve a table crowded with drovers. She looked harried but happy in her task.

Squirming with excitement, Jodee waited by the door.

The minute Hanna realized she was there, her freckled face split into a grin. "Ceddy!" Hanna bellowed, rushing forward, open-armed. "Look who's come home!"

This was the welcome Jodee had missed in Arkansas.

Cedric Bailey emerged from the kitchen,

wiping his hands on his apron. His seamed face folded into a broad grin, too. He looked nothing like the lonely surrey driver Jodee remembered. He looked new. "Miss Jodee! We thought we'd never see you again!"

Hanna caught Jodee in a fierce hug.

"This is *your* restaurant?" Jodee asked, studying Hanna's happy face. "What's Mr. Bailey doing here?"

"Why, girl. Me and him, we're married! I'm Hanna Bailey almost two years. We opened this place when Artie moved on. You won't know this town, it's changed so." Hanna's expression clouded suddenly. Hastily she untied her apron and propelled Jodee outside. "I'll be back in a minute," she called to her daughter and husband. "Why, just look at you, girl, all decked out. You're still thin as a drowned rat, but prettier than ever. You made it back to Arkansas safe and sound? I knew that's where you'd go. It only made sense. And you done well there?"

"Well enough," Jodee said, not wanting to talk about that yet.

"You found your grandmother? Your aunt and uncle? Your cousins?"

Jodee nodded. "My grandmother remembered me." Jodee still found that a marvel. "She was glad I came back. She passed on a month ago. She left me her house, the barn where my grand-father died, and a hundred sixty acres. I gave the

340

place to my aunt and uncle. I didn't need it, but they have a big family. Six children, a new grand-daughter. My uncle gave me some of his savings in trade. I tried to refuse, but—let's just say I'm well set." She shook off tangled emotions. "I'm so glad to see you, Hanna," she said to change the subject. "Aren't you the sly one? Married to Bailey. I never guessed you and Bailey were even friends."

"Surprised a lot of folks," Hanna said with a smirk. "You surprised a few yourself, clearing out like you did so sudden-like. And just when we were all getting used to you." She grinned.

"Folks must've thought I was running away. I wasn't, really. I was—"

"Don't think a thing about it," Hanna said. "What folks think ain't no never mind."

"I brought gifts," Jodee announced as she walked. "Do you think Avinelle's receiving today?"

Hanna linked her arm with Jodee's. It took only a few minutes to turn up the street and see Avinelle's house with its wide front porch now crowded with rocking chairs. A sign hung at the gate: *Boarders Welcome.*

Jodee stopped. She couldn't believe her eyes. "Whatever's happened here?"

"Avinelle went back east. We ain't heard a word since."

"She went back to find her family, I'll bet," Jodee said, feeling faintly relieved.

"And Miz Ashton, she cleared out, too. Took Maggie with her. California, we think. The stage line shut down. For a while folks had no way of getting back and forth to Cheyenne City until the railroad came through. That was a big to-do! Their house was sold at auction. Boteller bought it, found himself a new bride, a rancher's daughter, moved into the carriage house and opened the place to boarders. There's eleven of them now. Artie moved on. Quimby, too." She nodded. "Lots of changes."

Jodee's heart sank. With Quimby gone there was no hope of buying back her father's gun or her mother's locket. "I can't imagine Reverend Boteller living in that carriage house with all those children."

"He farmed out the older ones to work, enclosed the stable to make an extra sleeping room. He does a good business."

Steeling herself, Jodee looked at Hanna, and Hanna looked back with a hard, clear stare.

"So what brings you back after all this time, honey?"

There was no use explaining that with her grandmother gone there was no affection lost between herself and the aunt and uncle who cared nothing about her. That part of her life had been laid to rest.

"Tell me how Corbet is," Jodee said softly, thrilled to at last speak his name. "I was certain

I'd come back to find him married to Avinelle."

Hanna started back toward the restaurant. "I could use another serving girl." She tossed Jodee a big smile. "Are you looking for a job?"

Jodee shook her head. "Corbet didn't get himself killed, did he?" Her heart stood still at the terrible words.

Hanna slowed. "The day you left town, he quit marshaling. Brucker's the marshal now. We don't have any trouble with him in town. But Corbet's gone. He bought his spread and proved it up. Built a cabin and grew a beard." She laughed but had to dab at her eyes. "One day Ceddy and me remarked we hadn't seen him in a while. We rode out to pay a call and found him gone." She brightened. "But you came back to us. That's something. What do you plan to do now that you're here?"

Jodee hadn't imagined Corbet gone. "I don't know," she said. She was too surprised to cry.

In her hotel room that night Jodee sat a long time by the window, wondering what she might do now that Corbet was gone. She didn't have to work. She had enough cash money to last years.

Word spread quickly that Jodee McQue— Jodeen McQuerin—was back in town. Patsy was the first to send an invitation to dinner. Jodee accepted with pleasure. She marveled at Patsy's new house and Henry looking so darling and learning to talk. Best of all, Virgil was up and about although much changed from the robust deputy he'd once been. Thin and serious, he was manager of Wilson's Mercantile.

One day as she was shopping, Marshal Brucker hailed Jodee on the street. His grin was as insolent as ever. She stopped to talk with him, but he was called away and she was glad.

What might she do with the lace blouse she brought for Avinelle or the silver sugar and creamer on a matching engraved tray for Widow Ashton? Or the thread assortment for Maggie? Jodee packed the things away, supposing she'd never see those women again.

Eventually Jodee did what she knew she must do—she rented a buggy and drove out to the place where Corbet pitched his tent that long ago day when she and Hobie rode out there. Hobie was back east at college. His brother Warren was the hotel desk clerk and had no end of praise for his big brother.

Jodee found Corbet's cabin abandoned. She pulled the latch-string and went inside. Corbet had built a rope slung bed. The mattress stood on end to keep dirt from settling on it. Except for the earthy smell and empty feeling of the single room, Jodee felt Corbet's presence in the very air she breathed. It felt as if that invisible tether that once held them together was still there.

Outside, she circled the cabin, delighting to

see the carefully set foundation stones. She imagined the hours of work Corbet spent, selecting, felling, and peeling the logs, levering them into place single-handedly. The creek was a babbling ribbon of silver water slipping between the boulders and brush nearby.

Jodee's heart swelled with love for the place. Corbet built the cabin thinking of her, she knew. His love was in every notched log, in the perfectly set window and in the heavy hewn door. There was even a flat boulder where she could sit in the sun and remember his smile. She could picture him lashing ropes between the boulder and his horse to drag it into place.

Corbet's spirit lived all around her. The feeling was so strong that Jodee almost felt afraid sometimes, believing he might've died somewhere and no one knew about it. She feared she might wander down the valley some afternoon and find his bones among the boulders. How could he have gone off, saying nothing to those in town he cared for? Even Virgil was hurt to think Corbet left without a goodbye.

Surely, Corbet left some memento, Jodee thought that first afternoon when she sat in front of the cabin, feeling the crisp mountain air dry her tears. She looked over the cabin inside and out, trying to imagine what Corbet's life had been like after the roof was on. She dragged the mattress into the sunlight to air, imaging him sleeping on it. She looked for words carved into the windowsill; she looked for a hole in the floor where he might have hidden a strongbox. Nothing. Not a hint. She sat in the red glow of the sunset, pretending to be Corbet and thinking his thoughts. Where had he gone?

Checking out of the hotel the next day, Jodee rented a buckboard and moved her trunks to the cabin. She bought supplies at Wilsons, telling Patsy where she'd be should anyone inquire. Then she set up housekeeping in the cabin. It was better than any place she and her pa had ever known. She felt some afternoons as if her father was there with her, fishing just around the bend in the creek where the water was deep. When she did her washing in the yard, she thought she could hear her mother's skirts snapping in the breeze.

Jodee laid out new linens on the bed—Hanna and Bailey presented her with a beautiful Jacob's Ladder quilt. Patsy gave her a worn nine-patch. The stone fireplace drew perfectly. Jodee felt safe at night with a pine plank snug in the brackets, barring the door.

She took care, gathering her kindling by day, watching for rattlers and varmints like in the old days when she followed her father from campsite to campsite. She had a grand vantage point, overlooking the valley and the creek. On

Saturdays she joined Hanna and Cedric for supper at the restaurant. She had Sunday dinners with Patsy, Virgil, and little Henry, who was soon joined by a baby sister they named Sally.

Summer waned. Life settled into a pleasant, relaxing pattern. Jodee even received a letter from her Cousin Addee in Arkansas, announcing her betrothal. Jodee wrote back, detailing her life in Corbet's cabin. She thought her penmanship, improved in Arkansas with Addee's assistance, still looked terrible.

In the fall Jodee took the train to Cheyenne City to visit her father's grave. In the paupers' yard, his was the only grave marked by a stone. She stood in the cold, remembering the desolate day she found his grave for the first time and imagined him laying under the ground in his stocking feet. Her grief had been so intense she hadn't been able to leave her hotel room for a week, but when she finally gathered her courage, she knew what she needed to do. She had bought her ticket east. By chance, she met a cavalryman's wife traveling east with two small children. The woman needed a traveling companion and helper. Avinelle's letter of reference on Ashton Babcock letterhead secured Jodee safe passage with the woman all the way to the Mississippi River.

Leaving a new pair of boots and a buff-colored hat on her pa's marker, Jodee returned to Burdeen that afternoon. By nightfall, she lay in her bed in Corbet's cabin, listening to the crackling fire in the fireplace, smelling the cold of winter coming on, and hearing the yip of a coyote far off in the mountains. *Wherever Corbet might be,* she thought, closing her eyes, *she hoped he remembered that she loved him.*

Snow came in November. Bailey urged her to move into town for the winter. They had a spare room. Jodee told him she was content alone of an evening, learning to piece a quilt with fabric scraps gathered from several ladies in town who were coming to accept her. Hobie's brother Warren furnished her with a primer so she could practice reading by lamplight.

That was where Jodee sat, with the wind lashing the door one night when she heard a horse approaching outside. Cedric and some friends had built her a corral and lean-to shed so she could keep a horse. Thinking he had come to insist she move to town, she got up from her rocker and laid her rifle alongside the door. At the window she lifted the heavy shutter and looked out.

There in the darkness came a hulking figure of a man, hat pulled low, slipping in the snow. His horse waited by the lean-to.

Her heart stood still.

For a second Jodee thought Hanna was right. She had no business living there alone. The man might be anyone. When the door rattled with a pounding knock, her heart leapt.

"I got a rifle aimed at your gizzard," she yelled in a gruff tone.

When she heard nothing more, she backed away, afraid the intruder might try to kick the door down.

"Jodee?" came a flabbergasted voice, thick with astonishment.

With a cry of disbelief, Jodee discovered her hands all a-fumble. She couldn't lift the plank from its brackets fast enough. When she finally got it free and dropped it to the floor, the door nearly slammed open into her face. Snow blew inside and swirled as far as the fireplace.

There stood Corbet, his face a study in wonder, his dark eyes wide, his cheeks red with cold. "Jodee?"

Was it really him? Jodee couldn't believe her prayers had been answered.

Corbet lunged forward and grabbed her. He held her close, hard and tight, as if he didn't believe it, either. "You're here?" he said, holding her out at arm's length to gawk at her.

She pushed the door closed against the cold.

Corbet's lips pulled back over his teeth in that remarkable smile. She didn't need to wonder. She didn't have to ask. He still cared.

She grabbed handfuls of his coat and pulled him close. His mouth came down on hers in a fierce, passionate kiss. She staggered back, felt him steady her, then draw her in against him again to lock her mouth with his.

When he pulled back for air, she laughed.

"Tarnation, Corbet! Where the hell have you been? Sometimes I think you must be as stupid as me, going off somewhere without telling anybody where, same as me, when we should've been here all along."

He laughed so hard it almost looked like he was crying. "I went back to the farm where I grew up. I inherited it, but there wasn't anything for me there, not without you, so I sold the place. How long have you been here?"

"Since summer."

He looked around. "It looks like home." When he looked back at Jodee she saw the anguish she knew only too well at having been parted from him for two years. He had felt it, too. "I was nothing without you, Jodee."

"Are you back to stay?"

"After you left I nearly went crazy. I never should've let you go. I realized I didn't know where you went. I couldn't guess where to look for you. I didn't tell you how much I love you. Will you stay? Will you live with me here?"

She nodded.

"As my wife?"

She went up on tiptoe and kissed him with every particle of her being. She wrapped her arms around his neck and held on with all her might. This time she wouldn't let go. She had found her way home to love.

FINES
5¢ PER DAY
FOR
OVERDUE BOOKS

Center Point Large Print
600 Brooks Road / PO Box 1
Thorndike, ME 04986-0001 USA

(207) 568-3717

US & Canada:
1 800 929-9108
www.centerpointlargeprint.com